"Can I ask you something?" Elsa said.

"Yeah," Clio said reassuringly. "Sure."

"You and Aidan," Elsa said slowly. "You don't . . ."

"Don't what?"

"Do you *like* him?"

"What?" Clio said. "Aidan? No. I . . . no."

"It's just that you two are so alike. Sometimes it feels like you two should be together."

"Aidan?" Clio asked, her heart pounding. "And me? God, no. Elsa, no."

The denials were coming out of her mouth much, much faster than her brain was moving. But even hearing Elsa make the suggestion was intoxicating. Disturbing. Very, very unsettling. It made no sense!

"Good!" Elsa let out a massive sigh.

Also by Maureen Johnson

Girl at Sea

maureen johnson

HARPER TEEN

An Imprint of HarperCollins*Publishers*

HarperTeen is an imprint of HarperCollins Publishers.

Girl at Sea

For information address HarperCollins Children's Books, a division of HarperCollins
Publishers, 10 East 53rd Street, New York, NY 10022.
www.harperteen.com

alloyentertainment
Produced by Alloy Entertainment
151 West 26th Street, New York, NY 10001

Library of Congress Cataloging-in-Publication Data
Johnson, Maureen, 1973–
    Girl at sea / Maureen Johnson. — 1st ed.
      p. cm.
    Summary: High school junior Clio Ford has to give up her dream job and a potential
first kiss to take a working vacation with her estranged father on a yacht in Italy, where
she falls for a research assistant, stumbles upon an archaeological revelation, and finally
reconciles with her father.
    ISBN 978-0-06-054146-0
    [1. Boats and boating—Fiction. 2. Fathers and daughters—Fiction. 3. Archaeology—
Fiction. 4. Interpersonal relations—Fiction. 5. Artists—Fiction. 6. Italy—Fiction.]
I. Title.
PZ7.J634145Gir 2007   2007003925
[Fic]—dc22   CIP
                                                                      AC

Typography by Andrea C. Uva
❖
First HarperTeen paperback edition, 2008
09 10 11 12 13 CG/RRDH 10 9 8 7 6 5 4 3

For Mary Marguerite Johnson,
the world's greatest mother,
arguably its best nurse,
and the person likely to find
the most safety violations in this story

Acknowledgments

Many thanks are owed to:

Abby McAden, Lexa Hillyer, Josh Bank, John Crowther, and Kate Schafer, all of whom were instrumental in making this book happen.

All the divers who lent me their expertise and answered my many questions.

And Hamish Young, who supplied his life background, his seafaring family, and one memorable descent into the depths of Queen Elizabeth Lake.

ITALY

Adriatic Sea

- Civitavecchia
- ✪ Rome

- Naples
- Pompeii
- Isle of Capri ● ● Sorrento

Tyrrhenian Sea

Mediterranean Sea

London, May 1897

Lightning flashed over Big Ben, and a bruise-like darkness draped over the dome of St. Paul's. On the streets of London, sudden claps of thunder caused horses to start and carriages to collide. The British Museum was packed with people seeking shelter from the oppressive weather within its massive halls, among its great stones. Unfortunately, too many people had the same idea; there was hardly room for them. The pressure in the air grew as screaming children ran between the display cases and tables, knocking into them. Crowds bumped around the priceless Elgin marbles from the crown of the Parthenon.

Eighteen-year-old Marguerite Magwell slipped through easily, not really noticing the chaos that was going on around her. She was even unaware of the ominous sky outside. If you had asked her at that moment if it was hot in the museum, she would not have been able to answer. Her own body was bone cold. The humidity that dampened her cornflower blue dress simply made her colder. She was hatless and gloveless. Her blond hair was loosely pinned up and curled wildly in this intense weather. Her appearance was not a concern; she didn't know what she looked like, didn't care. The only thing that mattered was the small slip of paper she clutched in her right hand. In her mind there was one thought only: *go to Jonathan*. Jonathan Hill had been her father's favorite student, besides herself. Jonathan needed to know. Jonathan could help her now, at the only time in her life when she truly did not know what to do.

Other people noticed her. Even in this state, Marguerite was striking, equal parts wild and delicate, with a face whose fine proportions could have been immortalized in marble. People eased aside as she pressed her way forward to the statue of Ramses II in the long Egyptian gallery. The statue occupied a place of pride in the columned hall. Marguerite fixed her eyes on the cold, pupil-less ones above her, the eyes of a king dead for thousands of years. She had never understood until this moment why the Egyptians tried so hard to preserve themselves after death. How wonderful it must have been for them to believe so strongly that the dead lived on, that they could be reached, that they would need their bodies!

No time to think about that.

She continued on, pushing between the overstuffed display cases and people, moving from room to room, feeling like she had less and less air to breathe. The door she was looking for was unmarked. Most people would not have been able to tell that it wasn't just a wooden panel between two cases of monkey skulls. The curators worked behind these secret doors, unseen by the populace, in offices even more crowded than the museum floor itself. Having practically grown up in the museum, she knew exactly what she was looking for. Marguerite moved aside two little boys who leaned on the panel she required and pounded on the door with the flat of her hand. A moment later, a familiar face appeared, smiling, slightly dazed. Jonathan's sandy hair was in need of a barber's touch, and he had ink all over his long fingers.

"Marguerite!" he said, shifting his collar nervously. "What brings you to the museum today? Sorry, I've been writing all morning; I don't want to cover you in this . . . Oh, I've just gotten it on my neck, haven't I? Never mind. . . ."

Marguerite could not bring herself to say why she had come just yet. Her throat was dry, and it felt like a hand had grabbed it and was squeezing it.

"It's very hot today," he sputtered, noticing her distress. "Would you care to take a walk around the courtyard with me? They're selling lemon ices in the square."

"Lemon what?" she asked abruptly.

"Ices?" he repeated.

"Oh. Ices."

There was a darkening at the windows, and a great crack of thunder broke above the museum, causing several ladies to cry out. A moment later, there was a pounding on the roof as the rain came down.

"Listen to that," Jonathan said, looking up at the ceiling. "It's like the great flood out there. I suppose that rules out the possibility of the lemon ices. Let me get the porter to start turning on the lights so that they—"

"I have news of my father," she interrupted.

"Wonderful!" He touched her hand lightly. "How's the work in Pompeii going? When does he arrive home? Did I get ink on you? Oh, I did, didn't I? Here, let me—"

"He doesn't," she interrupted him again.

"What do you mean?" he asked, already grabbing for his hand-kerchief and dabbing the spot of ink on her hand unsuccessfully.

"His ship," she managed.

"His ship?" he repeated. "What about his ship? Marguerite, are you well? Do you need to sit down? You've gone very pale."

She held out her tightly closed fist, the paper sticking out of it. Jonathan carefully pried it loose. She watched him take in the words. He reached up and held the doorframe, then looked at her.

"Marguerite, I—"

There was another enormous crack overhead. The heavens were screaming. It was as if the waters were coming for her as well. The whole world would drown.

"He's gone," she said.

The Secret That Dare Not Speak Its Name

Ollie was in aisle five of Galaxy Art Supply stocking oil paints when Clio Ford emerged from the manager's office. From her vantage spot by the modeling clay, she could watch him for a moment, drink it all in.

Ollie Myers. Absurdly tall at six-foot five. His hair was shaggy today. He was wearing a deep navy blue button-down shirt and a wide, seventies-style tie. He looked down over the slots that the little tubes went into, carefully making sure that the right colors went into the right places. He cared about that, and it killed her. It really did. She could watch him putting paints away all day. Sad, but extremely true.

Time for the show.

She was standing straight, so she slumped a little and arranged her face into a mask of minor melancholy. She approached slowly.

"Hey," she said.

Ollie turned. Good reflexes. (He used to do all-terrain skateboarding. Very badly, he said. Very, *very* badly. Humble as well. Could you ask for more in a man? No. It was impossible. All human wants had been fulfilled in him.)

Which was why this could never work. She had to be dreaming.

"Well?" he said.

"Well . . ." Clio began. "I'm only a junior in high school, and apparently, most Galaxy employees are in college. And I have no retail experience. No job experience at all, actually."

"Oh," Ollie said. His face fell.

"But . . ." Clio went on. "I have this."

She held up her arm, showing the long tattoo that wound around her right forearm: an electric-blue-and-pink zipper with three yellow-and-black stars flying out of the toggle.

"You got the job!" he said.

"You know it!" Clio said, feeling herself beaming.

Clio had prepared for the interview with her typical precision. White jeans, gently streaked with lavender paint from when she repainted her room. A pink short-sleeved T-shirt from a manga publisher. A chunky belt she'd made herself by attaching laminated matchbook covers to a plain old leather belt from a thrift store. Long, honey-brown hair worn up, pinned in place with two green cloisonné chopsticks. And the master stroke, her tattoo boldly on display. No long sleeves, no arm warmers, no sticking her arm behind her back. No excuses. The freak flag was flying at full mast.

Her cell phone buzzed in her bag. It had gone off four times during the interview. She ignored it.

"I'm still amazed," she said. "I didn't think they liked to see

6

tattoos at job interviews. Unless you're applying to work at a meth lab. Or a tattoo parlor. I guess *that* would make sense. . . ."

"Or an art store," he said. "I told you that tattoo would do it. Daphne loves Masahiro Sato. You were in the second she heard he drew that."

"She did get excited," Clio said, remembering the glow in the store manager's eyes when she said the name of the man who had drawn her tattoo. He was one of Tokyo's most famous manga artists. He had a massive cult following.

"This may be a historical moment," she said. "This is the first time one of my dad's insane impulses actually worked out for me."

"Your dad wanted you to get the tattoo?" he asked.

"Not exactly," Clio said. "It's a long story. A long, boring story."

"I doubt that," he answered. "I guess I'll have to make your name tag. I can even make it now. Want a name tag?"

Ollie was from Texas, and he had a voice that dripped low and slow into Clio's ear. He could draw out the words *name tag* and make it sound like something you would deeply want and cherish forever. She found herself nodding heavily. He took her to a back corner of the store, where there was a small cabinet and a computer. He reached into the cabinet and produced a little machine.

"Okay," he said. "It's *C-l-e-o*, right?"

"*C-l-i-o.*"

"Is that a family name or something?" he asked.

"Not exactly," Clio said. "I was named after a Muse."

"A Muse? As in the Greek Muses?"

7

"Yep," Clio said. "Weird parents. What can I tell you?"

"You're a muse," he said. "I've always wanted a muse. Can you help me paint?"

"I'm the muse of history," she said. "Is that any help?"

"A muse is always a help," he said, typing into the label maker.

Muuuuse. How had she never noticed the magical power of the Southern accent before? In the eight months that she had known Ollie, she had realized that it was attractive, but she hadn't heard it much. Their exchanges took place at the counter, when he was telling her how much stuff cost. Even still, he could make things that cost "eight dollars and sixty-four cents" seem worth every penny.

It wasn't until this last month, when he started talking to her as he restocked the shelves, that she got to hear the accent in all its glory. He was a painter and a freshman at Penn. He shared her obsessive love of beautiful, rich inks. He usually wore a vintage pinstripe jacket, rode an old purple bicycle, and smelled like an art studio—a faintly chemical, extremely familiar and homey smell. He missed his sisters in Austin, had no spare cash, and wasn't above attending openings of art exhibitions he didn't like just to get the snacks.

Clio, on the other hand, was a high school junior with a past and yet very little to say about the present. She tended to make her own clothes. (Out of other clothes, so it didn't really count. It wasn't like she was wearing homespun or sweaters she had knitted herself.) She lived in a massive, messy Victorian right near the Penn campus. And once upon a time, her parents had been married, and she and her father had invented a little game called Dive!, which turned into a very big deal. Once upon a time, she had been almost rich, not exactly famous, and totally happy. Her life had been unusual. There was a lot of traveling. A Japanese comic book artist had drawn on her arm. Things like that.

But an unusual life is not, by definition, a great one. And now, at seventeen, she felt the deficiencies had been made painfully clear. And there was one that was bothering Clio more than any other.

She had never been kissed.

It was shocking. It was embarrassing. It was largely inexplicable, but Clio knew the general place where the blame could be cast. But that was a long story, too. One that was about to end, she hoped.

The phone buzzed again. She shoved it farther down in her bag.

Ollie carefully tore off the clear sticky strip with Clio's name printed on it and stuck it to his cheek as he went rummaging in a box for a blank tag. Once he found one, he applied the sticker to it with extreme care. The tag was tiny in his massive hands.

"Here we go," he said. "Do I get to pin it on you?"

"Sure," she said, struggling to keep her voice from cracking.

He leaned down to her, which genuinely took some effort, considering he was a foot taller than she was. Now he was at face level with her. He gently pinched up some of her shirt, choosing his spot carefully, just under the left shoulder, directly above her heart. She watched his face as he delicately pierced the fabric; he bit the corner of his lower lip while he worked. The pin shut with a snap, but he didn't move. He just looked her right in the eye.

Was this it? The kiss? The one she'd been waiting her whole pathetic life for? Here? Now? In the aisle of an art store? Was that possible? It certainly looked like he was in the right position. Levels correct. Expression correct.

Pretend you know what you're doing, she told herself quickly. *This is a good general rule in life. When in doubt, pretend that you know what you're doing. Just go with it. Do something. Fake it until you catch on.*

A man came around the corner and stood behind Clio, waiting patiently. Ollie looked at him over Clio's head and backed up.

"Have to help the next person," he said, a trace of regret on his face. "When do you come in again?"

"I start training tomorrow," she said.

"I'll train you myself," he said. "If that's okay. But you already know your way around pretty well. Probably better than anyone here."

He smiled that slow, Southern smile.

Her phone buzzed again.

"Someone really wants to talk to you," he said.

"Yeah," she said.

"I get that," he said, closing with a smile before turning his attention to the man, who was already mumbling something about looking for a reliable adhesive for small tiles.

The phone continued to buzz and shake and generally rattle itself to pieces as Clio walked home. She looked at the display.

10

Unknown caller.

Unknown caller.

Unknown caller.

Mom.

Jackson.

Unknown caller four more times.

She was popular today, at least with the unknown caller, who wasn't unknown at all. That was her dad. Unknown caller plus insane repetition equaled dad, every time. He could get on a calling jag and be relentless about it. He was like a little kid— once he got an idea in his head, he made a big fuss until he got what he was screaming for.

Well, he could wait. She needed time to savor this blissful moment. It was a light, gorgeous late afternoon in the springtime, and she wanted to play her favorite fantasy in her head. . . .

They were at the beach, she and Ollie. They were sharing that brown-and-orange blanket that Clio had gotten in Peru for five dollars—the one she thought would make such a good beach blanket, except she had never taken it to the beach. It covered the bamboo chair in the corner of her room. Ollie wore long, blue trunks with a pattern of flames coming from the bottom of each leg. She wore a red bikini. She didn't own a red bikini, but she was wearing one. Sometimes her brain misfired in the fantasy and gave her red boots as well, and she would have to fix the image and start again.

Anyway, they were on the beach, sharing the blanket. Clio's best friend, Jackson, was there on a towel next to them. Jackson would be trying to read her magazine, but every time she looked

11

up, Clio and Ollie would be kissing again. Obviously, because he was so tall—he was like Mr. Torso—he would have to crane his neck down to kiss her.

"Seriously," Jackson would say. "You guys. You have to stop."

"I can't," Ollie would say. "Come on, look at her! I can't."

And then something would happen—Clio couldn't figure out what, but something—that would pull Ollie away for a minute. Maybe he would rescue a small child from a giant tangle of killer New Jersey seaweed. Jackson would move closer and say, "Sorry. It's just jealousy. You guys are so perfect together. It's not fair."

"Yeah . . ." Clio would answer. "I know."

Long sigh here.

"You were right to wait seventeen years for the perfect, kissable guy," Jackson would go on. "I just dated whichever guy crossed my path. I feel dirty now. Cheap. Like a balled-up napkin from a coffee place that you find at the bottom of your purse, and it's kind of . . . hard. And you don't know why. That's what I feel like. The mystery napkin."

Clio would smile benevolently.

Admittedly, the real Jackson would never say this, not in a million years. The real Jackson considered herself a connoisseur of kisses. In fact, she classified them using the same method normally employed by wine tasters. She claimed this was the best way. A look test. A sniff test. A taste test. A consistency test.

Some guys, she explained, had a thin, smooth technique. Quick, darting moves. They tended to taste of mint because they were obsessed with technique and chewed gum compulsively if they thought they had any shot at all. Some were more full-bodied. With them, it was a slower experience, one that Jackson always said had "woody aftertones."

She stopped short of the swilling-and-spitting part of the wine-tasting metaphor because it kind of fell apart there.

The phone was ringing again. Unknown number. Clio had reached her house by this point. The call could wait. She had good news to deliver first.

Where There Is a Balloon, There Is Always a Pin

This was a Thursday night, and Thursday nights were Clio's mother's date night. Date nights had been going on for the last eight months—basically, since the start of the school year, when Rob (the date) turned up on a tour of the Philadelphia Museum of Art that her mom had been leading. Thursday was the only free night they had in common, so it became the night that Clio got the house to herself, plus twenty dollars to spend on Thai takeout. Thursdays smelled of jasmine and ginger and were washed down with delicious, sugary Thai iced teas. Jackson would probably come over at some point, and they'd do homework or watch TV. Or they'd just blast music and mess around online.

Thursdays were beautiful things, and this was the king of Thursdays.

But her mom was home, and she didn't look even remotely date-ready. She was standing at the kitchen bar in one of the oversized men's dress shirts she always wore when she'd been working in the studio. Her hair was in pigtails. Suki, Clio's orange cat, sat on one of the stools looking deeply shocked about something. Clio picked him up, set him gently on the floor, and took his seat. There was nothing to eat at the bar but a jar of sesame seeds her mom had left out after cooking last night's stir-fry. Clio shook some into her palm and licked them off.

"I'm thirty percent more lovable than when I left," she said, picking the last spare seeds off her hand and popping them into her mouth triumphantly. "Ask me why."

"Impossible," her mom answered. "You're already too lovable. Did your dad call?"

"Yes," Clio said. "About sixty times. But I'm about to get unbearably lovable. Go on. Ask me why."

"Did you talk to him?" her mom asked.

"Not yet. Go on. Ask me why. 'Why are you so lovable, Clio?' The answer will amaze you."

"Okay," her mother said, sighing just a little. "Why?"

"Because I think I just got a job at Galaxy. That means thirty percent discount. I did the math. Between us, we spend about three hundred dollars a month there. With the discount, that's a hundred bucks for nothing. A hundred bucks! Or ninety. Whatever. Plus Ollie says that sometimes we get opened containers that they have to accept as returns."

"Who's Ollie?" her mother said, still not looking quite checked in. This news should have brought a lot more enthusiasm.

"Just some guy who works there," she said quickly. Of course, this summer was when he would become much more than that,

15

Clio hoped. But no announcements until it was all official. "Did you hear the part about the discount? Because I can repeat it. I can even throw in a few dance moves to really bring it home."

"Do you want a cup of coffee?" her mom asked. "I just put the pot on."

The coffeepot hissed and dripped in the corner as if to prove its existence and role in the conversation. Clio looked at it, then at her mom, who still wasn't smiling. Her expression was kind of like the one she'd worn after she'd had laughing gas at the dentist, just before she'd started having a heated, emotional conversation with the sofa.

"What's wrong?" Clio asked. "Why aren't you jumping up and down? Why aren't you on a date? Why are you making coffee at five in the evening? You didn't . . . break up, did you?"

"No, it's not that. It's something else."

Clio's brain went searching for what "something else" might mean, and the answer readily presented itself. Her mom and her boyfriend, Rob, had been dating for eight months. Her mom had come home every time, and Rob had never stayed over. It was only a matter of time before she got the "Clio, when a man and a woman love each other very much . . ." or "when one lives in University City and one lives in Society Hill . . . sometimes, there must be sleepovers" talk.

"Maybe I'll get some coffee," Clio said dismally as she got up to take a mug from the counter. "Do we still have that fancy vanilla creamer?"

"No. You drank it all. Listen, Clio. Sit down a minute."

Clio sat on one of the stools at the kitchen island, where they ate all of their meals. She steadied herself and told herself that in a minute's time, she would need to smile graciously and accept the inevitable. It was time for breakfast with Rob. There would be a man's razor in the bathroom again. There could even be a boxer shorts sighting.

"I got a letter today," her mom began.

Clio loosened. This was going in a strange direction, one that didn't sound like it had anything to do with Rob's underwear.

"A few months ago," her mom went on, "I applied for some funding for school. A real long-shot fellowship through a private benefactor. I never thought I'd get it. But I did."

"That's amazing!" Clio said. "You were scaring me back there! How much is it for? Does it give you a salary?"

"Yes, it does. A good one. And it pays for the rest of my research fees. It even pays off one of my loans."

"Okay. You completely beat my thirty percent discount. I give."

"The catch is," her mom said, "I have to do a ten-week special project this summer. The foundation that gave me this money just bought two sixteenth-century Dutch paintings. They're in very bad condition. They were lost in the Second World War, and they've just come to light. They were stored in houses and warehouses and knocked around. They're a mess. I have to work on them."

"That doesn't sound like a catch," Clio said. "That sounds like your job. The thing you like to do."

"It is. It's a very exciting opportunity, actually. The trouble is . . . the paintings are in their private facility, a new workshop space they just built. That's where the work has to be done. And it's in Kansas."

Clio felt her stomach plunge.

"Kansas is far from here," she managed to say.

"It gets slightly more complex," her mom went on. "The reason your dad was calling . . ."

Clio cocked her head. This made no sense. The way her mother said this, her voice going up in pitch, the words slowing down, her eyes no longer looking into Clio's . . . If Clio hadn't known better, her mom was about to suggest that she stay with her dad. And that wasn't possible.

"He had an idea," her mom went on. The inflection was even more sad and guilty.

"I know this sounds crazy," Clio said, "but it *almost* sounds like you're about to suggest that I spend the summer with him, wherever he is. And you know that is a horrible idea."

"Clio—"

"But you would never suggest that," Clio went on. "You would never, ever, in a million years betray me like that and send me to stay with Dad. Or let him stay here. You'd do something sensible instead, like stick me in an orphanage."

"Look—"

"I have full confidence in you, Mom," Clio said, her anxiety increasing as her mother failed to deny the fact. "I know you wouldn't do it. So go ahead. Tell me the clever plan you've come up with that lets me stay here. I'm ready for it. Hit me."

"He called after I got the news," her mother said, leaning heavily on the bar. "Just by coincidence, to see how things were. I told him the news. I had to—he's entitled to know. You two get four weeks every summer as part of the custody agreement."

"I acknowledge that you were fulfilling your legal responsibility," Clio said. "He knows you will be in Kansas. Fine. He's in the loop. Now, where am I staying?"

"He had a counteroffer. A good one, Clio."

Clio fell silent. The coffeepot hissed. Her mom quietly poured herself a cup.

"Define 'counteroffer,'" Clio finally said.

"He wants to take you to Italy for the summer. He has a boat there."

"And you said 'no way' and hung up the phone, right?"

Now her mother fell silent, poking at her coffee with a spoon. Clio put her head down on the kitchen bar. She felt crumbs adhering to her forehead.

"Why is this happening?" she mumbled.

"I think this could really work," her mother babbled on.

"Fine," Clio replied, picking up her head. "Whatever. I'll go to Kansas. Obviously, that's what you've been trying to get me to say. You were trying to show me that it could be worse. Very smart."

Clio looked up at her mother. The laughing-gas look was gone. It had been replaced by the expression she had when Clio was seven years old and her mom had had to tell Clio that her dog, Ziggy, had died while she was in school that day.

"The problem is," she began, "we're not even going to be in a city. We're going to be way out, in a converted farmhouse. I talked to someone who'd just been out there. He said there was nothing around."

"You're not taking me? You're just going by yourself? What about . . . Rob? Your *boyfriend*?"

This question seemed to cause her mother the most pain of all.

"He's offered to come with me."

It was like Clio had been slapped. Slapped hard. Crumbs started raining from her forehead.

"You're taking Rob but leaving me?"

"It's not like that," her mom said firmly. "This is just one of those situations where things come together in a weird way. Rob has decided to go freelance for a few months. He can work out there. With you out there . . ."

"You're picking Rob over me?" Clio said in disbelief.

"No. I was saying that there's nothing for you to do out there, Clio. Plus your father has a legal right."

"You have *met* my dad," Clio said. "Haven't you? I thought we agreed that he had given up any rights he had. If he wants to see me for four weeks, he can come here or to Kansas or wherever. But there is no way that I am spending ten weeks with him."

"It's Italy, Clio!"

"Who cares? Remember Greece? Remember how I got this?"

She held up her arm, twisting it so the tattoo was facing her mother.

"You don't need to remind me of anything," her mother said firmly. "Do you think I would do this if I thought it would hurt you in some way? You're out of school for the summer, so it doesn't affect that. And you're older and smarter now. You can stop him if he gets out of control."

"I can? *You* didn't seem to have much luck."

That was a low blow, and Clio knew it. But it was true. The

argument had reached a painful impasse. No matter what, all her dreams for the summer had just been crushed. The job, Ollie, the kissing, the beach, even the nonexistent red boots . . .

Once again, her parents' problems had run through her life like a piece of heavy equipment, smashing everything in their way.

Mementos and Omens

Clio curled up in a ball on her favorite chair in her attic room, ruminating on the disaster that was now her summer. A couple of hours earlier everything she had wanted had all been within reach, and now it was being ripped away—like every other good thing that had been screwed up by her father. This now included her kiss.

Clio couldn't really explain why she had never been kissed, but she knew it had something to do with her dad. No, Clio's father had never *physically* stopped her from being kissed. He didn't leap into the scene and deliver a kung fu chop between her pursed lips. Her father had a bigger, more total way of ruining her life. It was a comprehensive thing.

Their house was a good example of how things worked. The house was wonderful and Victorian. Three stories. Two turrets. It was beautiful and in the middle of Philadelphia to boot. It was also falling to pieces. It leaked. The wind whistled through it.

One turret was home to bats. The other was rotted and in serious danger of falling off. And the whole structure leaned about four inches to the left, which couldn't be good.

Her father had wanted it, though. The idea had been to refurbish it, return this little slice of Philadelphia history to its former glory. Her mother had opposed the idea but caved to his infectious enthusiasm. The house was theirs, but the transformation never happened. The money and the time just vanished, and now Clio lived in what was left. Her situation had been unstable, destined to fall apart from the start. And her father was the architect of this destruction.

People would call her lucky because she was going to Italy. If she tried to tell them that Italy wasn't going to be so great, she would look like the ultimate spoiled brat. "Daddy's taking me to Italy!" Pouty lips.

No one knew what being with her father was like. No one could see the evidence littered around her. Not just the house, but this room was full of evidence, little pieces of the story. Everywhere she looked, signs of her own former and now impending doom.

The raspberry soda can from Peru: purchased on one of the very first trips after Dive! was made. Not content with the person offered by the hotel, her father hired an "expert" guide to take them through the rain forest. He got them lost for four hours. This soda was the thing she bought when they finally made their way back to a town.

The Japanese ramen bowl: it had contained the ramen that she ate after getting her tattoo done. It was raining. The tattoo burned and itched like crazy. She and her father ran across the street to one of Tokyo's countless ramen bars. Clio could remember every moment of that day. She and her father were tucked into a small blond-wood booth, with red paper dividers separating them from the world and giving their little corner of the city a warm glow. It was good soup too, with fresh roasted pork and green onions. Her father was talking about his next plan. He had an idea for opening a school, a radical place, with no buildings. It would just offer constant experience, like the life that Clio was leading. He had taken her out of normal school by then. Clio loved the idea of other kids joining her. She paid for the bowl so she could keep it. She loved the shade of red. It was a slow day, so her father paid the chef to let Clio come to the back and learn how to chop and cook a little. They used to buy a lot of things then.

They arrived home from Japan to find two things. One, the massive tattoo on Clio's arm was a bridge too far for Clio's mother. And two, her father's "business partner" had defrauded them. Whatever money hadn't been spent was essentially gone. The party was over.

It took her father a while to get the message. He refused to believe it. Refused to go back to work. Tried to keep on doing things as before. There was a fight every night. He grew sullen. Her mother grew quiet. And finally, they sat her down to tell her that sometimes parents don't get along and can't be married anymore.

Clio took Suki to her room and stayed there for a day. She even dragged Suki's litter box and food inside. When she emerged again, her father had gone. Her mother said that he had moved to an apartment with his friend from work, Martin. Clio didn't know that dads could just move out of houses and in with friends. Apparently, they could.

He kept in touch, of course, swinging into her life at all the wrong times. He'd fall silent for weeks and then turn up outside her school expecting her to come along with him for some insane weekend battle reenactment or a quick trip up to New York to do the underground tour of Manhattan's abandoned subway stations.

Suki sat on the edge of the drawing table now, looking out the window. This was his favorite spot. Who would look after Suki if they weren't here? Would Suki go to Kansas? Clearly, her mother had to go to Kansas. Even Rob could go to Kansas. Clio could fight this if she wanted to. She could tell her mom no—that she was coming along. Kansas. A dry, flat line. No friends in sight. Her mom would be busy in the studio, and she . . .

She envisioned herself standing on a lone plain, looking out at hundreds of miles of empty farmland. The tallest thing in sight. A surefire target for lightning.

No. Maybe there would be some kind of silo. One lone silo in the distance. That would draw the lightning.

No matter what, she wouldn't be here. There would be no Ollie. She flipped open her sketchbook. She had started her eighth picture of him. The plan had been to give him one. That was how she was going to try to start it off. It made her want to cry. In fact, she started to until she heard footsteps on the creaking stairs that led to her room. Clio blotted at her eyes as her mother carefully pushed open the door and held out a takeout menu.

"I thought maybe we could order something together," she said.

"I'm not very hungry," Clio said. "The sesame seeds were very filling."

Her mother sat down on the step.

"I'd be angry too," she said. "I'd be furious. I would have been slamming doors and running out of the house. I think you're taking this really well. I'm proud of you."

Nothing was more annoying than your mom giving you credit. It was a total angst diffuser.

"What's he doing this time?" Clio said. "What kind of freaks does he have with him on his boat? Is it a pirate society? Do I have to bring a parrot? Eye patch?"

"He just said bathing suits and shoes with rubber soles."

"It's going to be something weird," Clio said, looking her in the eye. "And you know it."

Her mother sighed, a long, painful sigh.

"I know you don't believe me right now," she said. "But this could be really good for you, Clio."

Clio just looked at her mom for a moment.

"There's something I have to do first," she said, holding up the name tag from Galaxy. "I have to return this since I'm not going to be working there."

"So, I can call your father? Tell him yes?" her mom asked. There was a horribly perky note in her voice.

"Yeah," Clio said. "You might as well."

The store was dead, so they were pumping Johnny Cash over the speakers. When Clio had first started coming here, Johnny Cash was just some very old, very annoying singer tormenting her as she picked up her supplies. But she had come to love the deep voice and the simple guitar because they were the backdrop to some of her best conversations with Ollie, when the store was quiet. He liked the music, and she found she was able to like it too.

Ollie wasn't up front. Clio scanned the registers. The newest girl was working at one of them. She had short black hair and wore a silver mesh drape over a white T-shirt with a tag that said *Janine.* Clio suddenly hated art store girls, even though at this moment, she technically was one. Art store girls would do *anything.* They would be all over Ollie in her absence. This Janine girl in particular would go after him. She was new—he was nice. He would end up showing her something she didn't understand, some trick with the cash register, and that would be that.

Clio shook her head. This sudden paranoia . . . not good.

She firmly held the theory that everyone gets at least one very stupid superpower. Hers was a weak kind of homing beacon. She could find people or things really easily. If she was looking for Suki, for instance, she always seemed to know exactly where he'd be. And she also seemed to know when Ollie was in Galaxy and where exactly in the store he could be found. It wasn't that impressive. The store wasn't *that* big.

She cast out her senses to find him. He was here. Somewhere off to the side of the store. What hadn't been supplied for a while? She headed for aisle two, Turpentine and Solvents, one of the darker and less pleasant aisles.

"Back already," he said. "What's up?"

Clio opened her mouth but was unwilling to speak. She didn't want this to be true. She wanted her phone to ring and her mother to tell her that it was all off. But there was no ring. Now the stupid phone was silent.

"I can't take the job," she said quietly.

"Why not?"

"It's a long story," Clio said. "My dad . . . he's got visitation rights. I have to go and see him."

"Is he far?" Ollie asked. "Different state or something?"

"Italy," Clio said.

"Oh. That's far. But . . . nice for you, huh?"

Once again, her father's magical ability to make things suck was shining through.

"It's not quite what it sounds like," Clio said. "But yeah, it's far."

He let out a deep sigh.

"This is no good," he said.

"Maybe I can escape," she responded, looking at his eyes, hoping he understood what she was feeling.

"It doesn't sound like something you'd want to escape from," he said. "What? To come back here?"

Had she given away too much?

"No," she said quickly. "I guess you're right. I'm not coming back. I mean, I'm coming back *home*, but . . ."

He nodded slowly.

"I'll tell Daphne if you want," he said. "It's a shame."

She put out her fist, which held the name tag. He put his hand on it.

"Why don't you keep it?" he said. "Maybe you'll need it."

"Or forget my name," she said. "Always good to have a name tag. In case I forget who I am."

"I'll remember for you," he said. "Promise."

28

Your Kind of Crowd

For Clio, getting off the plane at the Rome airport was like being thrown directly into an Olympic relay event. There was a marathon line to the passport control, in which she was moved, shuffled, butted in front of, and pushed. Then there was a scramble for the bags and a run for customs, which all led to the final release into the airport proper, where everything became a total free-for-all.

At least she had her speedy suitcase.

Back before, when they had lots of money and were traveling a lot, Clio had purchased an incredibly expensive pink suitcase with a pattern of rose and green circles. She bought it with the very first Dive! check that arrived in her name. It was made of some advanced kind of lightweight plastic and had better wheels on it than a Mercedes. It was just one of those things in life that gave her tremendous satisfaction every time she looked at it. No matter what happened to her, she had a great suitcase. A light, fast suitcase. She could outrun anyone with this suitcase, no matter how heavily it was packed.

Running seemed like a very good idea. With every step Clio took in the direction of her father—getting off the plane, getting her passport stamped, getting her bag—she felt her heartbeat become heavier and faster.

And then, finally, there he was in the throng of people just outside the arrival doors. Her father was always easy to spot. He was the blond one that some woman was slyly eyeing. It was always a little weird to know that you had a handsome dad. His hair was sandy, always a little too long. He was (it pained her to think it) fairly built. He looked perpetually thirty, even though he had long passed that age.

Today he was easier to spot than normal. He wore somewhat tight, ragged jeans cut off bizarrely at the meridian of the kneecap, a deep blue dress shirt with rolled-up sleeves, black Converse sneakers, and, most disturbingly, a white fisherman's cap, one size too snug.

"Oh dear God," Clio said to herself, stopping in her tracks.

She couldn't do this. She couldn't. A boat. A tiny fisherman's cap. No. No, she had to turn around.

It was the crowd that forced her on. Only fifty paces and a glass wall separated them now. The suitcase glided along the floor with the grace and speed of an Olympic skater.

Come on! it seemed to be saying. *Let's just keep going. Hop on me and I'll get you out of here.*

I can't, Clio's mind replied.

Why not?

Because there's nowhere else to go.

The world's a big place, Clio. We're in an Italian airport. We could pull out your credit card, get on another plane, go anywhere.

My credit limit is way too low.

You know things are pretty bad when your mind is having crisis talks with your suitcase. Clio soldiered on, and with every step, her father's grin grew wider. He had a huge mouth too. His smile was practically as big as her foot.

"Please," Clio said, maneuvering the pink suitcase through the crowd, "please let him be *kind* of normal."

"Hey, kiddo!" he yelled. "Ciao! Italy, huh?"

"Yeah," Clio said, bracing herself for the huge embrace that enveloped her. "It's Italy."

"Our flight to Naples is in an hour and a half, so there's time to grab a bite. Give me that, kiddo."

He reached for the suitcase.

"I've got it," she said.

"You must be exhausted. Let me have it."

"I'm fine." She tightened her hold.

Something in her refused to give over control of the suitcase. It was hers. Her suitcase, her stuff, her life. She would have insisted even if her hand was broken. Even if she was *dead*. Her zombie would pull the suitcase before she would let her dad have it.

"Come on," he said. "Let me help you with that, kiddo. You relax."

Clio had already skittered ahead a few feet, taking the pink suitcase with her. Victory.

"We all just flew down from London," her dad said breezily as he followed her along.

"Who is *we*?" Clio asked.

"You'll love them. This is your kind of crowd."

She seriously doubted that the "we" was "her kind of crowd." She didn't have a crowd. Or if she did, it was the crowd called normal human beings. And her name wasn't kiddo. That was the newest annoying thing, just developed at his secret annoyance labs.

"We have a table at one of the restaurants in the concourse. There's just enough time for some dinner. Everyone is dying to meet you. They know all about you. From Naples, there's a car to take us all to Sorrento, which is down the coast about an hour. Your backpack's open."

Clio stopped to pull off her backpack before her dad reached it, only to find that she'd been tricked. He triumphantly grabbed the handle of the suitcase and raced ahead. Clio watched her precious pink luggage running ahead.

"Gotcha!" her dad said over his shoulder.

Clio looked at her large red watch. Four minutes. That's how long it had taken for her to want to go home. *Ollie, Ollie, save me!* a frantic voice cried in her head. But there was no time to dwell on this, as her father was rushing ahead and rapidly slipping out of sight in the throng of travelers and picker-uppers and car drivers that flocked by the arrivals gate. He dipped into a restaurant with a front display made of Chianti bottles.

"There they are," he said.

He nodded at a small table at the back. Three people sat there. Clio recognized one of them instantly. He was already standing up and coming over to greet her.

"Martin's here?" she asked.

Martin she could take. That was a good sign. Martin had been her father's colleague back when her father worked for a software company as a writer. He was a short man, older than middle-aged, with a salt-and-pepper beard. He had never married or had any kids, so he spent his time doing whatever he liked. Martin also had *two* PhDs and had retired early, simply because he could.

"Clio!" he said, hugging her. "You managed to get here."

"Just about," Clio said. "You look a little different."

"I've lost weight," he said. "All the swimming I've been doing."

The other two people were female, and they were strangers. They looked almost nothing alike, yet Clio could tell they were related. The younger of the two was a girl with very thick, long blond hair knotted at the top of her head. She had a full body, very curvy, in a Marilyn Monroe kind of way. She wore a deep blue tank top and tiny white shorts that showed off her apricoty tan. Her eyes were absolutely massive and sea blue, but her mouth was tiny. She was gorgeous and glowing. No makeup. Clio had the strange flash that this was what the person who invented cheese must have been like—a blond dairy goddess.

Clio suddenly felt very overdressed in her jeans (thready though they were) and her oversized blue hooded sweatshirt, covered in stars and Japanese letter patches. She'd done that herself—cutting them out of old T-shirts and sewing them on by hand. Her clothes, ordinarily a source of pride, seemed out of place here. The sweatshirt had felt good on the cold plane, but now she was in Italy, where it was quite hot, even in the airport.

33

Taking it off would mean revealing the normally acceptable pink tank top she was wearing underneath. (Unfortunately, there had been a salad dressing incident when they hit an air pocket somewhere over the mid-Atlantic. She had cleaned herself up as best she could, but she was still just a little too ranch-dressingy for her own liking.)

Off it went, though. Maybe no one would notice.

Next to the cheese girl was a woman who wasn't blond at all. Her hair was red and cropped short in a perfect pixie cut. She wore a snug one-piece black shirtdress that showed off her bone structure and a string of African beads around her neck, with a fairly alarming miniature mask set in the middle. It glowered at Clio when the woman stood to greet her, as if warning her not to come any closer. Aside from that, there was one empty chair at the table with a blue messenger bag slung across the back of it. One more person was coming. This was the group.

"Clio," her dad began, "this is Dr. Julia Woodward of Cambridge University and her daughter, Elsa Åkerlund-Woodward. Julia is a professor of archeology."

Julia was the redhead. Elsa was the cheese goddess. And she had a different last name from her mother.

"Hello," Julia said politely.

"You're Clio!" Elsa said. "We heard so much about you!"

Julia's accent was crisp and English. Elsa's was sort of English, occasionally lapsing into something Clio couldn't quite place.

"Have you taken care of the ordering?" her dad asked Elsa.

"It's all sorted. I just got you a pizza, Clio. And a Coke. I thought that would be okay."

There was a niceness about this girl. Clio could tell that she'd really tried to pick something that Clio would like, even though she didn't know her yet.

"Pizza and Coke is great, thanks," Clio said.

"Elsa speaks Italian," her father said. "She handles the talking for us."

"I'm the translator," Elsa said with a smile. She had large, rounded teeth. Clio could tell that she'd never had braces because her teeth were just a little unevenly spaced, a few of them slightly crooked. But they were naturally nice and real. Unwhitened. Unfussed with. Dairy goddess teeth.

"We have everything we need," her dad said, looking at Julia. "Translator. Artist."

"We don't actually need an artist," Julia answered. "Not that we don't want to have one along."

There was something lurking at the back of this remark, something in the limp smile—something that told Clio that Julia hadn't been too excited when she heard Clio was coming along. She was grateful when her little glass bottle of Coke arrived. It was kind of warm, and the glass that came with it only had two ice cubes in it, but it was still liquid, and it gave her something to do. She reached for it.

"That's quite a tattoo," Elsa said.

Clio winced. She hadn't been paying attention. She was usually conscious of her tattoo and careful about how she first presented it to people. Everybody always made a big deal about it. Except for Ollie. He had simply admired it and moved on.

"Oh yeah," she said. "It's . . . bright. I know."

"It's really nice," Elsa said. "Is it new?"

"No. I've had it for a few years."

35

"A few years?" This was Julia. It was so obvious when one parent was judging another.

"There's a very interesting story behind that," Clio's dad said. "Clio was in a bit of an accide—oh. What's up?"

He was addressing someone right behind Clio.

"I had to stand out in the taxi lane to get wireless connection," said a male voice behind them. "We're all set to go. Everything will be waiting for us to load in at the dock."

A guy had appeared by the side of the table. He noticed Clio and stopped. Cold. Just stared at her. He had to have been expecting her, but her arrival seemed to startle him.

"This is Clio," her father explained. "Clio, this is Aidan Cross. He's Julia's assistant."

This was an interesting development. There was a guy in her father's gang. He wasn't massive, redwood-tall like Ollie. Compared to Ollie, no guy could ever really look tall again. He was just a few inches taller than Clio. All of his clothes were just a few sizes too large. His red polo shirt hung loose and free. His jeans were slightly too big at the waist and knees, and they spilled down over his ankles onto his Chuck Taylors, also red. He had matched his shirt and shoes, whether or not he meant to. His hair was light brown, and his haircut had either been incredibly expensive or done for free by some drunk friend with scissors and a misguided sense of his own talent. With the right styling products in it, it would have looked like one of those cutting-edge magazine cuts that go in about nine directions. But it didn't have any of those in it, so it traveled in its many directions without any support.

But none of those things were really striking about Aidan.

What *was* striking was his face. It wasn't exceptionally handsome. It wasn't warm and welcoming like Ollie's. It was just slightly oval, kind of bony and severe, and it looked to her like it required a bit of an effort to keep itself still—like it might do things without his knowledge or consent. His eyes were round, dark green, and extremely bright, almost hard at the center. Those eyes didn't miss a thing. She was sure of it.

Those eyes were taking in Clio now, and it put her on her guard.

"So . . ." he said, shifting his focus to her father. "We got the—"

"We'll talk about that later," her dad said quickly.

"Got the what?" Clio asked.

"Oh," her dad said, trying too hard to sound casual. "Just some things for the boat. Your mom told you about the boat, right? Just boat stuff."

Now that the introductions were over, the real awkwardness could begin. Julia's eyes lingered on the spot where the ranch dressing had been. Aidan's gaze landed on her tattoo.

The realization was settling in—they were all about to get on a plane and then a boat together. Clio watched as everyone looked around quickly, unsure of what to do next. There were varying levels of familiarity. She and her dad. Her dad and Martin. Her dad and Julia. Her dad was the common denominator in all of this, and that was some bad math.

A waiter came and started setting down plates. Most of them contained pasta or small pizzas. There was one exception. Elsa's plate was ringed with oysters still in their rough shells. The shells clinked daintily as they were set down.

"Eating raw shellfish is an act of insanity," Aidan said. "Especially in an *airport*."

"I guess I'm crazy," she said with a smile, offering an oyster to him.

"And I guess I just don't want neurotoxic poisoning," he said, putting up his hand against the offending oyster. "I'm weird like that."

"I'm still alive."

"For now," Aidan replied easily, his green eyes moving from Elsa to Clio. He raised an eyebrow.

"Oyster, Clio?" Elsa offered. "Clio looks like an oyster girl. Oysters are the food of love."

Out of the corner of her eye, Clio saw Julia flash her watch at her dad.

"Oh," her father cut in. "We're actually in kind of a hurry. Everybody eat fast."

Elsa and Aidan were still looking at Clio and the wobbly, faintly purplish oyster that Elsa was holding up.

"Take it in one go," Elsa said. "Drink it back. All of it. Try not to chew it."

It seemed to matter a lot to both of her onlookers whether or not she was going to eat that oyster. Impulsively, she reached over and glurped it back. Her instincts kicked in enough to yelp, *Chew!* But it was too late. The oyster was glooping down her throat. So she started to cough and choke as it slid.

"Oh . . ." Elsa said lightly. "You're choking. It's okay; it happens."

She pressed the bottle of warm Coke into Clio's hand. The soda calmed the reaction a bit and washed the oyster farther down, where it couldn't cause any more trouble. Clio quickly wiped at her watering eyes.

"You all right there?" Aidan asked, leaning back with his arms across his chest.

Clio nodded. It was too soon to speak. Her voice would have come out very hoarse and gaggy.

"Warned you," he said, smirking.

"But look! She's alive!" Elsa said, licking her fingers. "Isn't that *amazing*, Aidan?"

"It's the law of averages. One probably won't kill you. Probably."

But he was smiling just a little as he said it. Clio couldn't tell if she was invited to this quasi-flirt fest or if she was just a prop.

"I knew you were like me," Elsa said. "An oyster girl. I *knew* it. We'll get along."

There were a few minutes of concentrated pizza-eating after this bizarre interlude. It was good pizza. The crust was thin, and the cheese was smoky. There were large leaves of fresh, peppery basil on top. After eight hours on an airplane, during which she'd only had a greasy (and small) chicken casserole and a wilted salad (the cause of the ranch-dressing incident), this pizza was heaven. Clio had to stop herself from eating too fast and searing the inside of her mouth. She carefully sliced the pizza into tiny bites.

Aidan wasn't taking the same precautions. Clio looked up to find that he had sliced his into two halves, folded them, and eaten them in about five bites each, washing each one down with a swig of his Coke. The whole thing was over before Clio had even started into hers properly.

"You're the girl from the Dive! box," he said, pushing his plate away.

It had been a long time since Clio had been called the girl from the box, but she couldn't deny it. She'd been featured on the box of the board game *and* the spin-off video games.

"When I was twelve," she corrected him. "It's not me anymore."

There was an announcement in Italian. Elsa perked up.

"That's us," she said. "We have to go. They've already started boarding. How did we miss that first call?"

"Let's hit it!" Clio's father stood. He pulled out his wallet and took out a large handful of euro notes, dropping them on the table. "That should cover it."

They grabbed up their stuff quickly. Clio was the last to leave the table. As she walked off, the waiter came over and took the money. From the joyous look on his face, Clio could see that her father had overpaid by some ridiculous amount.

Some things never change, she thought.

Dangerous Contraptions

The thing that was standing ready to take them to Naples could hardly be called a plane; it was more like a flying minivan. Clio and her father's little gang, sitting in groups of two, took up about a third of the seats. Clio and Elsa sat together. Their seats were directly off one of the tiny wings. Instead of jet engines, there were propellers.

Clio knew from experience that tiny planes often made for bumpy, crazy rides and was about to say this when the propellers whizzed to life, filling the cabin with a low buzz and a slight shake. Elsa leaned down and looked out the window.

"Oh my God," she said. "What is this thing? How old is this plane?"

"I guess they couldn't use a big plane because it's such a short flight," Clio said. "We'll be there in half an hour."

"I don't really like to fly," Elsa said. "My mum tells me it's all in my mind, but I really hate it. I don't know if I can do this."

The look of fear in her eyes was real.

"I'll get you through it," Clio said, taking Elsa's bag, an elegant white circular thing that kind of looked like it might contain a large-brimmed hat, and shoving it into the microscopic overhead compartment. It didn't want to fit in there, but Clio finally managed it. Then there was no room left for her own backpack. Behind them, Aidan and Martin were stowing their own bags. Aidan just had a computer and a novel. A thick one. It looked like sci-fi. He was pretending not to listen to the conversation, but Clio saw his eyes flashing in their direction.

"Can I share?" she asked.

"Sharing is good," he said. "We should all share more."

"I meant, can I put my backpack in your bin?" she said, rolling her eyes.

"Well, I guess you could, but I don't know what to do with this parachute in here. That's weird. . . ."

Elsa spun around fearfully.

"Shut *up*, Aidan," she said, her voice getting more high-pitched and British but not sounding terribly angry. "Don't be such a prat."

He smiled. It was a slowly unfurling smile, revealing a wide expanse of thin lips. Clio hadn't noticed how wide his mouth was before. It was like he had a stash of reserve lip length for when he wanted to lay on one of these seriously self-satisfied grins.

Clio pulled out her sketchbook and shoved the bag into his arms. He put it in the bin and slammed it shut.

"Will you take the window?" Elsa asked. "There's no way I can watch."

"Sure."

Clio stepped over and sat down in the window seat.

"I've been on some bad flights," Clio said. "The trick is to get distracted."

"How?"

"Let's just talk. School. Where do you go to school?"

"I just left school myself on Thursday. I barely had time to get home before we were on our way here."

"You're in college?" Clio said.

"Public school," she replied.

Clio quickly did the mental conversion. In England public school actually meant boarding school. As the plane started puttering toward the runway, Clio kept Elsa talking with a constant series of questions. Elsa's school was private but not too fancy. Languages were her strong suit. Next year she would be taking five A-level exams. She had to play one sport as part of the school curriculum, so she played field hockey, but she didn't like it. She loved watching football (soccer, she clarified for Clio). She had a roommate named Jenny, whom everyone called Binkie. She was Elsa's opposite—very skinny, dark-haired, brilliant at maths, bad at dancing, good at football. Binkie had once drunk twelve pints of beer and two toffee vodkas on a dare and ended up in the infirmary.

Elsa delivered all of this information in one steady, breathless stream as they went past massive jets like the one Clio had just gotten off. Her own stomach flipped a little. This was a *very* small plane. Elsa tightened her seat belt until it couldn't give any more.

They were on the runway now. The propellers were going full speed.

43

"Can I hold your hand?" she asked.

"Sure," Clio said.

"It might be kind of hard. Oh God!"

The plane dragged itself forward. It didn't have the speed and thrust of a jet as it went down the runway, so the takeoff was unexpected. The plane suddenly seemed to jump into the sky, throwing itself higher and higher in graceless little hops.

Elsa started mumbling under her breath in a different language. It was too low to tell which one. Once they were in the air, it was a little hard to hear.

"You must already think I'm insane," Elsa said, squeezing the blood supply out of Clio's hand. "It's just planes. I'm not scared of anything else. At least not much. I took one of these planes in Sweden once. Going to see my dad. It was horrible."

"Your dad is Swedish?" Clio asked.

"Yes. I'm half and half."

"Is that what you were just speaking?"

"I pray in Swedish when I'm scared," she said. "I'm still scared."

"So keep talking."

"I have photos," Elsa said, carefully reaching for her purse under the seat. "Would you like to see?"

"Sure," Clio said.

The plane bounced a bit as Elsa was reaching, causing her to bump her head on the seat in front. She snatched up her purse and clutched it to her chest, closing her eyes. Once the plane grew stable again, Elsa peeled them open and pulled the purse away from her chest. She reached inside and removed a book. She shook it, and a clump of photos fell into her lap. She passed them to Clio.

Three of them featured the same view: a massive, very green playing field and, in the background, a large building that looked like a Gothic church, with a dozen or more spiky spires bursting out along the roof. Different people stood in front of this view, all in similar uniforms—white shirts, red ties, gray blazers. Everyone in the pictures was laughing or making faces. A few other photos had obviously been taken at parties in small dorm rooms. There were various hot and sweaty guys, just after a soccer game.

Elsa was in most of these pictures, usually at the center, looking curvy and happy. She wasn't wearing makeup in any of them, but her skin had that glow, her lips naturally pink, her smile huge. It was like Elsa rolled out of bed every morning and directly into some kind of hilarious team effort. There she was in the middle of a crew boat, laughing it up at the crack of dawn. Later that day, clinking oversized coffee mugs in a library. Nightcap, seven people on her bed, smiling even as they filled their heads with Latin or calculus or whatever it was.

The last picture was of a rabbit. Clio held it up.

"That's Alex," Elsa explained. "He's our house rabbit at school. He's sort of my baby. I named him after my boyfriend. Former boyfriend. I like being able to say, 'Back in your cage, Alex! Stop pooing on the floor, Alex!' Anyway, what about you? I've been talking all about me. What's that book?"

"Just one of my sketchbooks," Clio said.

"Can I see?"

Some people didn't like having other people look in their sketchbooks, but Clio had no problem with it. Of course, looking at it over Elsa's shoulder, she realized that it did make her look like a bit of a stalker. The same people and faces turned up again and again. Jackson, her best friend. The guy who ran the Turkish takeout truck. That guy Henry from trig. Her cat, Suki.

"Who's this?" Elsa asked, flipping to the eighth picture of Ollie in a row.

"Oh," Clio said. "That's Ollie. He's . . ."

What was he? A dream. A goal. The prize for surviving the summer. A missed opportunity. The future. The past. Some guy at an art store.

"He must be your boyfriend," Elsa said. "He's handsome."

Clio realized that she should correct this statement, but she couldn't. It sounded so nice. *Ollie, my boyfriend.*

Maybe it could have been true if she hadn't been dragged here. But maybes didn't mean anything. To have an actual something, you needed some kind of concrete proof. Like one date, or one kiss, or even the exchange of words that promised one date. She'd almost gotten a job where Ollie worked, which wasn't usually thought of as one of the signs of a budding romance. Still, he'd said he would remember her. Did that mean he was waiting for her? It had to.

The moment to deny had long passed and she still hadn't spoken. The plane dipped again, sending Elsa back into her peaceful place with closed eyes, mumbling in Swedish.

Clio peered out of the window to see a surreal sight. The landscape made a kind of sense, but the colors were all backward. The sky was the color of a ripe, late-summer peach. The clouds were a kind of faded ink blue. The Bay of Naples, which stretched before them, was a dusky lavender. In the distance, there was a huge formation coming out of the water. It looked like a camel that had submerged itself, leaving just its humps exposed. Clio knew what this was instantly: Mount Vesuvius, the volcano that ruled over the area, the same one that buried the city of Pompeii in ash and lava two thousand years before. It was still, she knew, very much active. It had been suspiciously quiet for some time and could very well wake up again soon.

Landing wasn't so good for Elsa. The plane dipped and peaked, tossed by the crosscurrent as it got closer to the ground. Clio had four deep purple finger marks on her arm by the time it was all over but also, she could tell, Elsa's lifelong friendship.

As Elsa got her bag out of the overhead bin, Clio looked through the gap in the seats to the people behind. Aidan was directly in her line of sight. He saw her looking and fixed her with a look of his own, smiling strangely. He stood up and leaned over their seats.

"Good flight?" he asked.

"It's over," Elsa said. She was still a little shaky but smiled. "Clio got me through it."

"I heard."

Clio looked back to see what her father was doing. He and Julia were leaning in to each other, talking closely, whispering.

What is this big secret? Clio thought.

In the next second, she would regret this question. The answer came in the form of her father ever so quickly putting his tongue somewhere in the vicinity of Julia's ear. Julia smiled and laughed softly.

Clio spun around, her heart pounding hard in her chest. She

felt a huge rush over her cheeks, every blood vessel in them flushed and full. There was a painful pulsing in her neck, and her hearing got tinny. It really felt for a moment like something *very bad* might happen to her head from all the pressure. She could hear Aidan making more pathetic jokes about his imaginary parachute to Elsa.

"You okay?" Elsa asked.

Clio stared at her helplessly. No longer frightened, Elsa had gone back to being the luminous dairy goddess, and Clio was just a confused girl in a small airplane seat, about to hyperventilate.

"Head rush," she managed.

She wasn't standing up and turning around until she was sure that her father and Julia were finished and out of her sight. Aidan leaned over from behind, lording down from over her shoulder. This blocked any view she might have had but also left her feeling very boxed in.

"Nice tattoo," he said, examining the zipper from above. "What do you keep in there? Change?"

This wasn't what she needed right now. And this was exactly the kind of thing that Ollie *wouldn't* say. Ollie wasn't a jackass. Ollie was perfection.

"A little souvenir from my victims," she said, getting up quickly. "Usually a severed finger."

Clio didn't have to turn around to know that he was giving her one of those raised-eyebrow, "whatever you say, strangely scary girl" looks. She stood up and reached as far into the overhead bin as she could, taking as long as possible to pull her backpack out of the otherwise empty space.

"See?" Elsa said, her British voice purring. "That's what you get when you don't behave, Mr. Cross. Now make way. We're getting off this death trap. This is *over*."

Clio was happy for Elsa, but she knew that her torment had only begun.

Mental Scarring and Jokes That Aren't Funny

As they walked out into the blinding Naples sun, Clio found herself clasping her own left ear. She couldn't stop. It was as if by covering it, she could stop the horrific ear-penetration image from getting into her head.

Things would never be the same now that she'd seen her father tonguing some strange woman's ear. Never. That was the kind of thing that wormed its way into your brain, nestled itself between the warm, gray folds, and *bred*.

"What's the matter, kiddo?" her father asked, coming up alongside her and removing the comforting hand shield. "Ears won't pop? Try swallowing."

Somehow *swallowing* wasn't the word she wanted to hear right now.

"I'm fine," she replied, walking ahead.

Their transport was a small, unmarked white van. The driver looked hot and bored and pulled at his damp shirt. He loaded their bags into the back while they all got in. The bench seats had cigarette burn holes. Clio found herself wedged between Elsa and Aidan in the backseat. Her father, Julia, and Martin sat in the front. Like most guys she knew, Aidan took up a bit more room, sitting with his legs farther apart, his computer between his ankles, pressing his left thigh up against her right in the process.

The van let out a belch of diesel exhaust and rattled as it was turned on. This was *not* followed by a burst of refreshing air-conditioning, as she had hoped it would be. The driver cranked up the radio, which was tuned to a call-in show that she couldn't understand. The noise and the heat canceled out any conversation before it even started. Aidan put in his earphones, and Elsa laid her head lightly against the back of the seat and closed her eyes.

The first stretch of highway passed by some dusty and run-down housing developments, lots of uninspired billboards for local restaurants, and the occasional overheated car. There was a lot of concrete and scrubby brush, interrupted occasionally by a perfectly square plot of green, vined plants or a small grove of trees. Then it was more concrete buildings covered in laundry, trucks, highways, exits, signs. She had never been to Italy, and she had been expecting a bit more than this. This couldn't be the place that people always raved about.

Stuck in her little hot box with two silent companions and a front-row seat to her father's date with Julia, Clio had little else to think about. She kept her eyes trained on the back of her father's cap, as if holding him in place with the intensity of her stare. There had *better* be no more ear canoodling. She decided

51

that if they tried anything at all, she would start screaming and flailing and claim there was a bee in the van.

One thing was clear: this was going to be the worst summer of her life. No one would be able to fault her for that when she went home and handed out the explanations. Trip to Italy? No sympathy. Going along on her dad's date? People would get on board with that. Maybe she could even call her mother and tell her the second they stopped, and her mother would be outraged and rescue her. Better yet, she'd call Ollie. He would understand everything.

Meanwhile, Aidan was moving his head ever so slightly to the music. A heavy beat pulsed out of his earphones, just audible over the wind and traffic noise coming through the half-open windows. Elsa was fast asleep and had slumped farther down; now she was leaning against Clio.

She hadn't felt like she was going far away on the plane because planes didn't give her that feeling. You can't really tell where you're going on a plane because you usually just see sky or clouds, and that never changes. If you can see the view, there's something about the height and perspective that makes it all seem like a joke. Just a ride. But being in a hot van with strangers on a long ride on actual Italian highway—that felt far. Ollie, her mother, Suki, Jackson . . . everyone faded from view.

She replayed the final moments with Ollie in her mind. She needed to hold the name tag. Clio pulled her bag up on her lap carefully, reaching into the pocket to where the pin was stashed. There was no way she was letting Aidan see her do this, because it was unquestionably odd. Elsa would get it. Aidan would mock her. This much was already obvious.

Ollie had given her the tag to keep, and he'd said he would remember. And she had said . . .

Wait a minute—she had fallen over herself to say that she *wasn't* coming back. It occurred to Clio in one horrible flash that in her attempt to be smooth, she'd actually told Ollie that she wouldn't be back. Why had she said that? Why hadn't she realized it up until now, in a *van* in *Italy*?

She fumbled around inside her bag, found her cell phone, and switched it on. No signal at all. And even if she had gotten one, making a call home would probably cost a hundred dollars a minute or something horrible. It was still worth it, but it would hurt.

They turned off the highway, and it immediately became shadier and greener. Tree branches scraped the roof of the van. They entered a town with narrow roads full of Vespa scooters and tiny-but-determined little businesses housed in what were probably once magnificent buildings. Lots of long, shuttered windows, verandas, and peeling paint. This was more like it. Europe decayed so well.

As they turned the corner around a laundry, the van coughed and died. This jolted them all. Aidan took out his earphones.

"Hey!" her dad turned around and said. "Don't mind pushing, do you, kiddo?"

"Can you stop it with the *kiddo*?" Clio said. "I have a name. It's kind of weird, but you gave it to me. Why don't you use it?"

He smiled, though a bit more weakly than his usual, and turned around. Another look from Julia, with a half-turned head. *So this is your daughter*, it seemed to say. *What a brat*.

Clio bit her lower lip. Her dad made her snappy. He brought

out the worst in her. She had to try to hold this in. There were too many strangers here and not nearly enough space. Aidan had replaced his earphones, but she knew he'd heard her little outburst. Great, now *she* seemed like the annoying one.

She took a deep breath and looked up at the ceiling of the van. The upholstery there was peeling away and sagging. It reminded her of a stormy sky. She tried to file the color and the undulating way the cloth draped in her mind, in one of the many files she kept for future drawings. It was a good distraction.

The driver did some fancy gear-shifting and tried the ignition a few times. The van made a low, painful noise and continued its miserable effort.

The road did nothing but snake. It snaked through towns, along cliff edges, down hills. They drove into a tunnel cut through a mountain, and when they emerged, outside, all was blue. There was nothing to the right of the van but air, followed by a sharp drop down the side of a cliff to the sparkling sea. The coast was fully visible, stretching in front of them in a great wall of jagged rock. The land itself was thick with trees. On the horizon, there were occasional umbrella pines—strange, cartoon-like trees that were all trunk until they exploded into wide awnings of green. They stood massive and alone on the edges of the cliffs, in sharp relief against the sky. Everywhere, the water was punctuated with boats. Tiny fishing boats, like periods. Great, hulking cruise ships, like exclamation points.

This view brought the occupants of the van to life. They all looked out as they made their way along the edge of the coastline cliffs, constantly scraping low-hanging trees, occasionally getting stuck behind a massive tour bus that looked too big for the road. They passed through three or four more towns, each one a little bigger and prettier than the last, but none were too huge.

Finally, they came to a large intersection that was clearly *somewhere*. The buildings didn't peel here—they were big, in bold colors, with white detailing. There were grand cafés with crowds sitting outside. There were banks and shops and masses of tourists enjoying the late afternoon. The van turned down a road that had been cut into a split in the cliff. It folded in on itself in this crevice until it reached the bottom. They stopped at the water level, near a utilitarian ferry port. The town was a hundred feet above them now, its hotels built right to the very edge of the rock, adding to the height of the cliff. The water before them was peaceful. Big restaurants with huge signs welcoming tourists sat on pylons over the water.

"This is Sorrento," her dad said. "We've arrived!"

The van died as soon as it heard those words.

"Like Pheidippides," her father said, looking at Julia.

"Like what?" Clio asked, sliding out of the van.

"The first person to run the marathon," he said. "He ran from the city of Marathon to Athens to report the outcome of a battle. He ran the whole stretch, gave the message, and died. True story!"

He looked to Julia again. Obviously, now that he was dating a professor of archeology, he was going to be doing this kind of thing a lot. Wonderful. Clio looked to Martin, who smiled and shook his head.

"Actually," Julia replied, stretching her arms above her head, "that's probably a myth. There's no proof of it."

She said it plainly, not cuttingly. But still, in her prim English accent, it made her father seem dim and overeager.

"I need to get in touch with home," Clio said to her dad. "I need to tell Mom I got here safe. I need a phone or a computer."

This was true. This could not be denied. But she also had to fix this Ollie thing, *now*.

"In a little while," he said.

"It's important," Clio said. "I have to call soon."

"Relax, kid . . . er, Clio." He extended a hand to help Elsa get out of the van last, sleepy and slow. "Something to see first."

"Is this it?" Elsa asked Clio. "I've been absolutely out. I didn't realize how knackered I was."

"I think so," Clio said. "But I don't know what *it* is."

"Leave your bags, everyone!" her dad said. "Follow me!"

"I guess *it* is that way," Clio said.

"Can you tell the driver that we'll need at least an hour to unload?" he asked Elsa. "I'll pay him for it."

Elsa communicated this in Italian, and the offer was accepted.

Her father led them down a concrete path until it ended abruptly and four steps took them down to the dark-sanded beach. Clio looked over at the cliff face next to them, but couldn't quite understand what she was seeing. It was like the world's most extraordinary layer cake.

At the sand level, built entirely into the cliff, was a three-story building with a grapefruit-yellow front. The paint was worn to white in places, but the long windows were framed in bold and spotless red. If it had been up on a street, the building would have looked like an old hotel, but it actually had a large banner on the front announcing in English that it was a dive shop. In the space above it, where a normal building would have air and sky, was the middle of an entirely different building, again built flat into the cliff. This one looked like an ancient fortress of gray brick, complete with tiny openings for archers to shoot from. The structure was interrupted again near the top of the cliff, turning into a true and unmistakable grand hotel, also yellow, with pristine white archways that faced out to the sea and dripping greenery along the edge.

Clio wanted to draw it immediately, if only to understand it. She could only admire the insanity of the people who made such a thing—or three things. But her dad had started doing a little tap dance on the sand.

"Ladies and gentlemen," he said, swinging his arms open. "Welcome to your new home for the summer!"

There was some looking around at the water, the cliff, the Vespas parked along the walkway.

"You're not talking about this, are you?" Aidan said, his voice thick with dismay.

Sitting on the sand in front of them, directly behind her father, was a fifty-foot-long decaying wooden boat. It was moored in place on a dangerous-looking diagonal with metal barrels and lumber shoved under it, just about holding it upright. About a third of it was covered with a tarp, but the remaining two-thirds consisted mainly of smashed-out windows and rot.

"I realize it needs a little work," he father said. "But the potential!"

"This is our boat?" Julia asked. "This isn't going to . . ."

Elsa's eyes had gone wide. For once, strangers knew what Clio had been feeling all her life. That was a nice realization, but it didn't take away from the wreck of reality in front of her.

"Ben," Martin began. "I don't think this is going to work."

"That's kind of an understatement," Aidan said.

Her father looked at them in genuine confusion.

"Really?" he asked. "I got such a good deal on it."

"I imagine you did," Julia said.

Clio fixed her father with a deadly stare.

"With a little work," he said, "it'll be great. It's not nearly as bad as it looks."

Silence from the group. Martin let out a polite cough.

"Oh!" Her dad laughed, looking over his shoulder. "I'm sorry. I was facing the wrong way. There's our boat. Right there, on the end."

They rotated as one toward the gently lapping water.

Before them, no more than fifteen feet out—swimming distance, maybe even walking distance—was a row of five fabulous boats. At the very end of the row was the biggest and baddest of them all, definitely a yacht. Something about this boat screamed, "I am a very popular model in the world's oil-bearing regions. I cost more than your soul!"

"Welcome to the *Sea Butterfly*, everyone," he said, smiling one of the broadest, scariest smiles Clio had ever seen.

The Sea Butterfly

It was clear that her father had prepared that joke well in advance and was reveling in its perfect execution.

"You should have seen your faces," he said.

No one was answering. They were still taking in the white yachty magnificence before them. It was at least eighty feet long, with two visible levels, plus a tinted wraparound glass wheelhouse and more antennas coming off it than a skyscraper.

"How do we get there?" Elsa finally managed.

"Using this."

Clio's father pulled off his shoes and walked a few paces out in the water, which only came to mid-thigh. He grabbed an orange raft with a tiny motor on it that was tied to a post in the water. "We'll have to make a few trips to get everything on."

He dragged the raft over to the nearby dock, waving the others in that direction.

"Clio!" he said. "You come first."

He helped her down into the little raft, which sagged under their weight. After two tugs on the pull cord, the motor putt-putted to life and they made the very short trip to the *Sea Butterfly*, approaching it from the back.

"You bought a yacht," Clio said to him.

"To be fair, *yacht* technically means a lot of things."

"It means this. You bought a yacht. We can't afford a yacht. Dad, we can't even afford to get the roof repaired."

"Funny story behind this," her father said, smiling that crazy smile at the *Sea Butterfly* as it bobbed in the water like a giant bleached tooth. "I was going to just rent a boat. But then I met this woman in London who was getting a divorce. Very rich. This boat was her husband's plaything, so she took great pleasure in selling it to me at a fraction of the cost. I'll sell it off when we're done and make a killing. This girl is going to pay for herself *ten times over*."

"*Sea Butterfly?*" Clio said. "That's kind of a weird name."

"It's better than the old one," her dad said, bringing the raft up to the platform. "It used to be called the *Foxy Lady*. The guy who owned it was named Fox."

"That's a really gross name," Clio said.

"I know. This one is much better. Anyway, here we go."

He tied the raft to the back platform of the boat and held it steady. Clio scrabbled onto the back platform, a slippery sheet of fiberglass covered in water. She walked up the three steps to the deck proper.

"Okay," he said. "Stay right here. I want everyone to take the tour at the same time."

She watched as he brought the others over, two at a time. It only took a few minutes. Before long, they were all standing on the massive back platform of the boat. The first stop was the Jacuzzi, which had a cover that slid back at the touch of a button.

"This was broken," he said. "So I had it sealed up. We can fill it with water or whatever we need when we . . . We could fill it with water and fish and have our own tank to get fresh seafood from! Pretty great, huh?"

Nearby were some sliding glass doors, part of what was essentially an all-glass wall. He opened the doors and they passed through. Clio couldn't see anything yet, but the carpet told all. Whatever she was standing on was so thick and soft it felt like she was effortlessly balancing herself on a sponge bed on the bottom of the ocean.

"The lights are complicated," her dad was saying, fumbling with something on the wall. "Oh. Here we go."

Carefully focused lights lit up in a dozen strategic points all over the ceiling, revealing a long, elegant living and dining room. Everything seemed to be made of cream-colored leather. The spongy carpet was honey-colored and extended in all directions. The air-conditioning made that gentle noise kittens make when they sleep.

"Living room," her dad said, holding out his hands toward the sofas and the plasma TV. "Over there, dining room."

"This is amazing," Elsa said.

Julia stepped closer to Clio's dad, not quite hooking her arm through his but getting close enough to show her approval.

"We can all come together in here," he went on. "After a hard day at sea. The galley—kitchen—is through here."

61

Her father led them to a full kitchen with sleek silver-and-black built-in appliances. Half the Williams-Sonoma catalog was stuffed in there. Clio picked up an icing tube that sat on the marble counter.

"For all of those fancy pastries we like to make?" she asked.

"It all came with the boat," her father said quickly. "All of it. You haven't even seen half the place. Come on."

Just past the kitchen was a tight circular staircase extending both up and down. They went down first, ending up in a surprisingly long hallway. The walls were made of shiny, violin-colored wood and there was low-key lighting running along the floor, like in movie theaters. Along this hallway were several doors. Her father opened the door to most of them using a single master key, revealing four snug bedrooms. Clio felt a little too much emphasis was put on showing her that Julia had her own room. He passed by a few doors and proceeded to the end of the hall.

"What are in those?" Clio asked.

"Oh, just supplies and stuff. Speaking of . . . it's starting to get dark, and our loading hour will be up soon. You guys should probably go get your things from the van; then I can show you the rest."

They went back up the stairs, and Martin, Elsa, Aidan, and Julia went back to the raft to transport themselves to the dock. Clio's father watched them through the glass doors, then leaned over to Clio conspiratorially.

"I wanted to show you this in private," he said. "It's the best part."

"Is it the part with the phone or the computer?" she asked.

"Nope. It's your room. Upstairs!"

They went back to the circular stairs and walked up. They

ended up in a very small vestibule with a highly slanted, half-windowed wall that looked out over the back of the boat, the black water, and the moon. Behind them there was one honey-colored door leading to the only room on this level of the boat.

"Go on in," he said quietly.

The room behind that door was about three times the size of the rooms downstairs. The carpet was thicker here, a plush, fuzzy lawn, softer than slippers. Her father flipped a switch, and a dozen unseen lights came to life, bathing the room in a soft, almost rosy light. The walls were wallpapered in a champagne color, in a pattern embossed in tiny circles. It was as if the room was very impressed with itself and going *oooooh*, in a slightly drunk kind of way.

"This is evening lighting," he said. "There's also . . ."

Extremely bright, yellowish light, bright as day, then half of that, then a few pinpoint lights illuminating various corners of the room. They zeroed in on two sleek dressing tables that had been built into the walls, one on the window side and one opposite. The bed was wide. Its padded, semicircular head-board was firmly attached to the wall, and the base seemed to be solidly joined to whatever was underneath the coffee-colored carpet. It wasn't going anywhere, no matter what this boat did.

"The best part is through that door," he said with a proud grin.

There was a wood veneer door on the side—the super-shiny and extra-swirly wood she had never seen outside of a car dashboard. The door slid back into a groove in the wall, revealing a not-huge bathroom, but still one much larger than a boat bathroom was ever likely to be. It had two sinks, with gleaming brass fixtures that emptied into perfectly scooped-out basins. There was a wall-length mirror surrounded by round bulbs, dressing-room style—so bright that it caused Clio to step back in alarm as her reflection blasted at her. On the wall there was a panel of controls—fans, a dimmer, volume control for an unseen sound system. The gleaming, ladder-like heated towel rack was large enough to accommodate the thickest towels available. The centerpiece of the bathroom was a bean-shaped tub with a dozen or two gold jets around its side and base. It was large enough for two people and encased in folding glass panels. There was a slight bulge on the side, presumably to give visitors a place to sit or a place to set the wine bucket. A gold-colored, wide-mouthed showerhead extended straight down from the ceiling, like some heavenly trumpet poking into the scene to announce that this . . . this was the bathroom spoken of in the beginning, and yea, it was good.

"This is for me?" she asked. "This room?"

"I know you came a long way to see me," he said. "I know what you think. I wanted you to be happy."

This was just weird. It was a nice thought, being given the nicest room on the boat and the shiniest of shiny boat bathrooms. But it was still a boat far, far from home, a boat that he could never have afforded. Clio felt her head get fuzzy and unfocused. It had been a very long day—her night had disappeared sometime during the flight and the time changes. And there was no phone or computer in this room.

"What do you think of the *Butterfly*?" he asked. "She's named after you, after all."

"What?"

"Clio," he said authoritatively, "is the name of a family of sea butterflies. Sea butterflies are beautiful, colorful creatures."

"I thought I was a muse," she said. "The history muse."

"You're *also* a sea butterfly."

"Which is what?" she asked.

He bounced at the knees a little and looked a little frustrated. She knew she wasn't giving him what he wanted—daughterly praise about his toy—and it was starting to irritate him. That's what he had expected. She could see it clearly. He had thought that the second she saw his yacht, everything would be good between them.

But Clio wasn't biting. She walked over and sat on the bed, bouncing on it a few times. Like the carpet, it was sproingy in an expensive way.

"I'm kind of tired," she said. "And how do I call home? Where's the computer? Aidan had one. Is there another?"

Now he looked annoyed. He walked around the edge of the room, touching the tiny round light fixtures in the ceiling.

"We need to get stuff on board," he said. "I'll get you a phone. We need to talk anyway. Get yourself settled and meet me on the dock in twenty minutes. I'll bring over your suitcase."

When he was gone, Clio flopped backward, letting the deep down comforter envelop her. She closed her eyes. Her eyelids ached for some reason. This bed was nice, and if she just kept her eyes closed, she would fall into a deep sleep and none of this would bother her.

She forced her eyes open and pulled herself up off the bed, out of the door, and back down the narrow stairs. There was a

65

lot of activity on the back deck, with things being passed up. She retrieved her suitcase from the thick carpet of the living room and dragged it along. The spiral staircase was really only wide enough to allow one person, and not even that large a person, to pass. It was also quite steep. She had to prop her bag in front of her, hoisting it step by step, adjusting it each time the stairs turned. After a few steps, she realized she couldn't let go of the bag for a moment or it would fall on her.

Five minutes later, she was still only halfway up and swearing not so lightly under her breath, when she had the feeling that someone was watching her.

Aidan was leaning in the galley doorway, holding a large plastic file box.

"You seem to be having a little trouble," he said, not making much of an effort to conceal a smile. Once again, she was struck by his bright eyes.

"No," she said. "It's going really well."

"Want a hand?"

"I can manage it."

"Your dad asked me to tell you you're supposed to meet him outside."

"Can you tell him I'm trapped?"

"So, it's *not* going well?" he said. "That's weird, because you *seemed* to have this under control. But I can understand if you're not used to carrying your own bags."

"I . . ." Another push. Unsuccessful. ". . . am used . . . to carrying my own stuff."

"Obviously. You know, it might help if you turned it the other way. But I'm just saying . . ."

Clio looked at the position of the bag. He was right. If she could wriggle it loose and flip it, it would move. It was simple and obvious. So simple and obvious that she couldn't just flip it in front of him and give him the satisfaction.

"You okay?" he asked.

"Great," she said. "Just taking a breather."

"Me too. It was a long walk from the deck."

He knew what she was up to, and he was waiting and watching.

"So," he said. "Boats, huh? You must like boats."

"Not really," she said.

"But you made a boat game. Have you guys owned this boat for a while? Nice boat. Very fancy."

"It's new," Clio said, her annoyance coming through. "Very new."

"Is this bigger or smaller than your last boat?"

Clio could take it no more. She flipped the bag. His smile grew broader.

It took her several more minutes to get the suitcase up and, with one final shove, to throw it into the vestibule in front of the door. Clio let her suitcase drop onto the thickly carpeted floor. It barely made a noise.

When she got back on deck, Aidan was picking up a computer monitor that must have just come off the raft. There were a few computer bits there—a plastic box full of wires and connectors, a silver case that looked like it contained equipment of some kind. Martin was on the floating platform, passing scuba gear to Julia. There was a lot more than they would need for a few casual dives.

"So," she said to Aidan, "what *exactly* is all of this for?"

He tottered a bit as he tried to manage both the monitor and the box.

"Don't ask me," he said. "I'm just the help."

Out of the corner of her eye, she saw Julia and Martin looking at her, then turning back to the tanks and bags. There was a stiffness in Martin's jaw and a fixed expression on Julia's bony face. Martin was normally a talkative guy, so this silence was odd.

Her dad was coming up on the raft with Elsa and her bags.

"Come on," he called to Clio as he pulled up. "Get in. Let's go up to town."

Clio stopped to help Elsa up into the boat. Martin picked up her white bag and hoisted it over the back wall. Clio stepped down into the raft. It was a lot harder to get into than to get out of. It was squishy and it kept bumping away from the boat, plus there was nothing to hold on to. Her dad didn't seem to notice that she almost tumbled right over the side as she stepped in. It was Martin who reached over and steadied her.

"We're going to a phone?" she asked.

"Sure," her dad said, keeping his eye on the dock. "And we'll get a gelato. There's a great place up there."

He said this a bit more loudly than was necessary. It sounded like it was for someone's benefit.

"Dad," she said as they puttered away from the *Sea Butterfly*. "What *is* this?"

"Let's go up to town," he said again. "We'll get an ice cream, and we'll have a little chat."

There was only one little chat Clio wanted to have at this point, and it wasn't with her dad over ice cream. She had to be careful when she reached Ollie. She couldn't let her desperation make her sound crazy.

Then a new, positive thought came into her mind as she gripped the side of the raft. Maybe this little break in their as-yet-not-existent relationship had helped her. Maybe she had pushed it forward faster by making Ollie miss her. Maybe he was missing her right now. Distance was supposed to make the heart grow fonder—not that there was a lot you could do once this happpened. Because distance also makes it impossible to see the person you like.

Clio shook her head hard and looked up at the cliff. Too many thoughts bouncing around in her head. Now she just had to concentrate and get up the cliff, without (if it was possible) wanting to push her dad off it.

Just one thing at a time.

The Sea Rules

The town was definitely *up*. To get there, Clio and her father had to take an endless set of pedestrian steps cut into the stone. The climb was fairly serious and took their breath away. This worked well, as it prevented them from having much of a conversation until they reached the top.

They emerged on a busy square that fed into the main street. Every shop was open and bright. Clio scanned the signs for any that advertised computer access, but none did. This street was about shopping and eating, not getting in touch with would-be boyfriends over e-mail. She started to panic.

Just a few paces into the road, her dad stopped in front of a slender storefront with a large sculpture of an ice cream cone in front of it. The front of the store was open, revealing a long case full of astonishing colors.

"They have hundreds of flavors," he said. "Best in town."

He was smiling and still trying to impress, but his demeanor had gotten a little distant. Whatever this talk was going to be about, he thought ice cream would buffer the impact. Her father would never get that she wasn't little anymore and that ice cream wouldn't fix everything. Not that it had worked then either.

Still, Clio couldn't help but be entranced by the variety. She had a weakness for brightly colored desserts and exotic flavors. She surveyed the offerings for five minutes until deciding to go for a cone full of jasmine gelato, just because it sounded fragrant and strange. Her father annoyed the busy woman behind the counter for a few moments by insisting that she surprise him. She either didn't understand the English or she didn't want some idiot tourist to make her pick something only to have him say he didn't like it. Or she just had better things to do than choose other people's flavors for them. He persisted in his loud, cheerful way. He often thought that other people were having fun with him even though they *clearly* were not.

Clio decided to take matters into her own hands.

"This one," she said, stepping forward and pointing to the metal tray that contained a light yellow ice cream with a picture of a bee on the sign. "He'll have a medium. In a cone."

The woman looked grateful.

"What is that?" he asked as he accepted his ice cream. "Honey?"

"Do you even care?" Clio asked. "You asked her to pick it for you."

"No," he said. "I guess not. Let's walk and talk. There are some things you need to know."

"Is this the quiet moment you've chosen to tell me about this Julia person?" Clio asked. It was easier to do this on her terms instead of waiting for him to get around to it, building up to it with a long, heart-stoppingly awkward conversation about how adults sometimes had feelings about other adults. She had absolutely no doubt in her mind that he would present this as if she were twelve.

He stopped and gazed at her. He looked strangely young in the warm light of the street with his curly hair, his little hat, and his ice cream cone. It was disquieting.

"How did you know?" he asked. "Why am I even asking? You always know things."

"Yeah," she said. "I have magical powers."

"Is there something wrong with your ear?"

Clio removed her hand, which she had automatically clapped over her ear again.

"I know this is weird for you," he said. "If it bothers you, you know you can come and talk to me about it."

He definitely didn't sound like he wanted to talk about it. The words came out stiffly, like they were being read off a page by an inexperienced actor.

"What's there to talk about?" Clio said. "You're allowed. You don't live with us anymore. You left. It's all legal. You can do what you want."

"Clio, I don't know if your mother is—"

"And I'm not going to tell you," Clio cut him off. "It's fine. I just don't want to know the gory details of your dating life, okay? Is that too much to ask?"

Instead of laying into a complicated defense of ear love, her father simply nodded. They walked a few paces in silence. He reached into his pocket and produced a small, clip-on orange walkie-talkie. He passed this to her, then continued walking.

"This is your com," he said. "Everyone on board will carry one, and everyone has a number. You're number five. Always identify yourself by your number. There's a number list on the back."

Clio flipped the com over. There, stuck to the back, was a small sticker with the following list printed in an extremely tiny font:

Ben Ford: 1
Martin Young: 2
Julia Woodward: 3
Aidan Cross: 4
Clio Ford: 5
Elsa Åkerlund-Woodward: 6

"What are we doing that we need these?" she asked.

They parted temporarily to let a bicycle pass between them.

"Some archeological work," he said.

"So why the spooky secret-secret?" she asked.

"It's just a precaution," he said.

"A precaution against *what*?"

"Clio, all I'm asking you to do is take a com, use a number, and not to give out too much personal information. We have a nice boat with expensive things on it. That's all. This is a perfectly common safety procedure."

Clio seriously doubted this. Her dad always had to take things just the one step too far, to make a game out of everything.

"So why can't I just say, 'This is Clio, and I see a giant squid attacking the boat. Come quickly.' What's wrong with that? What's with the number? Do you just want to be called Number One, like they used to do on *Star Trek*?"

"The numbers are easier to understand."

"Not if I have to flip it over and see who Number Four is," she said.

"You'll learn the numbers."

"But *why?*" she said. "That's my question. I can't walk around all summer calling myself Number Five. 'Number Five got some sunburn today.' 'Number Five really liked that book you gave her.' It's stupid."

"Clio," he said, clearly running out of patience, "just follow the rules of the boat. Now, second thing you need to know. Your job. You are the official chef."

"The *what?*"

"You love to cook," he said.

"No, I don't," she said. "I'm the queen of takeout."

Her father turned on his heel and started back in the same direction that they'd just come.

"You're good at it," he said. "You always were. Remember that soup you always used to make, the one with the little meatballs? That was great! And the cooking class in Japan?"

"Just because I *can* do it doesn't mean I *like* to do it," she said. "I haven't made the meatball soup since I was ten. And the cooking class was one day. I learned how to cut a little faster. That's all."

"Everybody has to do something. Running the boat, setting the course, running the equipment . . . someone has to do it all. The galley is *your* domain. I'm giving that completely to you."

"What's Elsa's job?" she asked.

"Elsa is our translator."

"What is she going to translate?" she asked. "We all speak English."

"Look," he said. "Elsa is not my daughter. I can't tell her what to do."

"This is your way of telling me that Elsa has no job," said Clio. "Isn't it?"

"One last thing," he said. "I realize that you're . . . that age. And that you're going to be in close quarters with . . . a guy. But I just need you to know, *that* can't happen, okay?"

"I guess those rules don't apply to you, huh?" she said.

"That's different," he mumbled. "Clio, we're adults, and—"

"Did it ever occur to you that maybe I already have someone?" Clio went on. "And maybe I had to leave him behind to come out to this pirate-dance camp or whatever it is we're doing on the boat? Did you ever think of that?"

"Do you?" he fumbled. "I mean, your mother didn't say."

"Did you ask?"

"I figured she would mention—"

"No. Did you ask *me*? Have you shown any interest in what was going on in my life when you dragged me away from home? Do you even know who I *am* anymore?"

"Well," he said. "Were you . . . seeing someone?"

"Whatever," Clio said, having no idea how to answer the question. "I mean, if I'm lucky, he'll still be there when I get back. But that's not the point."

This seemed to satisfy her father. The conversational arrow had whizzed by his head. The actual point had missed him entirely. As usual.

"Of course he will!" he said. "You just need to know, this is not a party cruise. This is a working vacation. You have to take it seriously. You have a job. So, no drinking, no fooling around. And the bedrooms are off-limits. You don't go into Aidan's room, and he doesn't come up to yours. That's the bottom line."

"Whatever you say," she said. "I'll make sure to report myself if I'm ever having a good time. And I guess all the other usual things are out—dancing, playing cards, wearing red, smiling."

"You know what I mean," he said.

"No," she answered. "I really, really don't."

They both stopped speaking and looked away from each other, walking until they reached the point where they had started, the gap in the cliff, the twisting steps down to the sea.

"What about my e-mail?" she asked. "Or my phone call? Even people in prison get one phone call." The entire time they'd been walking, she'd been looking for a sign for an Internet café but hadn't seen one. There had to be a public phone somewhere.

"I already sent your mom a text saying that you got here safely when your plane landed in Rome. There's supposed to be a storm during the night. We have to get back and make sure everything is secure. We'll figure out your phone call when we get back."

He pointed to a heavy cloud lingering over the bay. It was only a few miles away, from the looks of it, lurking around the volcano. It had a lightning storm contained within it and silently cracked pencil-thin bolts at itself.

Clio had never seen such a clear omen of trouble in all her life. But her father was right—they wouldn't have much time to get back before it hit. Ollie would have to wait. Again.

The Champagne Suite

When she got back to the boat and opened the door to her bedroom, she found a strange sight. Elsa was standing at one of the mirrors, carefully tucking the pictures alongside the frame. Her suitcase was open on the floor, and clothes had spilled out of it in all directions.

"Hi," Clio said. "This, um . . . this is my . . ."

"I'm guessing your dad didn't tell you," Elsa said.

"Tell me what?"

"That we're sharing this room," she answered. "And yes, that means the one bed."

Clio slumped against the doorframe.

"He neglected to mention that," she said.

"Apparently the bed math was difficult," Elsa said. "It was assumed that we wouldn't mind sharing. Which I don't. It *is* a boat. Space is tight. And I'm used to sharing small quarters."

"I don't care either," Clio said automatically. "It's fine."

They were frozen in their politeness for a moment. Clio looked around. Utter chaos had already developed on Elsa's side of the room. There was a pile of thongs on the chair. The coffee-colored carpet was all but completely covered. Her clothes weren't covered in paint. They were short, bright, simple, happy. They were the clothes of a body-comfortable dairy goddess.

"I'm a bit messy," Elsa said. "Useless at cleaning. I'll try my best to keep it under control."

"No, no," Clio said. "It's all good."

This was just one more blow on an endless day of blows, and she had no fight left in her. She was going to have to start coping *now*. She took a deep breath, then popped open her suitcase and looked at her own clothes. Without even realizing it, she had packed standard artist issue. There were a half-dozen vintage T-shirts that she had cut apart and resewn herself, turning them into tank tops or lace-ups. A massive stack of pajama bottoms, her favorite summer item—all oversized and all loudly patterned with things like polka dots and skulls and crossbones. All of her jeans had paint on them. All of them. She had one skirt.

They each unpacked for a few minutes, Elsa randomly stuffing handfuls of little lacy things in the dresser drawers, piling clothes into the wardrobe. Clio was more methodical—stacking and folding, figuring out where things should go.

Elsa suddenly flopped in front of her on the bed.

"All right," she admitted with a laugh. "It's a bit awful. Even if it is the *nice* room. Let's just both say it. We'll feel better. This is *rubbish!*"

"It sucks," Clio said, her face breaking into a smile. And at that moment, she didn't even mean it. Elsa's demeanor lifted her spirits.

"I'm sorry if I've been a bit tetchy today," Elsa said "I've been in a mood for a while, and I wasn't very happy about this trip. I just wanted to apologize."

Clio couldn't hide the look of confusion she felt spreading over her face. Why was *Elsa* apologizing for being weird? She wondered if she had been acting so badly that Elsa was apologizing as a way of getting Clio to apologize.

No. That was *way* too convoluted and insane. Clearly, the jet lag was settling down on her brain.

"You haven't been," Clio said.

"I have," Elsa insisted, getting up off the bed and rummaging through her bag. "But I plan on making up for it. Here. I picked this up in the airport in Rome."

She pulled two bottles out of a plastic airport shopping bag.

"It's just a cheap sparkling wine," she said. "But we'll say it's champagne. Close enough. And it's warm. Let's chill it and drink it."

Clio's drinking experience consisted mostly of one very angry period after her parents' separation when she systematically downed everything in the house over a matter of weeks. No one noticed until one night she went a little too far and drank almost an entire bottle of pre-mixed margarita, warm, right out of the bottle, over the course of one afternoon. The vomiting that ensued had lasted for a day. Everyone had overreacted about it, but it *had* pretty much cured her of the drinking bug. It had never been an issue since.

But now seemed a good time to reconsider the option. It was

such a beautiful opportunity to flout her father's new command. And she was in Italy, after all.

"I'll go get the glasses and ice," she said.

Clio's dad was floating around in the living room. She dipped into the galley. There were heavy wineglasses in the cabinet, but Clio grabbed two chunky mugs instead. She found a plug-in teakettle shoved into the corner of the counter. That would work for the ice. She banged around, switching on the faucet in the dark, making it sound like she was actually using the kettle. Her father swung his head around the doorway.

"We could use a hand bringing in the food," he said.

"Elsa needs a cup of tea," Clio answered, making as serious a face as she could, pointing at the kettle. "She has cramps."

"Oh," he said quickly. "Okay. You do that. I'll get Aidan to give us a hand."

The one good thing about getting your period: it was dad conversation kryptonite. Clio smiled, though she wondered if she hadn't used that one too soon. She stuffed the kettle full of ice cubes and took it upstairs with the mugs.

They plugged the drain in one of the magnificent bathroom sinks and poured in the ice.

"Well done," Elsa said, nestling the bottles into the cold bath. "We'll leave that for a few minutes."

Clio sat down on the wide edge of the tub.

"Why did you think you were acting strange?" she asked.

"Oh," Elsa said, "there's no question. I've been a bit mental recently. And I wasn't too happy about this trip either. I didn't get much notice."

80

"Neither did I," Clio said.

"I imagine not. Did you even know about . . ."

Elsa waved her hand toward the floor.

"My dad?" Clio asked. "And your mom?"

"Right."

"No," Clio said. "That was something else he forgot to mention."

"Were your parents married?" Elsa asked sympathetically.

Clio nodded.

"How long ago did they split up?"

"A little over two years ago."

"The dating," Elsa said. "You'll get used to it. I promise. My mum's never been married, but she was with my dad for a while when I was little. He was on the board of the bank that gave her the grant to do most of the work for her doctorate. She was researching a crazy guy from hundreds of years ago who thought Atlantis was in Sweden. And got the grant, the degree, and me. Then she left. I really missed him for a while, but you do get used to it."

Elsa smiled and swished the bottle around. Clio didn't want to tell her that having your married parents, your *family*, blow apart wasn't quite the same thing as what Elsa was describing. But then, what did she know? Maybe losing your dad when you were little was even worse.

"The reason I bought this champagne," Elsa went on, still rotating the bottle slowly, "was because I was angry, and I wanted to celebrate."

"Celebrate what?"

"I'll show you," she said. "Come here."

She waved Clio out of the bathroom and over to the mirror, where the photos were. She plucked out two of them. One was of a girl, the other was of the rabbit.

"This rabbit? Alex? Named after my ex-boyfriend? He—the boyfriend, not the rabbit—dumped me three weeks ago to go out with . . ."

She switched photos and pulled out a different one, one that she hadn't shown before. Same backdrop, three girls. Elsa was on the right. She had her arm around another girl.

". . . this girl. Claire."

She said the name precisely, her Britishness deepening the *a* in the middle. Her eyes grew heavy-lidded as she spoke it. Never before had Clio heard a single name sound so ominous.

"One of my best friends," Elsa said. "*Former* best friends. And when I say 'dumped me to go out with her,' I mean that they had actually been seeing each other for a month when I caught them. It's hard to hide at school, when you all *live* together."

She carefully replaced the picture of the rabbit but hesitated with the one of Claire. This she eventually tossed under the table.

"British guys are *rubbish*," she said. "Really rubbish. At least at my school they are. British guys are obsessed with beer, sport, and cars. In that order. Some of the ones at my school expand this just a little to include money. If you find a smart one or a funny one, he's usually also depressed. Now, Swedish guys, much better. But I don't see as many of those. No. I spend my nights at the school pub with the wankers."

"You have a pub?" Clio asked. "At your school?"

"It's not that exciting," Elsa said. "They do it so that they can keep some control over the drinking. It's a sad little room with an air hockey table and a two-pint limit. I am *sick* of things being rubbish."

Even the worst of Elsa's experiences sounded a lot more colorful than Clio's general life at school. Living there, having a bar . . . it was like something out of a movie.

"An-y-way," Elsa said. "That's the anger. Here's the celebration. This summer? Things will be good. I've decided. In fact, it should start now. Let's have a party. Here. Tonight."

"A party? With who?"

"We'll invite Aidan. I've decided he's going to be my fling."

Clio let out a long sigh.

"He's all right, trust me," Elsa said. "I've only just met him myself this last week, but if he has to deal with my mum, his life is hard. He'll need a drink. It will be fun, I promise. And he's tasty, isn't he?"

"Right . . ." Clio looked away. "Think that bottle is cold?"

"It will be in a moment," Elsa said. "What do you think? Can we invite him?"

The words "this is not a party cruise" still jangled in Clio's head. The frustration they caused her overrode any that Aidan could possibly produce. And there was no way she could say no to Elsa.

"Sure," she said. "I've got it."

Clio pulled the tiny orange com from her pocket and looked on the back for Aidan's number.

"Number Four," she said. "You're needed upstairs."

Silence. Then a crackle and Clio's father's voice.

"Number Five? Did you need Number Four?"

"Uh, yeah. Copy that," Clio said, looking at Elsa and shrugging. "We need Number Four. He has something of Number Six's. We have Three approval. Over?"

Elsa tumbled to her side and laughed into her pile of clothes. Clio held up a hand to quiet her.

"Okay, Five," her father said. "Four's on his way."

"Roger, One. Over and out."

Clio clicked off the com and threw it triumphantly over her shoulder and onto the bed.

"*What* was that?" Elsa said.

"That was me telling my dad to send Aidan up here and saying that your mom said it was okay," Clio answered. "Your mom probably hasn't read the back of her com either, has she?"

"I *seriously* doubt it. That was brilliant. He's coming?"

"On his way."

Elsa went into the bathroom and produced one of the bottles. She ripped the foil from the top and unscrewed the wire casing that held the cork in place. The bottle popped triumphantly, with foamy liquid spilling out of the top. She quickly directed it at the mugs.

"Let's start," she said, passing one to Clio and holding it up to clink. "To our new room. The Champagne Suite! Chin chin!"

By the time Aidan showed up, five minutes later, she was already feeling the effects of the champagne. They were very mild—she just felt better. Talking was easier. She threw open the door.

"I was told I was needed," Aidan said flatly. He looked a little spent, half-moons of perspiration creeping out from under his arms, probably from dragging in the food that her father had just mentioned. Still, she noticed, guys frequently got a bit cuter when they'd been roughed up a little. A little sweaty . . . it worked. She could see why Elsa thought he was "tasty."

"You bet, Number Three!" Clio guided him inside, throwing Elsa a smile. He resisted just slightly, as if trying to figure out what was going on in this room before coming one step closer.

"You're having a drink with us," Elsa said.

"I can't. I have to set up the office."

"You can have a quick one," she said. "Stop being such a Muppet and sit down."

She came over and grabbed his arm, pulling him to the bed and plunking him down on the edge. He didn't put up that much of a fight. He looked around with that look of smug amusement Clio had already grown to dislike.

"So," he said. "You guys got the nice room. What a shock. But one question—who gets the bed?"

"Oh, right," Elsa said, walking over and throwing her arm over Clio's shoulders. "Just the one bed. We have to share. Remember that before you go to sleep—two floors above you, two lovely girls in one bed."

He narrowed his eyes a little but didn't give. He really did look like some kind of human computer, sucking in information and analyzing it.

Elsa walked over to the dresser and held up the bottle.

"You guys have *champagne* up here too?" he said.

This was directed at Clio.

"Elsa brought it," she said firmly.

"Only two mugs, though," Elsa said. "Two of us will have to share. Do you mind?"

She walked over and refilled Clio's mug, then sat down next to Aidan with hers and the bottle.

"I don't have germs," she said. "Promise. Or do you want the bottle?"

"The mug is fine," he said.

"You're not British," Clio said, almost accusingly. "Why are you at Cambridge?"

"I'm from Yale," he said. He was smugly matter-of-fact about it, as if it should have been obvious, like there was a big blue *Y* glowing on his forehead.

"Oh," she said. "You didn't get into Harvard?"

"You mean Cambridge Community College?" he said, accepting the mug and taking a sip. He tossed back the champagne like he was drinking a soda.

"That's very funny," Clio said. "Was that joke in your guidebook?"

A little more eye-narrowing. Clio had hit the nail on the head with that one. She drank triumphantly. This champagne was good for her.

"What do you do?" she asked. "You have lots of computers down there."

"I'm an engineer," he said. "But I also study archeology. I do the technical things—some weird, experimental stuff that's only being done in a few schools around the world. That's why Julia brought me over to Cambridge to be her assistant. I was supposed to go home for the summer, but then we got the call that this was happening. Suddenly, I wasn't going home."

"I was supposed to be working in an art store," Clio said.

He had no reply to this. The remark didn't seem to register at all. It was as if working in an art store could never be as important as what he had planned on doing. There was a little too much haughtiness in him. Yale. Cambridge. Sure, they were impressive, but he was *way* too aware of the fact. He didn't know how to be smooth about it.

"At dinner," Elsa said, swallowing a large swig of the champagne, "your dad started saying something about your tattoo. He said it was an interesting story. Was he about to say that you were in an accident? That's what it sounded like."

"Oh, right." Clio swirled the liquid in her mug and took a little drink. "I was. It was a long time ago."

"How do you get a *tattoo* in an *accident*?" Aidan said.

"I didn't get the tattoo *in* the accident." Clio heard her voice thickening just a tiny bit. "I got the tattoo afterward because I had a scar."

"Obviously," Elsa said, laughing a little too loudly and nudging him.

"What kind of accident?" he asked.

Clio took another drink. This story required a *lot* of explanation. But the two people sitting on the edge of the bed stared down at her, waiting to hear what she had to say for herself. And things were a little easier with the champagne.

"I got hit by a speedboat," she said.

Elsa let out a little yelp.

"How did you get hit by a *speedboat*?" Aidan asked.

"It's a long story," Clio said.

"We have time," Elsa said. "We definitely have the time for that."

Clio shrugged and drained her mug, holding it out for more. Elsa refilled it.

"Okay," she said. "When we first made the game, my dad had this idea that normal school wasn't enough for me. So he took us to Kos—the Greek island—to this colony where you had to live as ancient Greeks, circa 300 BC."

"This is not what I was expecting you to say," Aidan said. For once, he actually looked surprised.

"We wore sheets and lived in old buildings with no air-conditioning," Clio went on. "Most of the people there did it so they could drink wine and be naked a lot."

A giggle from Elsa.

"Every day I had to take Greek lessons. My teacher used to walk around because he thought that was more classical. So we'd have to walk for miles in the blinding heat, over rocks, with these slippery leather things on our feet. It was horrible. The only girl there my age was Hungarian, and the only way we could communicate was by throwing raw olives at each other. Mostly, I just tried to keep my sheet from falling off and avoid the tourists."

Her audience was enjoying her story. Her misery did at least make for good conversation.

"After about a week," she said, "my mom had had enough. We moved to a hotel, and I continued Greek lessons on the balcony, and we had room service and fluffy towels and things like that. But my dad—he was always trying to *expand my horizons*. So he signed us both up for diving lessons."

"Did you like diving?" Elsa asked. "I don't know if I would."

"Well, at first it was kind of annoying because there's a lot you have to learn. You have to take classes, learn about dive tables and decompression sickness and things like that. And getting into a wet suit isn't fun. But once they finally let you go in the water, it's kind of amazing."

"So you're a proper diver?" Elsa asked.

"I have my card," Clio said. The champagne made her feel like she could go on talking forever. "It's not that hard to learn. I'm a pretty good swimmer. Plus my dad was really serious about it. It was his new thing. We got lots of training, more than just the basics. I don't even know if I was allowed to do some of the stuff we were doing. Anyway, we were diving one afternoon. There's a marked-off diving area, but my dad saw these things he thought were columns. There's a lot of stuff under the water there to look at. So we left the area and swam out into the open water. Not far. Maybe fifty feet out or something. We got to the spot, and it wasn't columns. It was just some rocks. My dad gave me the signal that he was going up. I followed him. You have to go up in stages so that you don't get decompression sickness. So I was ascending with him. We were maybe ten feet apart. I got to the surface first, and there it was."

"The boat?" asked Elsa. She had grabbed a handful of Aidan's jeans.

"We were in the wrong place," Clio said. "But the guy who was driving had been drinking, and he was going way too fast. I don't remember it all that well. I know I tried to get out of the way. I think I did, sort of. It would have been worse if I had been right in front of it. I don't remember getting hit, but my dad says I flew pretty far. Maybe fifteen feet."

"Oh my God," Elsa said. "Clio! You could have been killed."

"Yeah. That's what they kept saying at the time, that I could have been killed. I was really lucky. It messed up my arm really badly, though. It was broken in eight places. I had to have physical therapy for a year. But it's okay now."

Elsa and Aidan were quiet for a second, both had their hands on the single mug of champagne. Clio was surprised to see that she had drained her cup again. She held it out for a refill. The bottle was empty. Elsa got up and grabbed the second one.

Suddenly, Clio was very tired. The jet lag had come fast, egged on by the champagne. She pulled herself up off the floor, taking her mug with her. She flopped down at the top of the bed and propped herself up on the pillows.

Aidan turned around and looked at her.

"Where does the tattoo come in?" he asked. All snarkiness had dropped away.

"Good question," Elsa said, popping the second bottle. More foam came gushing out, spilling onto the carpet, then across the bed as Elsa leaned across it to fill Clio's mug. Elsa stayed down on her stomach, clutching the bottle in a two-handed grip, like it was a lit candle, looking at Clio over it.

"We went to Japan the next year for a big games conference," Clio said. "Games and comic books, they tend to bring out the same people. So a famous manga artist was there. I loved his stuff. I met him, he saw the scar. I told him the story. And he drew over it because I told him I hated it so much. My dad let me get it tattooed in. My mom nearly killed him."

Clio rubbed at the tattoo thoughtfully. Elsa, seeing that she had finished, pointed to Aidan.

"It's your turn to tell a story," she said. "We're the girls. This is our room. We get to say who has to tell the stories."

"I don't have any stories," he said.

"You're such a liar," Elsa said, rolling onto her back and smiling. "Story. Now."

"About what?"

"Well, I don't know, do I?" Elsa said. "Were you ever in an exciting accident?"

"I fell off my bike once," he said. "I chipped a tooth."

"That's not very good," she said, making a face.

"My life isn't as exciting," he said, looking down at Elsa's sprawled figure. Elsa was good—absolutely natural, just being herself—and yet she was so clinically *hot*. That was what sexy meant. Clio had never really seen it before. Not super-skinny. Not throwing herself at anyone. Just curvy, natural, laughing, Swedish-English, kind of drunk . . . Like someone who had wandered out of some movie from the 1940s. Clio wasn't sure if she should be taking notes or giving up. It was too much for her head. How was it she had lived this long without being kissed? Why was she like herself and Elsa like Elsa?

Ollie . . . she still hadn't gotten in touch with him. Oh, right. There was a big reason.

"You have a computer," she said to Aidan.

"Yes, I do," he said, taking his eyes away from Elsa.

"I need to send an e-mail."

He sighed and set his mug on the floor.

"Nothing is set up," he said. "I should get back to that."

"What are we doing here, anyway?" she asked. "What's all that stuff for?"

"You're going to have to ask your dad," he said. "I just work here."

"Oh, come on, Aidan," Elsa said. "Just tell her."

"Tell her yourself."

"I have no idea. My mum doesn't tell me a thing. What's the big bloody secret? My mum and her drama."

"My dad and his missions," Clio said.

"Come on, Aidan," Elsa said. "You can tell *us*."

The sight of Elsa rolling on the bed, begging for information that he didn't want to give, was apparently a little too much for Aidan. He stood up.

"I should go," he said. "Thanks for the champagne. Let me know when it's caviar night."

When he had gone, Elsa rolled over and laughed into the comforter.

"A good start," she remarked, picking up her head. "A fun game. Just enough to play with. Good-looking, but a little slow with the social skills."

Clio felt her eyes starting to close. The combined effects of the champagne and the jet lag had finally landed on her.

"I think I'm tired . . ." she said.

"Oh yes," Elsa said with a laugh. "You're going out. Lightweight."

Clio was vaguely aware of her shoes coming off and the comforter being folded over her, and then a dreamless sleep swept over her like a wave.

London, November 1897

It was a cold, fine autumn night. The sky had gone a deep purple just before dark, and the lamps had just been lit along Russell Square. Marguerite Magwell put her hand against a pane of the glass and felt the chill through it. She pressed harder, pressed her nose to the window, wanting to drink in the feeling as much as she could before turning back to the warmth of the room.

She heard a bustle in the hall, a few last-minute injunctions to the cook. Marguerite turned her eyes to the side and watched in the reflection as her aunt came into the parlor. Since her father's death, her aunt had lived with her. For many years, Marguerite had been the only woman in the house. She hadn't had to deal with feminine fussiness. She could read and study without being scolded about her posture or her clothes; she could wear her hair loose without comment. Not anymore.

"There you are, dear," her aunt said. "Cook said that the bird is just ready and that it's a lovely thing. Such a big goose for three people."

Marguerite turned from where she was holding back the curtain.

"The staff can have the rest for their supper. Everyone deserves a good meal on a brisk night like this."

"Well, they'll enjoy that," her aunt said. "You're so like your father. He used to say the same thing. Has Mr. Hill come yet?"

"Not yet," Marguerite said. "I'm sure he's coming straight from the museum."

"Such a hardworking fellow. Oh, I *do* like him, Marguerite. And your father liked him."

"I know," Marguerite said.

"I think it is quite right of you to have him to dinner. I want to believe that this is a sign that you plan on going back out into the world. He's shy but so fond of you. But then, who isn't? And that dress! So few girls can wear black, but you can."

Marguerite automatically looked down at her dress, one of the many black dresses she had worn since her father's death. The view when she looked down was always black. Her aunt was just trying to be encouraging; it wasn't that nice.

"It's so very striking against your hair!" her aunt went on. "Although, my dear, I think it's time you started going back to some regular colors. For someone your age, it's not expected to wear mourning forever. It's understood that you have to meet young men, that you need dresses for dancing. Maybe a blue? A lovely deep blue."

Marguerite had much bigger ideas than blue dresses that

looked good against her hair, but her aunt would learn that soon enough.

The bell sounded in the hall.

"There he is," her aunt said. "Let's just fix you now, dear. You're a little bit out of place."

Marguerite lifted her chin patiently as her aunt adjusted the lace around her neck and tucked a few stray pieces of her hair back into position.

Jonathan appeared at the door. Tall. Too thin. Very bright and extremely shy around her. He had such a lovable way. It was a shame. He interested her. He was the only man who ever had. But she had to stay with her plan.

"Cook says everything is ready," her aunt said.

But instead of walking toward the dining room, Marguerite stood and went over to a table by the window. There was a piece of red felt laid over it and a collection of stones and papyrus fragments on top.

"Did my father ever show you these?" she asked Jonathan, spreading them out.

"No," he said, following her. "I don't think so."

He picked one up and looked it at closely.

"I've seen this script before," he said. "We have a few examples of it at the museum. None on display, since we don't know what it is. Where did he get these?"

"He received artifacts with writing on them from time to time. Most he could identify. These baffled him. Complex. Highly organized. A very distinct grammar. And do you want to know the strangest part?"

Jonathan nodded, his eyes fixed on hers.

"They are from everywhere," Marguerite said. "These from South America. Some from India and Egypt. Two from Japan. How can this consistent writing be from so many places?"

"I'm not sure," he said.

"Here is another strange fact. Almost all of these were found along coastlines or in the water itself. What would you make of that?"

"There are a number of possibilities," he said.

"What about flooding?" she asked. "The water is hiding something from us, something we cannot access, and it occasionally throws clues our way simply to taunt us. What if the people who made this language were drowned?"

"A flood would certainly have changed the landscape," Jonathan said. "And a flood could have destroyed the people who made this language."

She opened a drawer in the front of the table and removed a letter, passing it to Jonathan.

"On the morning of my father's voyage out of Naples, he sent this to me. It arrived a week after I heard of his death. I've only recently been able to bring myself to open it. But when I did, I found something of extreme importance. I want you to read it."

Marguerite carefully set the paper in his hand. She watched Jonathan's eyes run down the page and take in the contents.

"I really think we should go to dinner," her aunt said. She wasn't understanding this talk of floods, and she certainly didn't want Marguerite dwelling on her father's death tonight. "You know how cook gets. The last time we were late, she threw a spoon at Jenkins."

Jonathan didn't seem to hear any of this, or at least he didn't seem to care about Jenkins and the spoon at the moment. He was staring at the letter.

"A vast, ancient society, lost under the waters," Marguerite said.

There was a thoughtful silence, filled only by the smell of the waiting goose and Marguerite's aunt's pained looks.

"I asked you here tonight because I had something to tell you," she said. "I have to finish what he started. I leave in a week's time for Pompeii."

At Sea

Clio woke up when the world shook. She looked up from her fluffy pocket of comforter. There was bouncing. Big bouncing.

This was no good. She wanted the world to be silent and still so that her head would stop spinning. She looked to her right. All she could see was a little tuft of blond hair coming up out of the folds of a second comforter.

She turned the other way and was blinded by a powerful bolt of sunlight coming in through the little window. She shielded her eyes and slipped out of the bed, sinking into the decadent carpet to look out at the view. Italy seemed to be gone, replaced by sapphire-colored water that stretched in all directions. They were moving through it very quickly, pounding the waves into submission with sheer velocity.

Clio took a quick inventory of herself and her situation. She wasn't exactly sick, like she had been after the margarita mix. She just wasn't feeling great. It felt like someone was tapping on her forehead. She'd had worse stomachaches after too many sweet Thai iced teas; this was only a minor annoyance. Mostly, she just felt confused. She needed a shower. That would help.

She stumbled over to the glorious bathroom. One empty and one half-full champagne bottle and two sticky mugs sat on the sink. The shower had a temperature knob in degrees Celsius. She took a guess as to what temperature she wanted and was promptly scalded, then frozen, then scalded again. She ended up backing up to the very edge of the shower stall and cautiously reaching in for the water. The boat hit some choppy waves, forcing her to cling to the bar on the wall. After this valiant effort, she gave up, bounced her way back into the bedroom, and put on a shirt and a pair of pink pajama bottoms.

Coming down the circular stairs was a much scarier process than it had been before when the boat was docked. There was no one in the galley, so she put the kettle away and left the mugs in the sink. No one was in the living room or the dining room or at the back of the boat. Obviously, someone had to be steering, so she went out to the deck and up the back stairs. The speed of the boat made the air cool, and there was a fine mist caught in it. She held on tight as she pulled herself up the steps to the wheelhouse.

The wheelhouse was at the very top of the boat, a tight room with three walls of darkened glass. Clio opened the door. The wheelhouse was just as posh as the rest of the boat—more leather seats and lots of fancy stuff. Martin stood in front of a massive panel of tiny screens and readouts, one hand on a steering wheel. Julia, her father, and Aidan were looking over a map that was spread out on the floor. Clio had seen maps like that before, back when they were working on Dive! They were maps of shipwrecks and sunken objects, ordinarily used by the military or commercial boats to prevent crashes. There was also a small box of rocks down by Julia's foot.

"We're moving," Clio said to the group. "Where are we going?"

"It's eleven o'clock," her father said, folding the map quickly. "Nobody's had any breakfast."

Clio looked at the four able-bodied human beings in front of her and wanted to ask them why they hadn't fed themselves, but from the look on her father's face, she got the impression that this might not be a good idea.

"When will we be back tonight?" she asked. "I was supposed to call Mom."

A look circulated the room.

"We'll talk about that at breakfast," he said. "Or lunch. Let us know when it's ready."

Clio was being dismissed. She wasn't arguing this one, especially not in front of Aidan.

"No problem," she said stiffly. "I'll get right on it."

The first thing she did upon getting down to the galley was make herself a little hat out of a piece of paper. She folded it up until it was like a miniature version of a fast-food hat. If her dad wanted her to play chef, she would play chef.

There was a lot more food in the galley now than there had been the night before. The yacht was packed like a UN provision ship. Eight loaves of bread were piled in the corner. Three cardboard boxes stuffed full of vegetables sat on the floor.

Another two of fruit. A paper bag revealed meat. Just meat. The refrigerator had been filled with fresh fish—heads and all—trapped in clear plastic bags. There was something murderous about it. Like the Mafia had taken these fish out. These fish slept with the fishes.

"Number Five does not like these fish at all," she said to herself. She moved them to the back, making a wall of meat and cheese to seal them off. She could still feel their stares penetrating the food wall, even through the closed refrigerator door.

Coffee. Her head required coffee. It took a few minutes to find the coffee itself and a few more to figure out the pot, but soon the galley was filled with the rich, roasted smell. It was too much to hope that someone had bought French vanilla creamer, Clio's favorite substance in the world. This was probably for the best, as she had a tendency to drink it straight out of the container.

Once she had a cup of coffee in her body and felt herself waking, her natural inclination for order and composition came out. She sorted out the various useless gadgets, like the lemon zester, the crème brûlée torch, and the candy thermometer. She arranged the fruit in a bowl, made a row of tomatoes along the windowsill, and put the bread into a more pleasing formation. As much as she didn't want to admit it, Clio did like to cook. And these were nice, fresh ingredients. She sifted through the boxes and came up with a pile of basics. She pulled out some eggs, smoked bacon, peppers, onions, garlic, and cheese and set to work. She would make a big frittata—a big omelet cooked in the oven. That would shut everyone up.

She beat the eggs in a bowl, fried up the bacon and let it drain and crisp, and grated the cheese in a fancy canister grater. She

101

had just gotten to chopping up the vegetables when Aidan slipped in behind her. He didn't say hello, or good morning, or even excuse me. He just squeezed in and started riffling through the refrigerator until he got what he wanted, which was a can of soda.

"You complain about oysters, yet you drink soda for breakfast?" she asked. "That's some interesting nutrition."

"It's got nothing to do with nutrition," he said, leaning against the sink and cracking open the can. "No one has ever fallen over dead from drinking a can of Coke. But raw seafood is an actual health risk. The oyster should be left alone so that it can get sand in it and get irritated enough to make a pretty, pretty pearl."

He had on cargo shorts and a T-shirt from some event at Yale called "Tuesdays at Mory's." (Clio guessed that he probably had a lot of Yale-related T-shirts.) Again, the clothes were too big. The hair was a little flatter today, coming down over his forehead a bit. Clio liked it better that way. He wasn't bad-looking at all. Just a little conceited and annoying. Elsa could take care of that, though.

"So you'd rather have a bunch of chemicals?" she asked.

"Everything's chemicals," he said dismissively. "I don't care. Give me a nice cold can of corn syrup and delicious caffeine any day. What's on your head?"

"My hat," she said.

"Do I get a hat?"

"Nope," she said. "You only get a hat when you get a job."

"I have a job," he said.

"What's that?"

"Can't tell you," he answered, smiling a little.

102

"Why?"

"Your dad said not to. He's the boss. He has a hat too."

Clio turned back to her cutting board and onion. She could feel him watching her steadily turn the onion into a pile of evenly sized squares.

"You look like you know what you're doing with that knife," he said.

"I took a cooking class in Japan once. They're serious about knives there."

"Oh, right," he said. "Must be cool to be rich."

"I wouldn't know," she said. He was bringing her headache back and reminding her that she was not having a good time at all.

"So you're telling me you're not rich?"

"That's what I'm telling you," she said, chopping evenly, rocking the blade back and forth on the board.

"We're on your dad's *yacht*. You probably see why I'm having a hard time with that one."

Clio pushed the onion into the frying pan, where the hot bacon fat sizzled. Then she wheeled around, still holding the knife. Aidan backed up.

"Two things you should think about," she said. "One, things aren't always what they seem. Two, never piss off a girl with a very big knife."

"I get it," he said. "Your dad is one of those rich guys who likes to keep it real. So you're not rich, rich. You're just *theoretically* rich. That's why you have a job and a hat. And a knife. Which *is* big."

This wasn't cute. It wasn't funny. It was insulting. Clio hated people assuming that she was rich, hated having to explain that they weren't. It wasn't that she was angry about not being rich; it was that the questions were so probing. They were about something very painful in Clio's life—the loss of all they'd made, her parents' breakup. *Most* people got the hint that maybe this wasn't a great topic. But not Aidan.

He watched her cook up the vegetables in the pan, slurping and smirking away.

"Leave some runny," he said, nodding at the eggs as he slipped back out. "I like them that way."

Clio clenched her teeth. She poured the eggs into a pan, carefully layered in the vegetables, crumbled in the bacon, and sprinkled on the cheese. It was a perfect frittata. Or it could be. But as she stuck it in the oven, she resolved to keep it in there until she was absolutely certain that the eggs were as dry and rubbery as erasers.

"These eggs are a little dry," her father said, poking at his slice of frittata. "Something wrong with the stove?"

The sun streamed in through the glass doors, causing the leather sofas to glow a pristine white. The group had gathered for the breakfast-lunch at the white lacquer dining room table. Aidan threw Clio one of his narrow-eyed looks across it.

"I'm not an actual chef," Clio said. "Results may vary."

It was a shame, really. It would have been so good. Still, it had been worth ruining the frittata to see Aidan have to chew a bit harder.

"So," her dad said. "Did you pick all of your classes for next year yet?"

"A few months ago."

"Did you give any more thought to taking Greek on the side?"

"Not really."

"What kind of Greek?" Julia cut in.

"Greek . . . Greek," Clio said.

"Julia knows three variations of Greek," her father explained. "Mycenaean, ancient, and Koine."

Clio wasn't sure how to respond to this. Not too many places to go with that one.

"Is that what you teach?" she finally asked.

"No," Julia said. "I teach conservation methods, how to deal with manuscripts, history. Not language."

"Julia's a working archeologist," her father cut in again. "Also a conservationist. Kind of like your mom."

Clio really didn't want to hear her mother and Julia being compared, especially by her dad. There had to be some kind of rule about that.

"It's wonderful that your father took you to learn Greek," Julia said, breaking the awkward silence that followed the last remark. "I heard all about it. You've led such an interesting life."

"You could say that," Clio said.

"Do you have ketchup?" Aidan asked, still poking at his eggs sadly.

"I don't think so," her dad answered.

The smell of food drew Elsa down from the Champagne Suite. Again no makeup, nothing fancy. Just snug, soft red shorts and a white shirt. Her hair tumbled loose and had curled up a bit. Even with no effort at all, she had the natural beauty thing going on. She dropped down at the table, shook her head at the eggs, and reached for the coffee. Clio watched Aidan's gaze automatically shift to her. It was natural, like being drawn to a fireplace on a cold day.

"We're going somewhere?" she asked, her British accent sounding both morning-sexy gravelly and chipper at the same time.

"You sound tired," Julia said. "Long night?"

A crackly mother-daughter vibe passed between them. Clio didn't exactly get what was being implied, but it looked like Julia knew about the champagne.

"Oh, right," Clio's dad said. "Are you . . . feeling better?"

Elsa looked understandably confused. Clio had never mentioned the monster case of cramps that she had bestowed upon her the night before.

"Where *are* we going?" Clio asked, changing the subject. "And when do we get back tonight? I never got a chance to make my calls."

"Right . . ." he said, pushing aside his plate. "Come up to the wheelhouse with me."

They got up from the table and went upstairs together to where Martin was waiting alone, driving the boat.

"I've got it, Martin," he said, taking over. "Go grab some breakfast."

"Can't wait," Martin said with a smile. "I've been smelling that for the last half hour. I'm starving!"

Her father assumed the controls haughtily. There was no doubt that the boat was full of fancy and complex widgets, but the truth was, the little tiny wheel and the lights on the panel looked like the controls of a complicated video game. Plus it wasn't like the boat required complicated steering. The GPS seemed to be telling the boat where to go anyway.

"Here's the thing," he said. "We're going to be out on the water for two weeks."

Obviously, he thought that if he just slipped it in there like that, all quick, it would somehow be okay. Like ripping off a Band-Aid.

"Two weeks," Clio repeated. "You just took off from shore without telling us that we were going to be gone for *two weeks*?"

"Well, you were sleeping," he said. "From what I understand, you were sleeping off some champagne. And I know about Aidan being in your room. Don't think I missed that. You've already violated three of the rules. You overslept and didn't do your job. So you can't complain."

Even if she had been busted, this was totally unacceptable by any standards.

"What about Internet access?" she said, her desperation increasing. "How do we get that?"

"We don't have it," he said. "Like I said, your mom knows you've arrived. What you need to do now is follow the rules, Clio. We're all in this together out here."

"I can't believe you," she said. "You just cut us off from the world?"

"It's only for two weeks," he said. "It's good for you. People spend too much time staring at screens, playing with devices."

Clio looked at the many, many screens and devices on the control panel. He was one to talk. No. No, this could *not* be happening. If she had to wait two whole weeks before calling Ollie, who knew what would happen? Who knew what that slutty Galaxy girl, Janine, could be doing to him at this very moment?

"Now," he said. "I could have yelled, but I think you've learned your lesson, so why don't you get back downstairs and finish breakfast with the others? Let's start fresh, from now. This is the beginning of a great journey."

Kidnapped

"He's kidnapped us," Clio said, staring down at the eggy plates that had been left on the lacquer table. "My father has *kidnapped* us. He's turned us into slave labor. That's illegal, right? That's insane."

Elsa yawned widely, rubbed her eyes, and reached for the coffee.

"I have to send an e-mail at least," Clio said. "This is war. I'm not kidding."

"You know," Elsa said. "I honestly don't mind. It's probably better this way."

"How could this be better?" Clio asked.

"I can't call. I can't write. I'm just gone. I remember reading something about how they used to cure people of things like heroin by putting them on slow boats. Like slow boats to China, where they couldn't get any drugs. They go through withdrawal, but they arrive cured."

"Alex?" Clio asked.

Elsa nodded. "You don't know what I'd give to be cured of him," she said. "I didn't sleep well. I haven't been able to for a while. I always dream about him. It's sort of easier not to sleep. That way I don't see him. But I always *do* fall asleep, and there he is. If I dream about someone every night, does that make me obsessed?"

"No," Clio said. "It just means you're upset."

Elsa smiled. Even with her eyes puffy and her hair tousled, it was hard to imagine how anyone could break up with her.

"So," Elsa continued. "As long as we're stuck out here, I can't make drunken phone calls late on a Saturday or send long e-mails about how I'm angry, or how I understand, or how he's a bastard. . . . It changes all the time, the stuff I want to write. Now I can't do anything. It feels kind of good."

"Well, now we both need Aidan for something. You need him to help you get over Alex. And I need him for Internet access."

"Your dad just said there isn't any," Elsa said.

"He was lying. I'm sure of it. Plus this boat is wired all over the place. You should see the wheelhouse. It looks like mini-NORAD up there. They just don't want us to use it because they are being very, very weird."

"Wow," Elsa said. "You're really observant. And I guess it's not surprising. My mom is kind of secretive about her work. This time, a little more so than normal."

Clio's com crackled to life.

"Number Five and Number Six!" it said. "Number Two is going to take you on a safety tour when you're done."

Elsa tried to help with the dishes, but she was tired and slow.

Clio stuck her on the sofa, where she promptly fell asleep. Clio looked down at her peaceful figure and tried to decide whether her bunkmate was an insomniac or a narcoleptic. Then she put in her earphones and plowed through the dishes. It took her an hour to restore the galley to order.

Martin came down, as promised, from the locked session in the wheelhouse. Aidan and Julia did as well, but they continued right downstairs.

"Where are they going?" Clio asked.

"We have a workroom down there," he said. "A little one. Come on. Let me show you the safety features. Your dad walked me through them last night."

There wasn't a lot to see. Their home for the next two weeks wasn't even the size of a small house. What had seemed like such a magnificent boat last night quickly shrank to a seagoing veal pen.

"There's a lot of white furniture in here," Clio said. Along with the white table and chairs, the two sofas and the chair and a half were covered in white leather.

"It all came with the boat."

"I don't really trust people who buy leather furniture," Clio said, looking at Elsa's sleeping figure on the sofa. "Furniture is supposed to be soft and welcoming. Leather is sticky and gets hot and cold. There's something *inhuman* about a leather sofa. And *white* leather. That's not designed for any kind of real life. It's too sterile. It's like something in a mental hospital. Where did this boat come from again?"

"There was quite an ugly divorce," Martin said, sliding open the glass doors and leading Clio outside to the deck. "A banker and his wife in London. This boat was the husband's toy, and the wife sold it off at a fraction of the cost. Still expensive, but . . . crazy things happen in divorces."

"I know," Clio said.

"Right," Martin said, catching himself. "Well, I think this one was a lot more uncivil than your parents'. In any case, let's look at some of the safety issues. I've always enjoyed those safety displays the airline staff does before takeoff. Tell me how I do. Now, the main issue at sea is obviously sinking. Fire is a concern, but there are lots of smoke detectors and extinguishers. You need to know what happens if the boat goes down. That right there next to the window is the EPIRB."

He pointed to a little orange cylinder attached to the outside wall of the cabin.

"It's a pretty cool device. It contains a unique registered serial number. If it's activated, it sends out two radio frequencies, one at 406 megahertz and one at 121.5 megahertz. . . ."

Clio felt her eyes glaze slightly.

"The 406-megahertz signal goes to a geosynchronous weather satellite, and the Coast Guard can get your exact position by tracing the serial number. The 121.5 and 406 also go out to any boats or planes nearby. Basically, the EPIRB allows rescuers to pinpoint you instantly. And it self-activates."

"How does it activate?"

"Hydraulically, in ten feet of water," he said, walking to the back of the boat. "So you don't really want to be here if it's working. Apparently, the rule at sea is that you're never supposed to get off your sinking boat until the water level is up to your waist and you can step right into whatever it is you're escaping into. Which would be this."

He tapped an orange box that was clamped just under the back of the boat.

"It's a six-person raft. It wouldn't be fun to be out here in this, but you should probably know where it is. Both walls of the deck back here are just life jacket and oar storage."

He reached for a handle that was cleverly worked into the wall so that it could barely be seen and opened up a ten-foot-long storage space neatly stuffed with orange jackets.

"I think we have about twenty or something," he said. "If anyone falls overboard, throw these and get on the com immediately. If the raft is needed, we'll all be in it, so there's no need to go through that."

"What about that raft?" Clio said, pointing at the little motorized one that had shuttled them back and forth to the dock and was now lashed to the back platform.

"Too small," Martin said. "That can only carry three people, and it offers no protection. That's about it. This is the end of your tour. I hope you enjoyed it. You don't have to tip."

She tried to smile.

"Now that I've fulfilled the very minimum in terms of your physical safety," he said, "how are you doing?"

"I'm alive," she said. "He could have *told* me he was on a date."

"He was worried," Martin said. "But he really wanted you here, and he was afraid you wouldn't come if you knew he was bringing his new girlfriend."

"I tried not to come anyway," Clio said.

She didn't have to lie to Martin. Martin had been the voice of reason all along, back when he worked with her father, back before.

"Well, he's really glad you're here. He misses you all the time."

"Then he shouldn't have left," Clio said before she could catch herself.

Martin sighed and gave her a "you know it wasn't that simple" look.

"I know," Clio said, sitting down and looking over the side. "Forget it. So, how did *you* end up here?"

"I'm between positions right now, and your dad needed help."

"For what? What are we doing?"

"It has to do with Julia's work," Martin said.

"But *what*, exactly?"

"He's asked me not to say," Martin said.

"What could we possibly be doing that he needs to keep it a secret?" she asked. "From me? Doesn't it strike you as deeply insane that he wouldn't trust his own daughter?"

"It's some kind of academic confidentiality."

"But you know. And Aidan knows."

"I know a little. Aidan works for Julia. And from what I can tell, that's not a fun proposition."

Clio looked up with interest.

"She scares me," Clio said. "Where did they meet?"

"At a conference. She was presenting. They seem to have hit it off." Martin stared out at the wake thoughtfully. He opened his mouth to say something else, then closed it again.

"And now my dad is paying for her work?" Clio said. "Martin, this makes no sense. He doesn't have the money for this boat."

"He's planning on selling it. It's an investment."

"Did he borrow money from you?" Clio asked.

Martin sighed again and rubbed his salt-and-pepper beard

with both hands. Clio knew that Martin had a good amount of money from things he'd developed, investments. When her father had crashed, it was Martin who had let him live in his house for a year rent-free.

"It was a combination," Martin said. "He had some Dive! money left over. I think that was the last of it. I lent the rest. But he really did get a good deal on this boat. He should make a profit."

"And Julia?" Clio asked.

He got up and walked toward the stairs to the wheelhouse.

"I'm sure she'll grow on you, Clio," he said, patting her shoulder. "You shouldn't worry so much. Just enjoy the ride. It's a great boat, a beautiful place. Your dad's okay. Trust me. Don't worry about Julia."

"Sure," Clio said, smiling halfheartedly. "Why would I worry? This all makes so much sense."

Confinement, Not Solitary

Over the course of the day, the *smallness* of the world of the boat began to really sink in. Clio paced around it for a while, like a zoo animal in an undersize cage. There was no television, nothing to watch. There was no phone. The only thing she found that was of any interest at all was the compact stacked washer-dryer in a closet next to the galley. When a washing machine is the best you can do, you know you're in for some trouble.

In terms of places to be, there were only really three: her bedroom (which wasn't even private), the horrible white living room, and the deck. The deck was beautiful, without question. It was sunny and hot, and they were going past massive islands that jutted out of the water, coastline dotted with grottoes and villages. But then those things got smaller and smaller as they headed out. And then there was water.

"I have to get out of here," she said to the view.

The view didn't offer up a reply. It offered only more of itself. Clio could only think that with every passing mile, she was getting farther from a chance of contacting Ollie. She was falling off the map.

Elsa, on the other hand, had woken up happy. She came shuffling out in the early afternoon, and the peaceful smile on her face told Clio that she had fully accepted that the *Sea Butterfly* was some kind of clinic for the brokenhearted and she was a patient. She wanted to be confined, sedated, and kept away from sharp objects. She wanted the outside world to go away. She settled herself down with a bottle of nail polish and painstakingly painted her toenails shell pink, then stretched out to tan.

Everyone else had something to do, and they kept well hidden. On occasion, one of them would come out of the wheelhouse, but they'd return just a few minutes later. Aidan came out the most, often carrying things back up with him. He never once lost that look of smug self-importance. Clio could just tell that no matter *what* Aidan did, he assumed it was the most important activity in the world. It was so important that he barely even looked at her.

Aside from her cooking, Clio didn't have much to do. She went upstairs and brought back down her sketchbooks. Clio usually drew every single day in the way that some people practice a sport or an instrument. She hadn't done it in the last few days, and already her hands felt stiff and strange. She sat on a deck chair and stared at the pictures of Ollie. She had gotten the shoulders and nose all wrong in most of them, but the eyes and chin were very good. Her drawing teacher would have been proud.

He already seemed less real to her now. Ripped out of her normal environment, she had already started to feel like a different person, like her life of just a week ago was a dream. Plus the boat bumped, knocking her hand across the page when she least expected it. She slapped the book closed. She couldn't even draw.

"What's wrong?" Elsa asked.

"Nothing," Clio lied.

"Come lie next to me. We'll get great tans out here."

There wasn't anything else to do, so Clio went up and got a few of their thick towels and made a place for herself. But as soon as she closed her eyes and the sun bore a hot spot into the lids, she could only see Ollie. Her head started to replay the fantasy of the two of them on the beach. This was all a cruel joke.

At four, Clio's com rumbled.

"Number Five!" it said. "You'll probably want to get dinner started. I think there's been a request."

"A request?" Clio said to Elsa.

Elsa shrugged.

It was something to do, anyway. She pulled herself up. On the black granite countertop in the galley, someone had left an Indian cookbook open to a page displaying a chicken korma recipe. A note written in a quick, sloping print also requested the cucumber raita (page 189), rice, and tamarind chutney. She quickly flipped through the book and examined the long list of ingredients.

"Great," she said, and shut the book with a decisive thump. "No problem. Anything else you want? Ice sculptures?"

She slapped on her hat. A thought struck her as she did this, and she ran up the steps to the Champagne Suite and got out her Galaxy name tag. She pinned it to her shirt. Not only was it a token of Ollie, it was a nice touch. Her servitude was going to be noticed.

Each time she went looking for something on the list—something unlikely, like coconut milk, or clarified butter, or cumin seeds, or fresh ginger—it was there. Someone had known they wanted curry, and that person had made sure the deck was stacked in their favor.

Still, it took Clio a full hour and a lot of double-checking to get through the recipes. There was jasmine rice to soak and steam, piles of vegetables to cut, spices to toast and grind. The actual cooking of the curry required a careful layering of oil, butter, spice, chicken, vegetables, coconut, all in a very precise order. The tiny kitchen grew warm.

She was extremely gratified to smell something distinctly curry-like coming out of her pot and to see that its contents had come together to form a thick, golden stew. The rice was white and fluffy. The raita looked thick, cool, and yogurt-like. She located the jar of English chutney, pulled half the kitchen apart to find enough bowls and dishes to serve all of it up, and managed to haul it all out to the table only fifteen minutes after she felt the boat come to a stop and heard people gather for the expected dinnertime.

As she had hoped, the name tag was noticed. No one commented on it, though. Everyone seemed genuinely impressed by the curry. There was a lot of fast eating. The sea air had made everyone hungry.

When they had finished eating, Clio's father stood, arms spread, in speech mode.

"Let's move these plates out of the way, Clio," he said. "We need the table."

No "thank you." Nothing about the work she had put in. Just an order to shift the dirty dishes. She stood up, unable to meet anyone's eyes, and wordlessly stacked the plates.

"Tonight," he said, "I was thinking we could all spend a little time together. We only have each other out here, after all. I thought, what better to do than play a little Dive!"

He reached around to the white leather sofa behind him and produced a well-worn box. From the expressions around the room, no one thought much of this idea except for Elsa, who would take on anything.

"How many of you have played before?" he asked. "Aside from the obvious."

Aidan admitted to having played the video game version on his cell.

"Kid . . . Clio, why don't you explain how it works?"

The boat creaked a bit as they shifted lightly from side to side. Her father was now commanding a group of people to play their board game. Clio felt something inside her die. Her spirit? Maybe.

"Come on!" he said.

"The object of the game is to get as much treasure as you can and get your ship back to port," she said dryly. "You try not to get arrested, attacked, or sunk."

"It's relevant," Martin said, trying to be helpful.

"The board is divided into seas, made-up ones. Not real ones.

All of these little tiles represent areas of water. Some have ship-wrecks under them, some don't. The goal is to get as much treasure as you can. There are a hundred and fifty treasure cards. You can dive for it or steal it. There are lots of ways of going about it."

"Everyone plays a little differently," her dad chimed in. "Some people barter a lot. Some people like to steal from other people. You can follow in the wake of a ship that's doing well. Your style of play really depends on you."

"How long does this take?" Julia asked.

"A while," her dad answered. "Two or three hours. It's great for something like this. None of us has anywhere else to go."

Julia fell silent. It was a throbbing kind of silence.

"Can we play teams?" Elsa asked.

"Sure!" he said. "Team play works well. Obviously, Clio and I need to be split up, so . . . I'll be with Martin and Elsa. Clio, Julia, and Aidan, you can be the other team."

The task of explaining the rules to Aidan and Julia was not an enviable one. Julia put on a flat, unmoving listening face. Aidan second-guessed the logic at every turn. But when Clio started setting out and explaining the cards, Julia sprang to life.

"Why is this worth a hundred points?" she asked, holding up a card bearing a Greek vase.

"Because it is," Clio said.

"This is a red-figure bell krater, a vessel used to mix water and wine. This one on the card happens to be in the Getty Museum. And this"—she slapped down a five-hundred-point card—"is a Hellenistic fish plate. And not even a very interesting one. Why is this worth five times as much?"

"Because I liked the picture of the clam on it," Clio answered.

"You can see why this makes no sense. But I know that's not the point. It's a game. And a good game, so I hear."

"Right," Clio said. "It's a game."

And it was a long game, the longest game of Dive! she had ever played. This group was surreal. There was her dad, trying not to flirt with Julia and failing. There was Julia, smiling the most uptight-yet-sultry smile back at her father. Julia's appeal was becoming devastatingly clear. She was petite, intense, obviously intelligent. She was like a more-commanding version of Clio's own mother. Still, there was something a little bit . . . *off* about Julia.

There was Aidan, leaning across to Elsa, not really hiding the fact that he was looking at her chest. There was Elsa, causing the problem by doing some kind of magical lift-and-separate move, making sure that her breasts hovered over the board at all times, like cloud cover. There was Martin, trying to pretend this was all normal.

And there was Clio, wearing a paper hat and a name tag, looking down at her past. It had been a long time since she'd seen Dive! There were way too many memories embedded in the box, the experience. There was the two-hundred-point bronze statue card. She'd made that one from one of her mom's old textbooks. There was the whirlpool in the left corner—an accident, really. The board had gotten wet when she was painting it, so she'd swirled the damp corner with her finger. And bang—a new challenge had been developed. Her dad had incorporated it right into the game.

They were smart back then. Smart and lucky. She wasn't feeling that so much now. Sitting there on that endless, terrible night, the smell of leftover curry taking over the entire cabin,

Clio had the sensation that she had already done the best things in her life. Eleven and twelve had been her peak years. She had a long time to go downhill.

And then the worst of it hit—she saw the board, the boat-shaped pieces moving around the squares of blue sea—and she saw her life, right now. How had she not seen this clearly before? Her dad was playing Dive! in real life. He was guarding his cards, moving his boat, gathering his treasure. . . . He had snapped. And he had taken them all with him.

But what treasure was he looking for?

Even though she was barely paying attention, she led Aidan and Julia around the board effortlessly, leaving them out of the decisions entirely. She couldn't help it. She knew every move. The trick to avoid the pirates was to stock up on lots of low-point cards. The trick to getting lots of treasure was to make lots of quick passes on the board. Her dad was just as good, and he had gotten the competitive glint in his eye. She fought back, her mind readily serving up a defense to his every attack.

"Are you two going to let anyone else in?" Julia said.

The cool British voice cut into the heavy fog that had descended over Clio's thoughts.

"There's no point," Aidan said, standing up. "You can't play a game with the people who made it."

Clio was grateful. She needed out of this room. She stood up and headed for the steps.

"Where are you going?" her dad asked as she retreated.

"Upstairs?"

"The dishes," he said. "The galley is your domain, remember? And we have to keep it shipshape."

On hearing that there was cleaning to be done, the others scattered. Clio stood there, limp with a helpless rage. She stepped back into the galley, where every surface was covered with remnants of the dinner.

It's fine, she thought, taking a deep breath. *You need time to think anyway. Just do this.*

Before long, the galley had turned into a miserable little sauna of soap and steam. This was when Aidan wandered in, laptop in hand.

"I noticed you're wearing your name," he said. "The spelling was unusual. So I looked it up."

He opened his laptop and balanced it in one palm. He had come to *flaunt* the fact that he could get online.

"Clio," he said. "Let's see here. One of nine muses, nine sisters. Daughter of Zeus, king of all the gods, and the goddess of memory. Invoked at the beginning of an artistic endeavor. Muses inspire divine madness. Without them, the creation—whatever it is—can be technically correct, but it will never be truly inspired or perfect. But . . . I see here that you are also a boat! Clio, the sea butterfly. I didn't catch that one before. We've been riding around in you."

"I know," she said flatly. "Not my idea."

"Ever see a sea butterfly? They're pretty. Also technically mollusks, so you're related to oysters. Your favorite. Also a *hermaphrodite*. That's nice. They start life as males and mature into females. Have a look."

He turned the computer around to show to her. This wasn't something she really wanted to see, but she leaned in anyway. As she did, he snapped it shut.

124

"Psych," he said.

He rendered Clio speechless. She stood there looking at him, one hand soaking in the soapy, curry-stained water, searching her mind for a word that fit this kind of behavior. He pushed away the hair that had flopped onto his forehead, smiled, and left.

A full five minutes later she was still standing in the exact same position, mouth slightly open, forcing her brain to fire up the perfect comeback, when she heard the last of the water sucking down the drain. She lifted her hand and examined it. It was pruned, covered in pearlescent soap bubbles tinged with yellow. No one except her father had ever rattled her like this before.

That was it. From now on, her purpose was clear. Get online. Get off the boat. And Aidan—he was going *down*.

The Snoop

The next morning, Clio woke up a bit earlier than she had the day before. Elsa was still out cold. There was a book on her side of the bed. She probably hadn't slept again.

Elsa had been awake last night, though, and had poured out the entire story of her breakup to Clio. It *had* been rough. Elsa had been madly in love with Alex, a guy she had known since she was twelve. They had dated for seven months when Elsa found him making out with one of her best friends in the library, and there was no escape.

Clio's dreams that night had been filled with images of English boarding schools—big ivy-covered buildings that looked vaguely like Hogwarts. There was an art supply store in the basement, but Ollie didn't work there. The strange thing was, Aidan did.

She woke up with absolutely no idea where she was.

The boat had stopped. She went downstairs and found her father and Martin in their wet suits, preparing their tanks.

"What's going on?" she asked, stepping out onto the deck.

"Just doing a little dive," he said. "Getting the lay of the land. We'll be back up in about an hour. Have some breakfast ready!"

"Sure," she said uneasily.

It had been a while since she had seen this process. There was so much stuff: air tanks and tubes and fins. There were even a few smaller pony tanks—tanks that divers carry in case their main tanks fail. The boat bobbed and rocked now that it was anchored in place, causing Clio's stomach to flip a little. She realized she was clutching her arm.

She went back inside and set up the coffeepot and stuck her hat on her head groggily. Day two, and this ritual was already a little old.

It occurred to her that the others had to be around somewhere, possibly in the workroom mentioned below. It seemed worthwhile to have a little look and see what they were up to.

She went down the stairs as silently as possible. Some of the doors along the hall were open, but the only one with any noise coming from it was solidly closed. She went up to the door and pressed her ear as hard against it as she could.

"We haven't started," Aidan said. He sounded defensive. "I haven't even put the tow fish in. He's going on some numbers alone, which aren't that reliable."

"Just *let* him," Julia said. "Let him do what he wants."

"I'm just trying to—"

"Enough," she said.

Clio backed away from the door quickly as she heard steps approaching it. Julia walked out.

"I just came down for breakfast orders!" Clio said chirpily. "It sounded like you guys were awake."

Julia seemed surprised to find her there, smiling, wearing a paper hat.

"Just coffee," she said. "Thank you."

"No problem," Clio said. "I'll take Aidan's order too."

It was completely obvious that Julia didn't want Clio going into that room, but she wasn't about to tackle her and throw her to the ground to stop her either.

"I'm just going to check on them," Julia muttered, heading down the hall.

"Okay!" Clio said brightly.

It was probably good to have your possible future stepmother think you were a little nuts. It would keep her on her toes and dissuade her from trying to sit her down and have touchy-feely talks. Not that she expected that from Julia. Julia looked like she might head-butt people in meetings.

Aidan sat at his computer in the corner of the tight little room, rotating slowly back and forth, his arms wrapped tightly across his chest. He wore a thinning, torn T-shirt, and his hair was still wet and shaken up.

"You want my order?" Aidan said, the annoyance still in his voice. "Okay. I'd like burned bacon, soft scrambled eggs, and toast, as long as the bread isn't whole grain."

"We need to talk," she said.

"Do we?"

"Yes. We do. You can get online. You came into the kitchen last night to make sure I knew this."

"No," he said. "I came to tell you the wonderful meaning of your name and to enrich your life."

"Here's the thing," she said, leaning over. "I need to send a note to someone. You can help me send that note."

The skin on his cheekbones got very taut for a moment.

"Could," he said. "But can't. Again, your dad's rules."

"Why?"

"If I told you," he said. "I'd be telling you. So I can't tell you."

"Listen, haircut . . ."

"Did you just call me *haircut*?" he asked.

"Yes. You know there's no reason we can't go online. It's crazy."

"Why'd you call me haircut?" he asked, touching his hair. "Is it because I have a great haircut?"

"You figure it out," she answered.

"I don't make up the rules," he said.

"Well, you can't stop me from sitting in here," she said. "I need somewhere to practice my Mongolian throat-singing. You know us rich kids. We take lots of weird lessons."

She started to warble a deep gargling noise.

"Okay," he said. "You're not going to sit in here doing that."

"You'd be amazed at what I'd do," she said.

"No. I really wouldn't."

"I won't tell on you. And you should remember this. I *make your food*."

She pointed to her hat. He got up and shut the door.

"Whether you like it or not," he said, "I work for Julia. Which means I now work for your dad. And I actually need my job. If I break the rules, I could lose my job. And I can't let that happen. Do you understand? *Please* don't mess this up for me."

The sudden seriousness stopped her. Whatever her dad was doing, maybe Aidan was as trapped as she was. Her father had tied up Aidan's job in this scheme, whatever it was.

"Are you joking?" she asked.

"Do I sound like I'm joking? Your dad figured out that we were drinking the other night too. I got a lecture from Julia for about an hour. I really don't want another one."

He pursed his lips and stared at the wall. Clio could tell that it had bothered him to say that. He wasn't as powerful as he would have liked to make out. He was being ordered around by everyone too.

"Fine, haircut," she said, getting up. "I won't make trouble for you. But you'll eat what I make. That's *my* job."

The dive lasted about forty-five minutes, after which Clio's dad and Martin emerged dripping from the water. All of the preparation and general hoopla didn't come to much. They peeled off their gear and wet suits and quietly went back to what they had been doing before.

Clio watched this from the glass doors, shook her head in misery, got her sketchbooks, and sat down on the plush living room carpet. Today she had a nice, complacent subject: Elsa, sleeping again. She stuck her earphones in and flipped to a new page. Without realizing it, she passed an entire hour doing the sketch. Time slid past so easily when she was absorbed in her drawing. She only stirred when Aidan passed in front of her carrying what looked like a massive toolbox. He certainly kept a lot of toys down there.

"Hello, haircut," she said. "Going fishing?"

There was a little stiffness in his demeanor now. And he was clearly working. She set the book down on the floor and followed him out onto the deck. He set down the box and removed a small cylinder.

"I guess that's some piece of equipment," she said. "Is it a camera?"

He said nothing.

"Come on," she said. "You're not really giving anything away by telling me that. I'm just curious what you put in the water. I'm not trying to get you fired."

A pause. The eyes flashed. He was still in serious mode.

"It's a tow fish," he said. "It's a reader that drags in the water and sends out the signal for our side-scan sonar. The sonar creates a picture of the ocean floor. Depending on conditions, we can usually get a fairly clear look. It doesn't take a photograph—more like a sonogram."

Clio eyed the long tube and the way Aidan carefully handled it.

"My dad didn't listen to you this morning," she said. "You should get used to that."

Aidan tugged on the cable connected to the device to check the connection but didn't reply. He stood up and lowered it off the side and carefully secured it.

"No one likes the tech guy," he finally said.

He cleared his throat and adjusted his massive watch. It was one of those silver-and-gold things with six dials on the face.

"That's a serious watch," she said. "Looks like an astronaut's watch or something."

"Do you really have to say something about *everything*?" he asked. He self-consciously stopped touching the watch and stuck his hand into his pocket. It was a deep cargo pocket; he got his whole wrist in there.

"You're one to talk," she said. She turned on her heel and went back inside, sitting back down with her sketchbooks. Her heart was beating a little faster. It was like she was allergic to him. She should just stay away.

He came in after a moment, quietly shutting the glass doors.

"I'd like pasta tonight," he said. "Lasagna."

Obviously, her remark had caught up with him and he didn't want to lose out on his game. She didn't look up. Instead, she fingered through her pencils intently.

"If by lasagna," she said, "you mean fish, you're in luck."

Aidan bent down and picked up her sketchbook, flipping through its pages.

"This must be your boyfriend, huh?" he said, dangling the book down, the page open to one of the drawings of Ollie. "Nice tie. Very *ironic*. I love people who dress all ironic. It's so deep, you know?"

"Don't be bitter, haircut," she said, taking the book back. "It makes your eyebrows come together."

Rules and Transgressions

Being trapped had paid off for Clio in the past. For example, being trapped in the rain. That was how Dive! had been made.

During the summer that Clio was eleven, the family went to the beach for a week. It rained every single day, turning the little yard in front of their rented beach house into a mud pool and forming dangerous swells on the ocean. They tried to go to the boardwalk a few times, but it was frankly pretty depressing to run from one waterlogged booth to the next or to drink frozen lemonades while soaking wet and freezing in the air-conditioning.

Clio's mother was studying restoration techniques on artifacts taken from the sea and spent most of that week curled up on the couch under a blanket, occasionally reading passages out loud. Clio started to trace the path of a boat on her sketch pad. Her dad watched her doing this. He suggested that since they couldn't go anywhere, they make something. A game.

Something based on what Clio had drawn. They were like that then, she and her dad. It was like they had one mind.

It was Clio who drew the board design, carefully working at it with a ruler and a set of drawing pencils. Her dad crafted the initial rules. They worked back and forth, taking each other's ideas. What started as a pastime for one afternoon became an all-consuming obsession for the remainder of the trip, and their return home, and the next three months. They started trying it out on family and friends. Everyone commented on how good it was. How *playable* it was. How amazing Clio and her father were.

This encouragement gave her dad an idea. He decided to package it up and shop it around. Clio could still remember the day that they got the phone call that it had been purchased by Botzoo, a major New York game company. The video game version was what really brought in the money. People were playing it on their cell phones and their computers. It was everywhere.

The fact that a popular game was made by a handsome man and his eleven-year-old daughter (and that they were even depicted on the packaging) made for a good story. For almost a year, Clio and her father were the subjects of newspaper stories, early-morning news programs, and endless online chatter. That was when her father decided regular school wasn't good enough for Clio, not when they had a sudden swell of income and opportunity. They would learn about the art and culture of the world directly. So, at twelve, Clio said good-bye to her friends at school. From then on, it was tutors and travel, drawing lessons and trips.

And in her memory, it had all been pretty great, right up until the end.

Sitting in the *Sea Butterfly*, Clio tried to reconcile this in her head. She remembered liking those trips then. Everything seemed perfect, like a fairy tale. Her life was charmed. The fall had come so fast, and since then, nothing had ever been quite right. This trip was just the most extreme expression of this "not rightness" so far.

When six people share a fairly small, confined space, two things become important. The first is personal space. Everyone had a few cubic feet to call their own, a place to retreat to. Even Clio and Elsa, who had no *true* personal space, came to an understanding. Everything on the right side of the room was Elsa's, everything on the left was Clio's. An invisible line divided the center of the bed, marked by the edges of their folded comforters. Sometimes Clio could take a long bath, just for the excuse of having a little room completely to herself for a while. Julia and her father kept up the ruse of separate bedrooms, and since they slept downstairs, Clio never had to watch them going into her father's room each night.

The second element of survival was routine. The routine got her from day to day, and if she could get from day to day, weeks would go by. And if weeks went by, she would get to land. And land meant contact with Ollie.

There was breakfast in the morning. Dishes. Elsa's morning nap. Lunch. Clio drew for longer and longer stretches in the afternoons, filling her notebooks. Preparing and clearing dinner took at least two or three hours in the evening, after which there would be some seriously awkward conversations. There were

135

attempts at card games and one disastrous night in which her dad suggested charades, and then people would scatter to their little corners. Night always came early.

Clio watched the routines of others. For those involved with the mission, the days were full. Generally, Aidan and Julia worked downstairs, though Julia could also be found reading or writing in the living room. Martin and her father spent most of their time in the wheelhouse, controlling the boat, or diving. There was a dive almost every single day. Nothing ever seemed to come of these dives, not that Clio knew what they were looking for. They would stop the boat, send up the diving flag, and Martin and her dad would go in. Then they'd come up, and more meetings would take place.

When not sleeping or talking about Alex, Elsa spent her time "revising for A levels," which Clio eventually figured out meant that she was preparing for some extremely serious tests that would determine her future. The floor of the Champagne Suite was often littered with notes in French and Italian. Elsa also had the habit of sucking on lemon wedges all day and leaving the remains on her bedside stand. Put her in the sun with a textbook, a lemon, and some suntan lotion, and Elsa was a happy girl. She didn't seem to care at all what the others were doing— the only thing she didn't like was that Aidan was elusive, frequently locked away with her mother.

The door-locking was something Clio paid very special attention to. The downstairs door to the workroom was constantly shut. When her father and Martin dove, she would sometimes go down and stand in front of it, and she would hear Julia snapping at Aidan about something. That room was definitely Aidan's territory and was definitely the source of all Internet access. He sometimes stayed in there in the evenings, maybe working, maybe communicating with the outside world.

And so the week went on.

On the tenth afternoon, Clio realized that everything she had been planning to use for lunch wasn't really edible. The bread had gone moldy, and there was only a tiny bit of meat and cheese and no more canned tuna. No soup or lettuce or pasta. No more lemons for Elsa to suck on. This was a clear, definite sign that they would have to return to land—but this fact had to be presented carefully. If she came out and told her father that there was no food, he would insist that there was. The trick was to put out really bad food, the dregs, and let him figure it out for himself.

"Oh yes," Clio thought, pinning on her name tag. "This is the sign."

There were so many dregs to choose from. Mushy olives. A handful of crackers. A single cup of the by-now-ancient curry. Some plain rice. A single slice of ham. Clio arranged it all very carefully, maximizing its misery factor. When it was all ready, she decided to go and get Aidan personally. She could take a little additional pleasure in walking him to his lunch of doom.

The door of the workroom was unlocked, so she pushed it open. To her surprise, no one was there. There was no noise anywhere on the downstairs level. She walked along and tried the doors, knocking on each one and trying the handles. No one was in any of the rooms. Only Julia kept her bedroom locked, but she clearly wasn't there.

Clio returned to the workroom. The only things on the main

table were two large charts that showed water depths and obstructions. There was a notepad on the side with a few numbers and letters scrawled in a jangled, masculine hand. This was probably Aidan's writing and clearly the writing of someone who ordinarily used a keyboard. The strokes were rough and jerky.

Aidan's laptop sat in the far corner, at his makeshift desk. There were crushed soda cans next to it. The screen was pushed halfway down.

Looking at someone's laptop was a clear breach of privacy under any circumstances. But in this environment, the crime was ten times worse. Then again, these were not normal circumstances. This could be it—the opportunity, right here in front of her. She could just quickly check her e-mail and send a message to Ollie. Maybe one to Jackson, too, asking for advice. Maybe Jackson would agree to keep an eye on what Ollie was up to at the store. Why hadn't Clio thought of this sooner?

She pushed the screen up carefully. The screen saver was on. She tapped the space bar gently, and it woke up. Aidan was running some program she'd never seen before—something obviously scientific. There was a graph on the screen, a little mountain range of a line spiking up and down. It probably had something to do with the sonar that he had dropped into the water. There was a key near the bottom that said *Bell Star* and a list of what looked like measurements. She briefly wondered what kinds of bells and stars Aidan would be studying. At the very bottom of the screen, though, were two little folded-up windows, one of which was Google, the other, a Yale e-mail system.

"Oh my God," Clio said to herself.

It was sad how exciting this was. She stood there, unsure of what to do. This was clearly her shot—but then again, that meant invading Aidan's privacy. It was possible that if she touched the computer, something would go wrong with the graph on the screen.

The temptation was painful. Truly, physically painful. She sat down and stared at the screen, trying to figure out what to do.

"What are you doing?"

Clio turned with a little yelp to find Julia in the doorway.

"No one was in here," Clio said.

"Please don't touch that," Julia said, nodding at the computer.

"I wasn't . . ." Clio said. And she hadn't been. "I didn't."

Julia wasn't buying that for a minute.

"I came down to tell you about lunch," Clio said. "There's lunch."

Aidan came up behind Julia but stopped when he saw Clio sitting at his chair.

"I wasn't," Clio said again.

"There's lunch," Julia said to Aidan. "Maybe we should all go up."

The sad buffet that Clio had laid out didn't go down so well under these circumstances. Her father was standing over it, looking deeply unimpressed.

"We need to talk," he said. "Upstairs."

Nothing in the world is more humiliating than being ordered around by your parents in front of other people. The only thing that would make it worse would be putting up a fight, so Clio shrugged and followed him to the wheelhouse.

"Julia is upset," he said. "And frankly, so am I. You used Aidan's computer. That's his property, and it's—"

"I didn't use his computer," she cut in.

"Clio. Julia found you."

"All I did was wake it up to see if it was online. I didn't look through it."

"This is serious," he said, sitting down. "You can't go snooping around."

"Snooping?" Clio repeated. "I went down to tell everyone that lunch was ready, and no one was in there. I walked into the room, I saw the computer, and I touched it. I didn't use it. I touched it."

"You expect me to believe that?" he said.

"Yes," she said. "I do. If you don't believe me, why don't you go and ask Aidan if there's anything weird about his computer? And you know what? I expect you to believe me over Julia. I'm your daughter."

Without realizing it, she had started to yell.

"That's enough," he said.

"No," she went on. "It's *so* not enough. I didn't ask to be stuck out here. I don't think you can call it snooping if I'm stuck on this boat. There are only so many places I can go. And why is it wrong to want to contact the outside world? None of this is fair. You practically kidnapped me."

"All right!" His own anger had broken through. Her dad got red-faced very quickly when he was upset, and his face was a bright raspberry color now. "I want you up in your room. Now."

"My room?"

"That's right. I think you need to spend some time up there."

"Oh, you have got to be kidding. How much more can you isolate me?"

Her voice was cracking with frustration.

"Some girls would be grateful that they got to spend the summer in Italy," he yelled.

"Some girls wouldn't be stuck with you," she said.

This remark was way too volatile. She hadn't really meant to say it—at least not like that. But now it was in the room, lurking like a poisonous snake. It was time to back up and get out.

"Fine," she said. "I'll go to my room. But just so you know? We have no food."

The Escape

Clio spent the afternoon up in the Champagne Suite, fighting down the most overwhelming urge to scream that she had ever experienced in her life. She wanted to rock the sonar and scare the fish and tear the skin of her own throat with the force of her effort.

But she did nothing of the kind, mostly because she wasn't crazy and partially because Elsa stayed with her out of protest and helped calm her down. Specifically, she brushed Clio's hair. She plunked Clio down on the floor, sat on the bed with a brush, and stroked away. It wasn't something that would have occurred to Clio to do or that she normally would have thought of as helpful. But in a matter of half an hour, her nerves were steady. Clio got the feeling that Elsa had been through many nights of freak-outs at school. She was just altogether too prepared.

Having Elsa was the one good thing to come out of this ridiculous experience. It really was like she had gained a sister.

For the rest of the afternoon, Clio sat at the top of the bed and drew another picture of Ollie, noticing that his face was getting less and less clear in her mind's eye. He'd surely become smitten with the art store girl, Jaimee or Janine, and forget all about Clio. Elsa stretched out on the end of their bed, copying Italian phrases in a notebook.

The boat lulled to a stop, and Clio heard the tiny whir of the anchor going down. The boat sloshed quietly back and forth. Several minutes later, Elsa rolled off the bed, stretched, and went into the bathroom. She came out and fussed with the things on her dresser, stirring in an obviously bored way. She walked over to the window and then let out a tiny squeal.

"Come here!" she said to Clio. "Look!"

Clio got up and joined her. Just off to the side, maybe a quarter of a mile away, was a town.

"Oh my God!" Clio said. "Finally!"

"Let's get dressed," Elsa said.

The sheer exhilaration of just being near a town drove them both into a near frenzy of indecisiveness. After several outfit changes, Elsa settled on a white tube sundress with a finely woven leather belt that she said had been her Swedish grandmother's. For makeup, she applied just the smallest amount of gloss.

Clio opted for her skirt and a special half-red, half-blue T-shirt. It was the most complex of all her creations, and she had yet to wear it on this trip. She kicked off her sneakers and changed into a pair of red, sparkly flip-flops that had yet to come out of the back of the wardrobe. It took her a minute to find her wallet; she hadn't used it since her arrival. She had gotten a hundred euros

143

before she left, in two fifty-euro notes. She'd never had an opportunity to spend any of them. They were shoved in the front pocket of the skirt.

She and Elsa headed downstairs to find out the plan, but no one was in the living room. They went out onto the deck. Elsa went up the steps to the wheelhouse while Clio went to the back of the boat and stared at the Italian town. She didn't know what town it was, just that it was a town. It was land. People walked on it. There were shops and cars and restaurants. And computers and phones.

Then she looked down.

The launch was gone.

"They're not up here," Elsa called.

"Elsa," Clio said, waving her over. She pointed down at the empty spot on the platform. "I do *not* believe this."

"Maybe someone's still here," Elsa said. "Downstairs."

All the doors along the hall downstairs were shut. Clio went along and banged on each of them. After a moment, Aidan's door opened. He stood there, shirtless, in stretched-out sweatpants that revealed several inches of his boxers.

"What?" he asked, rubbing his face. He had deep red sleep creases on his left cheek.

"They didn't take you either," Clio said.

"Who didn't take me where?" He shook his head and seemed to become aware of both the change in motion and the fact that his pants were falling off. He pulled them up. "I just took a nap. Have we stopped? Where are we?"

"Doesn't this bother anyone else?" Clio asked.

"Bother what?" Aidan asked. "What's going on?"

Clio could already see the hopeful light in Elsa's eyes. The three of them had been left on the boat, alone. Clio could almost see a ripple go through Elsa's spine, causing her to straighten, shift her hips just slightly to the left, and thrust her chest just an inch out and up. It was like some biological response, subtle and unconscious.

Clio couldn't stand that her father's ignorance might actually result in something pleasant for someone. The *Butterfly* had never felt as confining as it did at that moment. This was a buttery leather–and-teak prison, the most literal expression of everything that was wrong with her father. Excessive, unexplained, ill-conceived, thoughtless . . . and ultimately bad for Clio.

"I need . . . off," Clio said. "You guys do whatever you want. But I'm getting to town. I *have* to call home."

She squeezed between Elsa and the still-confused Aidan and went up the steps.

When Elsa and Aidan joined her, he had on a shirt and shorts. Elsa's face was strangely calm.

"Do you see that?" Clio said, pointing at the expanse of water. "Do you see how close we are? This is my dad's way of showing me that he's still in charge. *Dogs* do stuff like this when they pee in the house."

"They could be right back," Elsa said. Her voice got a little higher and chirpier. "And even if they're not, we could make the best of it. We have the whole boat to ourselves! Come on. We could have a . . . party or something."

Clio automatically turned toward the glass doors and looked at the boat. Nothing really mattered less to her at that moment than having the *Sea Butterfly* to themselves. The look on Aidan's face suggested he felt the same.

"What kind of party?" Clio asked. "The kind without food? Or fun?"

"Good point," Elsa said.

"When we first got on the boat, they left shore without telling us," Clio said. "They took off when we were sleeping. They kept us out here for *days*. And when we do get to land, they leave us out here. We're like prisoners. Isn't this a form of torture? Keeping people moving? Breaking off their contact with the world?"

"Yes," Aidan said, sitting down on the side of the boat. "It's Sudanese yacht torture. Rare, expensive, and evil."

Clio ignored this and turned to Elsa.

"He always does this," she said. "He doesn't think. He doesn't care. He just does what he wants to do. It doesn't occur to him that other people exist or have feelings or even just have *things to do*."

"So," Aidan asked. "What are you suggesting we do about it? They took the raft."

She turned back to water and gauged the distance.

"It's an easy swim," Clio said. "Well, it's a swim, anyway."

"Because that wouldn't be weird at all," he said. "You in your skirt, dragging yourself out of the water onto the beach, soaking wet. That's a good idea."

"I didn't say it was my idea," Clio said. "I was just thinking out loud."

"If I know my mum," Elsa said, "there's bound to be a decent bottle of wine or two around here somewhere. I say we get them open and enjoy ourselves. I don't really see what else can be done."

Clio's stomach burned with anger. There was no way she could sit back and take this, not when the town was so close.

There were computers and phones and, somewhere in her dreams, a possible means of escape. A seagull flew overhead, dipping into the water once before continuing to the beach. Another boat chugged past them, churning up a slow, wide wake that sent them rocking back and forth.

"That's it," Clio said, pointing at the boat as it made its way to the dock. "People are going in for the night. We bum a ride. We're only going over there. We can see our destination. Why not? You can do the talking."

"Oh, that's *brilliant*." Elsa laughed.

A minute or two later, a very small wooden boat went by a few yards off, carrying only one young man with a net. Clio started waving at him wildly. He stood watching them for a moment from a distance, then cautiously turned his boat in their direction and came up a few feet behind.

"What do I say?" Elsa said, looking at Clio and swallowing a laugh.

"Just say we need a ride," Clio said. "Say we need to meet our dad."

Elsa communicated this. The fisherman didn't look entirely convinced, but he seemed intrigued by Elsa.

"I don't know if this is going to work," Elsa said quietly.

"Here," Clio said, digging around in her pocket for the fifty-euro notes. She found them and slipped one out. "Tell him he can have this if he takes us."

Aidan gave Clio a sideways glance.

"Oh, you *are* good," Elsa said, taking the money. She held up the note, and there was another, briefer conversation. From the man's smile, Clio could see that the offer was happily accepted.

Fifty euros to go somewhere he was going anyway, somewhere that was actually in sight. That was too good to pass up. He pulled his boat around by hand, rowing to the back of the boat.

"Ride," Clio said, holding out her arm in the direction of the fishing boat.

"I can't believe you just hired a stranger in a fishing boat," Aidan said.

"It was better than swimming."

"How do we get back?" he asked.

"We bring the coms," Clio answered, holding hers up. "We call them."

Aidan sighed heavily, folded his arms, and looked back up at the wheelhouse.

"If we leave, there will be no one on this boat," he said.

"They should have thought of that before they left without telling us," Clio said, swinging open the hatch. "Nobody told us we had to stay. I'm going."

Clio handed the man his fifty euros. He smiled and nodded, folding the bill twice carefully and putting it in his pocket. Clio stepped off the back platform and into the boat. It was neither tied up nor entirely stable and there was a large gap between it and the *Sea Butterfly*. Also, it was higher than the back platform, meaning that she had to swing herself into the boat, no small feat considering she had chosen to wear a skirt. The only way she could guarantee that she wouldn't lose her balance and end up in the water or crash back onto the platform was by pitching herself forward into a pile of lumped-up nets. They were wet and smelly, with a little trash and a crab claw trapped in them.

She looked up at Elsa and Aidan, who were well above her

now, up on the deck of the *Butterfly*. There was a visible battle going on inside Elsa. Both options obviously held some appeal. But Clio could see that she was winning.

"Come on, Aidan," Elsa said, widening her eyes a bit. "What's more valuable? A boat or us? The daughters of your bosses?"

"In pure cash terms?" he asked.

"Do what you want," Clio called up. "You can sit out here alone, rocking back and forth slowly. That's probably how you spend a lot of your nights."

His lips twitched just slightly. Elsa looked between them, turning her gaze from one to the other.

"Yeah," he said, throwing up his arms. "Fine. I guess they can't blame us if they didn't tell us."

Elsa clapped.

"I'll get my purse," she said. "I'll be right back."

Aidan tried a large, heavy stride that rocked the boat and almost sent the fisherman off the side. He settled himself on the damp bottom of the boat and gave the fisherman a flat smile. The fisherman stared at him, then at Clio.

Where is the large-breasted, Italian-speaking blonde? his eyes asked. *She was the only reason I even came over in the first place.*

"*Momento,*" Clio said, and immediately regretted it. She was pretty sure that wasn't an Italian word. You can't just add an *o* to any English word to make it *foreign*.

Aidan looked into the plastic barrel next to him and quickly retracted.

"Crabs," he said. "I'm sitting next to crabs."

"See that?" Clio said. "You're with your own. This is working out already."

149

"I'm only doing this to make sure nothing happens to you two," he said.

"Liar."

Aidan's slender eyebrows shot up, but he quickly pulled them back down again and composed his expression into the usual calculating one. He leaned forward, balancing his elbows on his knees. The fisherman looked between them, clearly unsure of what was going on.

"We probably only got left behind because your dad was annoyed at you," he said. "You know, about my computer."

"I didn't touch your computer," she said. "Well, I touched it. And that was literally it. I didn't look through it or do anything to it. I just wanted to see if it was online. I didn't . . . go into any of your personal stuff. I wouldn't."

"I know you didn't," he said. "I could tell. But that's still probably the reason."

"So you're blaming me?" she asked.

"No. I'm simply stating a fact."

The doors opened, and Elsa ran across the deck, her shoes clomping hard against the fiberglass. She had obviously changed them while she was getting her purse. As she extended a leg off the platform into the boat, Clio saw the shoes—they were very high white wedges. They struck Clio as being very Scandinavian. She loved them.

Both the fisherman and Aidan attempted to help her. But since Aidan was sitting, the fisherman got there first.

"All ready, everybody?" Elsa said, flashing the fisherman a smile that would have melted a hole in a polar ice cap. "Let's go."

A Brief History of Floridian Girl-Lifting

The fishing boat didn't go to a dock; it went to the beach. The man waved his arms, and three other guys waded out to it. They stared at Clio, Elsa, and Aidan. A conversation was had in Italian.

"They're asking about us," Elsa whispered as they spoke.

The owner of the boat got out, and the four men together took a rope that was tied to the front of the boat and dragged it up to the beach. It was clear that their presence made the work a lot harder than usual. But there was a final tug, a yell, and the boat eased onto the shore with a thick sluffing sound.

"What do we do first?" Elsa asked after giving the fisherman their thanks. He looked after her and blew her a kiss. She smiled that easy, radiant dairy goddess smile.

"There's someone I have to get in touch with," Clio said.

"Your boyfriend!" Elsa said, squeezing her arm. "You poor thing! You haven't been able to talk to him all week!"

"Is that why we just jumped onto the good ship *Crabby*?" Aidan asked, looking genuinely unimpressed. "So you could call your *boyfriend*?"

This boyfriend thing had been getting thrown around too much for Clio to correct it now.

"No," she said. "We did it so that we could visit this beautiful Italian town. Wherever we are."

Like Sorrento, this town was above them, but not nearly as high up. If anything, the town seemed to be piled on top of itself in about eight layers of sherbet-colored buildings. They only had to walk up one set of steps to get there, and these steps were nowhere near as agonizing as the ones Clio had taken last time. They started making their way to them. Elsa pulled off her white wedge shoes.

Clio looked down at her red flip-flops in the black sand. This sand glinted bizarrely—there were tiny dots of color strewn throughout it, sparkling in the sun. She reached down and grabbed a large handful, picking out the colored bits. They were tiny, perfectly smooth pebbles in brilliant green, aquamarine, rust red, stark white.

"I think this is glass," she said.

"Wow," Aidan said. "Glass."

"No," she said. "Look. Have you ever seen a beach like this? How did all of this glass get into the sand? It's everywhere! And it's completely smooth."

"I guess it got sanded," he said. "Here. In the *sand*."

"But there's so *much* of it," she said, pointing to the long stretch of beach.

"I guess the Italians throw a lot of bottles into the sea," he said. Clio shook her head. Why did he have to be so sarcastic all the time? And why was she letting it get to her? Ollie would have appreciated all this beauty. But for some reason, Clio was really frustrated that Aidan didn't seem to get it. Was he *trying* to be stubborn?

Elsa wasn't paying attention to them. She was examining the view around them with a thoughtful look on her face; then she jumped in front of Aidan and Clio.

"You two," Elsa said. "You do not have the proper attitude right now. So I'll tell you what we're going to do. We're going to get something to *eat* and to *drink*. Then you can call home."

There wasn't a lot to the town, whatever it was. There was a stretch of pavement at the top of the steps with a smattering of restaurants, gelato stands, and tourist beach-supply shops. Beyond and above that were peeling buildings with large shut-tered windows swung wide open, revealing the insides of apartments, televisions on, and dangling laundry. In any other place, this probably would have been very unappealing, but in Italy, it felt right.

There were plenty of nice restaurants along the main street, but the trio needed something affordable, and it was Clio who managed to locate the perfect spot. It had white plastic outdoor tables with blue vinyl cloths on them, shaded by tipsy red umbrellas advertising something that Clio had never heard of. Each table was decorated with silk flowers arranged in empty Orangina bottles. The menu was one laminated page, written in both Italian and misspelled English, and it was all pasta.

None of them had a lot of cash, so they ordered three of the same dish, ziti with tomato sauce, the simplest, least expensive pasta on the menu. Elsa added something on at the end, pointing at a different section of the menu and giving the waiter a huge smile.

"We're celebrating," she said, passing the menus over.

The waiter brought over two carafes of red wine and three glasses and a basket of chewy, dark-crusted bread. Elsa poured.

"To our escape," she said, raising her glass.

They all sipped the wine. It was warm going down. And once Clio got over that initial strange flavor, the total lack of sweetness, she almost thought she got what people meant when they said "woody aftertones."

"I think he likes us," Elsa said, watching the waiter walk off. "This is a little bit nicer than what I think I ordered. Now. Our plan for this evening? Since we will have already annoyed the others, and by the others, I mean Clio's father, I think we should just go out fully. Agreed?"

"I agree," Clio said.

They clinked glasses on it.

Aidan said nothing. He just leaned back in his plastic chair, his hair flopping over his piercing eyes. He picked out a bug that had flown into his glass and drowned.

"Here," Clio said, retrieving her com and putting it in Elsa's purse. "I don't want to hear it when he starts calling for Number Five."

"Exactly," Elsa said, dropping her arm over Clio's shoulders. "*That's* better."

In no time at all, they were presented with three massive plates. Even though the pasta was simple, it managed to be the best Clio had ever had. It was very fresh and just a little spicy, with big pieces of basil. The pasta was chewy and perfect, and the whole thing was steaming hot, as if it had just been snatched off some grandmother's stove.

"You're not being very smart," Elsa said, toying with her pasta and looking over at Aidan. Aidan had already cleaned a quarter of his plate before they had really even started.

"Why's that?" he asked, his mouth full.

"Because you're sitting here at a table with two girls, two rather attractive girls . . ."

How did Elsa do that? Clio wondered. How did she just come out with that and not have it sound conceited? That was definitely a superpower.

". . . and you're doing absolutely nothing to impress or entertain us. And we need entertainment. We're both suffering."

"All right," he said, his eyes narrowing a bit. "I've got a story."

"Let's hear it," Elsa said, raising her glass.

"I used to be a ballet dancer."

Elsa's glass landed back on the table, and she let out a bright, loud laugh.

"You're lying," Clio said, feeling herself crack a smile.

"This is one *hundred* percent true," he said. "When I was a kid, we had an insane neighbor named Mrs. Chemonsky who started a dance studio in her basement. She used to come over and have coffee with my parents all the time. She was one of those people who no one really wants to have over, yet you can't seem to stop her. No one could say no to her because she'd just push and push and push. She ran everything in my neighborhood. So, she kept complaining to my parents about how she didn't have any boys, and how dancing really was a masculine thing to do, and how she really wished more parents were enlightened about it, and why didn't I come over and be in the class? She completely wore my parents down, and I ended up going there two times a week."

"In tights?" Elsa asked. "Please tell me there were tights. Please describe them fully."

"Oh yes," he said, reaching for more wine. "There were tights. They were green."

"And they had feet?" Elsa asked. "Full-length tights?"

"They had little green feet," he said. "It did really good things for my self-esteem."

The vision of Aidan in green tights cheered Clio up a lot. The more she pictured it, the more she realized that it probably wouldn't be too bad a sight. He had really dense legs, with muscles.

"It was only supposed to be for a little while," he went on, "but we couldn't stop, or Mrs. Chemonsky would come over and hound my mother. And my mother really hated being hounded by Mrs. Chemonsky, so I stayed in there for *three* entire years. I was in high school when I finally got out of it. You do not want to know what would have happened to me if the people in my high school found out I was in ballet class. I'm from Florida. You do not do ballet in Florida if you're a guy."

"So you can dance?" Elsa said. "And you're going to show us, right?"

"I can't dance at all," he said. "My dancing ability is *zero*. All I really did was lift. That's what guys in ballet do—they lift girls. I did a lot of girl-lifting."

"Not bad for you," Elsa said.

"You'd think so," he said, getting more animated. "Right? But

156

that's totally not the case. First of all, no serious dancers went to Mrs. Chemonsky's. It was mostly little girls. Little girls and me. It was okay when I was, like, thirteen and the girls were ten. But when I was fifteen and the girls were ten . . . then it was starting to get creepy. The whole thing only ever paid off in my Yale interview, when they asked me what my hobbies were. Not too many ballet dancers in the engineering department."

"Well, that settles it," Elsa said. "We're going dancing after this, and you're lifting us. We need to experience this very special skill of yours."

"If you want," he said with a shrug. "It's up to you. If you want to be lifted, I'll lift you."

"Oh yes," Elsa said, refilling all the glasses. "There will be lifting."

Clio realized that she hadn't spoken through any of this. It was all Elsa lifting and carrying the conversation, twirling around with it.

"Sure," Clio said. "Pick me up."

Aidan tipped his head in concession, his green eyes lit up for once.

"You want me to pick you up, I guess I can't refuse."

Now that she'd heard her own words said back to her, Clio realized her mistake. But he had gone with it, and strangely . . . she liked it. For the first time this whole summer, she really felt like she was part of a group, a group she wanted to be in.

When dinner was over and they'd cobbled together what money they had for the bill, Elsa hooked each of them by the arm and started off down the cobbled street, walking a slightly uneven walk. Clio couldn't tell if it was Elsa's high shoes on the stones or the wine . . . but she was definitely leaning on Aidan's side. This threw Clio off balance. But that might have been the wine too.

"Now," Elsa said, "here's what happens. We find a place where Clio can make her call. And then you and I . . ."

This was to Aidan.

". . . find a place to dance. You have a promise to keep."

Clio chose not to lean over and look at Aidan's reaction. She was suddenly a little less anxious to make the call. This made no sense—this was all she had wanted for more than a week. Yet the moment was here, and she found herself wanting to say that she would just go on with them, that they would look for a place to dance together.

Between a newspaper stand and a store full of shapeless clothes and table linens was a grubby little shop advertising phone and Internet access.

"Here we are," Elsa said, releasing Clio. "We'll be back for you in half an hour or so. Is that okay?"

"It's fine," Clio said. She didn't want them to go and leave her in this store. But obviously, this was where she was supposed to be.

There were two dusty coin-operated computers in the window and, in the corner, one much-used tan phone with a flat handset. Clio purchased a ten-euro phone card from the man behind the counter, who was watching a soccer game on a small television and smoking a cigarette.

The first thing she did was dial her mother's cell phone, but there was no answer. She quickly did the math—six hours' difference to home, one more to Kansas. It was around lunchtime in Kansas, and her mother was probably stuck in some corner of the studio. Clio left a message, trying her best to express that it hadn't been her idea not to call for more than a week. When she hung up, she still had plenty of credit on the card.

And now, Ollie. She had two options: she could buy some credit and sit down at one of the busted-up computers, or she could use the card in her hand and simply call him.

She pushed the card into the space between her two front teeth and bit down in thought. Now that she finally had her chance, she was flooded with doubt. Would it be too weird to call Ollie from Italy? How did she explain that and not make it look like she was obsessed with him? "Hi, I was just walking around Italy and thought I should call . . . because I'm completely insane."

Then again, he might really like that. She would need an excuse, though. She could ask if India Blue #7 had come in. They were always out of that ink. It was a stretch, but she felt like she could pull it off. She would make it sound like she had been working on a picture and really needed that ink and would ask him to set it aside. Then she'd work up the nerve to say she'd been thinking about him.

It wasn't bad, actually. Kooky, yet it made her look dedicated to her work.

Before she could think about it anymore, she reentered the code on the card and started dialing. One ring. Two rings. Three . . .

Three normally meant that the call wasn't going to be answered. She was preparing herself to leave a message when the call was answered by a strange voice.

159

"Hi!" Clio said. "Ollie? It's me!"

"Who's this?" a girl said.

Clio stopped speaking and dug her finger into a thick layer of dust next to the phone.

"Is this Ollie Myers's number?" she asked.

"Yes," said the female voice. "Who's this?"

"This is Clio."

"He's not here right now, Clio," said the girl. She didn't sound mad or curious. Very matter-of-fact. The voice was vaguely familiar. Clio had definitely heard it before, but she couldn't place it. It had to be someone from the store.

Her mind immediately leapt to the new girl in the silver mesh shirt. Janine.

"Oh," Clio said. "The thing is, I'm in Italy, and—"

"Did you just say you're in Italy?" the girl said. Now the voice was taking on a strange tone.

"Just . . . can you tell him I called?" she said. "I'll try . . . I'll try some other time. Thanks. I have to go."

She clapped the phone down. The gray-and-black display showed how much time had elapsed. Four minutes. She had been here for *four minutes*. The big moment had been squashed like a little bug.

Clio stood there and considered calling someone else. She could call Jackson. But if *Jackson* wasn't home either, then she would feel truly doomed. So she went and waited outside, in the hopes that Elsa and Aidan would come back for her early.

They were late. Five minutes late. And the one thing Clio learned in that time is that if you are a girl sitting by yourself for a full half hour in Italy, people will look at you. The dark was descending, making all the pastel-colored buildings on the street simply look gray.

It was either the wine or that phone call, but her head was whirling. She went through every female voice she had stored in her mind and tried to make a match but couldn't come up with anything. She tried to imagine why someone might just have Ollie's phone. Maybe he'd left it lying around in the store. And it wasn't like if you were seeing someone you would *give them your phone*. No. Clearly, it was just a fluke.

She tried to convince herself of this fact as she sat there, but it didn't really take. Her stomach started to hurt—maybe it was the ziti. Maybe none of this had been such a good idea.

"I thought you'd still be on the phone!" Elsa said, hurrying over, dragging Aidan by the hand. "Come on! We found the *best* place. You won't believe it."

Clio found herself staring at their locked hands. This was definitely something Elsa just *did*, but it also seemed like they might be . . . together. Elsa wanted that, clearly. But Aidan still had that slightly aloof expression, like he was above whatever might be going on with them.

"It's very classy," he said dryly.

She wasn't in the mood for his snarkiness right now, so she ignored this and took the other hand that Elsa offered her. She let Elsa drag her down the street in a daze. Nothing made sense. In her head she kept hearing the voice on the phone, saying, "Who's this?"

Eurotrash Springs Eternal

The club was called Fez. They had to walk down a narrow stairwell lit by brass lamps with multicolored plastic panes to get to it. It smelled lightly of day-old beer, cigarettes, and plastic— like the inside of a mask from a Halloween costume. A man at the bottom of the steps demanded five euros each before they could go inside. He stamped their hands with a neon green image of a camel.

Clio had never been to a real club before. She was expecting lots of tiny people in tiny dresses, barely able to support the weight of the cosmo glasses in their hands. This wasn't what she got.

There were maybe two dozen people in the club, and it was completely clear to Clio that every single one of them was a tourist. In the center of the room was a dance floor made of multicolored squares that lit up at random. No one went anywhere near it. To give the club the Moroccan theme that its name promised, there were massive frondy plants all over the place.

The club made up for the lack of people and activity by being very dark and very loud. It was currently blasting some dance song that Clio had never heard before. This was something she remembered from her previous travels—anonymous dance music was one of Europe's bountiful natural resources.

It was too loud to say much. Elsa signaled that it was time to go over and get some drinks. There wasn't really anything else to do, so Clio followed along. Elsa shouted something to the bartender, and three bottles of Italian beer appeared. Clio went into her wallet to get some money and was shocked to find just how little she had now. She had seen herself spending it, yet it didn't seem possible that her hundred euros had so quickly dwindled to eight. It immediately became two.

They drank the beers quickly and silently, looking around and making eyebrow conversation with each other about the lack of movement. Clio tried desperately not to think about the conversation she had just had and let it ruin her night. She felt the beer filling her with a numb buzz.

Elsa bounced a bit as she drank, piling her hair on top of her head with one hand and letting it fall down. She reached over and did the same to Clio, who had much more hair. It tumbled over her face and shoulders. Then she ruffled Aidan's hair. For some reason, this gave Clio another uncomfortable pang. The night was starting to feel out of her control.

"What's wrong?" Elsa said, as quietly as she could. "You have a funny look on your face."

"Nothing," Clio said, unable to meet her eyes.

Elsa bobbed her head in a deep nod to the music and ruffled Clio's hair some more.

The volume lowered a little as the tracks changed and a new beat took over.

"Time for our dance," Elsa said. "Mind if I go first?"

Elsa put down her mostly empty beer and pulled Aidan off his stool. Obviously, the dance floor was there for whoever had the courage to take it. Clio stood on the edge and watched as Elsa made Aidan demonstrate his technique. He really couldn't dance, at least he didn't even try, but he picked her up over and over. Elsa did her part laughing, putting in leaps and spins. She gave Clio the occasional wave or made a "watch this!" gesture. Aidan occasionally shot her a quick glance as he was setting Elsa down. The more times they did this, the closer they got to each other, the longer he held her—and the less he looked over.

And here was Clio, drinking the rest of Elsa's beer now, still wondering who that had been on the phone . . . the phone of someone who wasn't even her boyfriend. Someone she had no right to be jealous about. Someone who wasn't hers.

All the joy from before, all the feelings of being in a group, of being happy . . . it drained away, disappearing into the spaces between the gaudily lit squares. Something was deeply wrong with her. She finished Elsa's beer and watched as Elsa leaned over and said something to Aidan. She came over to Clio.

"Your turn," she said.

Aidan stood, his arms extended, patiently waiting for his next partner. He wasn't smiling or smirking. His expression was strangely flat. Maybe he didn't *want* to dance with her. This was too much.

"I have to go," Clio said, handing Elsa back her empty bottle.

"Go where?"

"I have to make another call."

"Are you sure you're okay?" Elsa asked.

"It's fine," Clio said quickly. "I just . . . I'll be back."

Clio hurried across the dance floor. Aidan reached out halfheartedly but then let her pass.

Out on the street, Clio took a deep breath of air. It was too warm and heavy. She made her way back to the computer place quickly. Her two euros weren't even enough to get her another call. It was just enough money to buy ten minutes on one of the computers. When she managed to log on to her e-mail, she found that she had a hundred and seventeen notes in her in-box.

She backtracked into the older mail. She had an e-mail from Ollie somewhere, from months ago. They had been talking about an exhibit that came to a small gallery in the city. It took her a few minutes and a few tries. The connection was slow, but it was there. She hit reply and stared at the screen.

As her precious minutes ticked away, she looked for something in her head, something to express what it was she wanted to say to Ollie. She didn't want to accuse him. She didn't want to freak him out. She felt dizzy.

She managed to start typing something about Italy and ink and how she was sorry if her call had been confusing. Nothing made sense. Her sentences wouldn't go together. She kept deleting and retyping and noticed only at the last second that the timer was at three seconds. In one panicked moment, she hit send.

"Oh my God," she said aloud. "What did I just do?" The short guy behind the counter glanced at her and shrugged.

As she stumbled back to Fez, Clio looked up between the buildings at the white, full moon. Someone had dangled a fitted bedsheet out of a window. It looked like a lazy ghost, empty and mournful.

Outside the door, Clio showed the host her stamped hand and descended into the smoky, sad depths of Fez. There were five people on the dance floor now. Things were more animated and had graduated to some flailing arm moves.

"It's a party," Clio mumbled under her breath.

Elsa and Aidan were not in this particular party. Clio looked around the bar, behind a potted palm. She saw them in a far corner. They had moved back a bit. She started to walk toward them, her head pounding from the music, then realized just how close they were standing to each other. In fact, they were *very* close. Elsa put her arm behind Aidan's neck, and the two started kissing.

Clio stood there, dumbstruck. This made perfect sense. She'd seen it coming from the very first moments. It was clearly what Elsa wanted and needed, and therefore, Clio should be happy. It shouldn't have been a surprise.

But she didn't feel that way at all. It was a shock—a cold, disgusting shock. Her stomach tumbled. She turned away from the sight and ran out of the club.

Kill It If It Moves

Clio sat on the damp black sand in her skirt, looking out at the cold black water. It was too dark to see the gemstones in the sand now. She was fighting back nausea and swallowing back a bile in her mouth that tasted like warm beer, pasta, and woody aftertones . . . all mixed with a hint of self-loathing.

So many issues to choose from. Ollie. Her dad. Aidan and Elsa kissing . . .

The kissing was something that should have been simple. It was something other people, like Elsa and Jackson and . . . okay, *everyone* . . . took for granted. Right now, this very second, the only two people she really knew here were making out. And she was alone, drunk on the beach. Unkissed. And struggling with all her might to keep the sob she felt lodged in her throat from escaping.

Jackson, for instance, was one of those annoying people who could go into any party alone and, if she set her mind to it (and she frequently did), make out with someone reasonably hot. In Jackson's mind, all guys were in a constant state of readiness to be made out with, and it was a female's prerogative to select and act. Jackson always said it was a question of focus, of knowing that was what you wanted. She said that Clio simply never committed to the task and that on some level she was sabotaging herself.

But could it have been self-sabotage if, as in Clio's case, you got pretty much right up to the moment at a party, and then someone set the fire alarm off as a joke, and when everyone had to leave, the prospective kissee's friends told him that they were leaving? And since he didn't have a car, he left with them?

No.

Or what about the time she had a long buildup of conversation with a guy at school (Michael Flannigan) that went on for weeks, and when they finally made a plan to go out for coffee, he not only got mono, but post-viral syndrome, and stayed out of school for the next six months?

No.

Or the time that Swiss exchange student had become fixated with Clio's tattoo, and things were looking good, but then she ate that tuna burger that had been sitting around in the fridge for maybe one day too many. When the barfing was over, he was back in Zurich.

Jackson still insisted that this all had something to do with Clio's will, a deep, internal resistance, but Clio wasn't seeing it.

She also couldn't really even see the boat from where she sat. It was a blue-and-red glowing dot out in the distance. As much as she had hated it only three or four hours before, now she ached for it. She didn't feel like having the inevitable argument with her father. All she wanted was to get into her side of the bed, pull the comforter over her face, and maybe slip into a coma for a while. Eight weeks would be good.

Clio was sitting on the sand at the edge of the water, letting it lap over her toes. She could just close her eyes and sleep here. Of course, that was dangerous for about a million different reasons, as well as being deeply unappealing. Or she could go and whine to her mother, but there was still no way out of this. She had to go back to the boat. She had been beaten.

The thought struck her, brilliant and simple. She could swim for it. Even if her father was there already, maybe she could just slip on board and make it seem like she'd never left.

She shivered at the thought. It wasn't the swimming that worried her. She could handle the distance easily. It was the boats. Once you've been *hit* by a boat, you see them differently. But the channel was clear. It looked like most of the boats had come in for the night. Far out, there was some kind of large tourist boat, probably a dinner cruiser. It wasn't going to pass between her and the *Sea Butterfly*.

She looked around. No one was in sight. The route itself was straightforward. Out, under the rope that marked the swim area, along the rocks, and then directly to the boat. There were numerous signs up, all in Italian, but not one of them had anything that stood out as being scary, like a big picture of a shark's fin.

"It's an easy swim," she said to herself. "Do it and shut up."

Before she could give herself any more time to think, Clio walked into the water. The flip-flops sank into the pebbles and stuck; she stepped out of them. They would have to go. The stones cut into her feet and made it slippery and hard to walk, so she kicked off and swam out a bit farther. Now her skirt was a problem, so she wriggled out of it and released it into the water. It was better to lose a few bucks' worth of clothes than face this night any longer, and her tank top and underwear almost looked like a bathing suit anyway.

There was no going back now—now that she had no shoes and no skirt. That sealed the matter nicely. Nowhere to go but out into the inky darkness.

It was a perfect night for a swim, really. The water was calm, and the moonlight spilled over it. Almost immediately, she felt her head begin to clear. It was impossible to worry about Ollie or wonder why there was something so devastating about the kiss between Aidan and Elsa. There was only a deep breath, then she was facedown in the water, her arms making clean, long strokes.

A few fishing boats like the one they had hitched a ride on were anchored just a short distance out in the surf. Clio swam around them and continued straight out, keeping her eye on a formation of rocks that extended into the water to keep her path straight. Once she had passed them, she bore right. The *Sea Butterfly* had transformed from just a blip of light to a shadowy outline. This was easier than she'd thought. After a few minutes, she was halfway there. She had finally done *one* smart thing today.

She flipped over onto her back. It was magical, actually—the dark sky and endless stars and big moon, the warm water. The swimming had cooled her brain and slowed the churning and the pulsing inside.

A wave rolled her a bit, spilling water onto her face and up her nose. She snorted it out and pulled her head up out of the water to focus on the moon. It was full and marble-white, and she could see faint shadows and depressions on it.

She tried to call the image of Ollie back up in her head. She could see him in his vintage pinstripe dress jacket that he wore with jeans. . . . She could see him riding down Chestnut Street on his bike, smiling at her as he pulled up in front of the store. Clarity. The water brought clarity.

She flipped herself over, checked her position. The boat was maybe fifteen yards off. It didn't look like the lights were on. Maybe she had gotten lucky. She could get on board, and no one would be the wiser. If she hurried right now, this night would end peacefully.

She started for it again, swimming hard. She hadn't gotten more than a few feet when she felt the flick against her leg, a burning slash.

A cramp, she figured. She slowed for a second to let it release itself.

Another flick, much hotter and more painful than the first.

"Ow!" she said out loud. "What just . . . ?"

There was another one. Then down near her butt. And again, in the same spot.

Then she saw them. They were so pretty, like translucent little purple water clouds with yellow lightning trapped inside. Pretty or not, no one wants to find herself surrounded on all sides by jellyfish. There were at least ten or a dozen directly behind her, a few more beyond that, another two to the side, another four to the other side. She had swum directly into them.

Another sting, this one on her elbow.

There was nowhere to go except in the direction that would get her out of the water fastest. The problem was, when she kicked and moved, her legs just chopped into the tentacles more and more. There was slashing and burning over her thighs, her butt, her ankles. As the throbbing got worse, moving got hard. Panic was starting to take over now, exploding into all of her thoughts. She was swimming frantically, feeling her body cramp up and burn. If she stopped, they would keep stinging her, her muscles wouldn't work, she would drown. Really drown. Her body would stop working and she would sink like a stone, right between the land and her father's boat. The possibility was very, very real.

So she pushed harder. Now it felt like someone had smashed in her knee with a hot iron. She couldn't bend it enough to swim as hard as she needed to. She willed it to bend anyway. She took in too much water as she opened her mouth to breathe, and she gagged. The panic made her breathe faster, harder. She took in more water.

There was so much stinging all over her body that it was impossible to tell whether or not the jellyfish were still with her. Her movements had become completely erratic. The only thing she knew for certain was that she had moved forward. The swimming felt unreal now. She had tunnel vision. All she could see was the water, the bobbing back platform, her arms swinging. The boat was close, just a few feet away.

Her legs stopped working once they got the message that the boat had almost been reached. She had to rely on her arms. She started breast-stroking, pulling herself through the water. She screamed out, but there was no one on board to hear her.

To her amazement, she had reached the platform. It was so

beautiful, this sheet of white fiberglass. She just had to get up onto it. She tried to lift herself with her arms, but they were worn out and burning now. More force. She needed more force.

"All right," she told all her muscles. "You have to do this. You have to."

With one massive effort, she threw her body with as much force as she could muster onto the platform. Her chin slammed painfully into it, making her bite her tongue. She cried out in pain.

She was still mostly in the water. She had to get up the steps into the boat. She tried yelling again, but her voice was giving out, and no one was there anyway.

She dug her fingertips into the ridges of the platform and pulled herself along until she reached the handrail. Clio couldn't stand. Her legs didn't want anything to do with her. She just managed to drag herself up, scraping her knees against the rough, tractioned surfaces of the steps. That was the least of her worries. When she got to the top, she rolled herself over and landed unceremoniously on the hard white deck.

Then she fainted.

The SS *Bell Star*
May 1897

The noise woke Dr. Magwell in the middle of the night. He was a light sleeper. He had been since his wife died. It wasn't a particularly bad noise or extremely loud. It was just wrong, out of place on a night at sea.

He sat up. He heard it again. A high-pitched note ... one that an opera singer might strike. An opera singer would definitely be out of place here.

He got up and felt around in the dark for his dressing gown. The first thing he noticed was that the boat wasn't moving. The second was that it was leaning quite far to one side. He stumbled, reaching for a chair that used to be closer to the side of the bed.

He found the gown, slipped it on, and opened his door.

The smell in the hall was unlike anything he had ever encountered. It seemed to be the smell of something that could not and should not burn. There was heat from the direction of the stairs that led down to the second-class compartments. The whining noise was the ship. Its fabric cried and whined.

He had always thought he would know death when it came. Maybe this was because he had watched his wife die after Marguerite's birth, and it had seemed so inevitable. A joy such as a child's birth almost had to be accompanied by a sorrow just as great. Or perhaps it was because he had worked at Pompeii for so long, chipping away the work on one single morning of destruction. He had constantly envisioned that morning in AD 79 when the mountain that sat above the town suddenly exploded, sending a column of ash and fire into the sky, blocking out the sun, raining down rocks and air that boiled the lungs that breathed it. The shutter had come down on Pompeii, stopping it midday. Its inhabitants had tried to hide in their houses, block it out. But it came.

There was screaming now, cries of both "fire!" and "water!" He couldn't tell if this last one was a request or an exclamation.

He stepped back into his room and shut the door. It took some reaching around, but he found and lit the oil lamp that was secured next to his bed. If he survived this, two things would need to come with him. The first was the object that sat on the small desk, wrapped in layers of rough cloth. The second was a small alabaster cameo on a gold chain. This was the face of his daughter, Marguerite. She always gave it to him to take on his travels. "For luck," she said. "So that you are never alone."

There was another, louder whine, and the *Bell Star* righted herself, then fell in the other direction, throwing him up against the wall. The bundle slid across the desk, and he just managed to reach over and keep it from falling to the ground.

"Somewhere safe for you," he said, taking it in his hands. "You need to go somewhere safe."

There weren't many options in his small cabin. The best of them was the space under the heavy dresser that was bolted into the corner. The bundle fit under there snugly.

He sat on the floor next to it, listening to the chaos outside his door grow louder. There was heat under his floor and weirdly cheerful popping noises, a long series of them.

"My dear," he said to the cameo. "I have a very bad feeling about this."

The cameo smiled its peaceful, sleepy smile.

"I've always wondered how it would be," he said. "The timing is very bad, though. I've just found it. I suppose the gods are unhappy. History wants her secrets kept."

He was not fearless, but he was resigned. There was no fight he could put up. He would wait for nature and the gods, for history herself, to decide his fate.

Rescue

Something was jumping around Clio's head. It was loud, loud like a horse. A horse was dancing around her head.

Except that wasn't right. She wasn't sure where she was for a second, and she hadn't yet opened her eyes, but she knew that noise couldn't be a horse. That just didn't make any sense at all. It had to be shoes. Very loud shoes. And behind that noise there was a language she didn't know. Something was being mumbled.

"Clio!"

She opened her eyes to find Martin, Elsa, and Aidan leaning over her.

"Say something," Aidan demanded. "Clio. Talk. Say something."

She found the strength to deliver one short, decisive expletive.

"Good," Aidan said approvingly. "Try to keep talking. Where does it hurt?"

"Everywhere," she gasped. "Legs. Back. Fingers."

That was enough talking.

She had known pain before. It had been very painful when she'd gotten hit by the boat. But this—this was something else. This was the pain of something that seemed to *hate* her. Something that was still seeping into her system and growing. It was oozy and wet, yet it burned. The contradiction was so pronounced that it scared her. Something deeply programmed in Clio's nervous system told her that this wasn't good for her, that she needed to be afraid. Her body was shaking, for about six reasons.

In a very loose way, she wondered if she was dying. The thought of dying was less scary somehow. Dying was something that kind of made sense. This pain was confusing.

"Do we have the key to the wheelhouse to call this in?" Aidan asked Martin.

"No. Ben has it. Clio?"

"She can talk," Aidan said. "But I think she's in a lot of pain."

Clio groaned another, slightly higher-pitched affirmative.

"This is useless," Martin said, clicking off his com. "They're out of range. We can get her to land, but then we'd have to figure out what to do from there, and it doesn't look like she can move much. I'll go and try to find a doctor or someone."

"I'll go with you," Elsa said. "I can do the talking."

"You'll stay with her?" Martin said to Aidan.

"I'll take care of her," he answered.

"We'll be right back, Clio," Elsa said, taking her hand. "Don't be scared, okay? We'll bring help."

They hurried off. She looked up at Aidan. His head was blocking out the moon, but his crazy haircut had picked up the white glow.

"Are you cold?" he asked, his voice sounding uncertain. "You're shivering. Hang on."

He was right. She was shivering. Aidan vanished for a moment, returning with a white chenille blanket that had been decoratively draped over the end of the sofa. He also had a cushion for her head.

"Listen," he said, tucking the blanket around her, "I'm going to find out what to do. I'll be gone for a few minutes. Will you be okay?"

She blinked. The blanket made things just a shade better. At least it felt like she wasn't alone and exposed. In some ways, though, it made the pain even more clear.

"It's okay," he said. "I promise I won't be long."

Clio lay there on the wet deck, cocooned in her little throw blanket, staring up at the sky. The air suddenly stank of fish. Aidan soon returned with the biggest kettle from the galley. He was carrying it carefully by the handle.

"This is hot water," he said, setting it down. "It's really hot, but it should take away some of the immediate pain. I'm going to pour this on you, okay? I'm going to start with your legs."

She looked at him and nodded slightly. He peeled off the blanket and threw it to the side. Clio felt the scalding water dumping over her, starting around the waist and going right down to her feet. It pooled around her, soaking the cushion under her head. After the first burn, she noticed that it did help. She heard a strange sound and realized that she was making a low wailing noise.

"I'm going to get some more," he said.

He returned with another potful and rolled her over. She put

179

her face down into the pooled water. It gurgled up her nose. She felt her shirt being pulled up a little and the water dropping onto the small of her back.

"God," he said. "They really got you. I've never seen anything like this."

"Can I go inside?" she asked. Her voice sounded small and weak. Kind of pathetic.

"Sure," he said. "Can you get up? Forget it. Here."

Before she could even try, his arms were underneath her. She was deadweight, but he picked her up without too much difficulty and got her through the glass doors. In her miserable state, the random thought that passed through Clio's head was, *I guess this is my turn to get picked up.*

It was way too cold and dark in the living room, and the leather sofa he set her on felt like ice. Her skin stuck to it. She felt welts popping up all over her body.

"Blanket," she mumbled. She didn't mean to sound so blunt, but it was all she could really manage. She couldn't be subtle and conversational. She had been reduced to a Franken-Clio level of speech. He rushed back out and got the blanket.

"It's all wet," he said. "I'll go get the one off your bed."

He brought Elsa's, which struck her as odd. But it wasn't like he should have known which of the two was hers. It smelled like Elsa too, an herbal smell, kind of like chamomile. He put it over her and switched on some of the lights.

Her body was coming back to life now. The pain was still strong, but the warm blanket that smelled of Elsa, the light—it all made her feel more human. A wellspring of emotion and fear, something huge that she hadn't felt since she was little, suddenly

180

blossomed inside her. She wanted her father. She wanted her mom. She wanted her cat.

She tried not to let it happen, but it was useless. There was way too much inside her—too many thoughts, too much fear, too much jellyfish. It was about to come out whether she wanted it to or not. She pressed herself hard into the crease of the sofa in the hopes that it might swallow her. Maybe there was a secret room in there where she could quietly die on her own. She could not lose it in front of Aidan. Enough was going wrong at this moment.

"Clio?" he asked.

This, apparently, was the cue for the crying to begin. In a second, she was going all out, her face adhering to the leather.

There was no movement from Aidan for a moment or two, then Clio felt him sit down on the sofa a few inches away from her head. Clio balled up one of her fists and managed to stick it into her eyes, as if that might make them dry.

"I'm . . . fine," she gasped.

"Yeah," he said, in his usual Aidan tone. "I can see that."

Clio took in a huge breath and tried to hold it. She managed to stop the tears for a few seconds and pull up her head.

"Fine . . ." she mumbled again.

He moved over so when she put her head down, it landed in his lap, just above the knees.

"Don't you ever give up?" he said, more quietly this time. "You're hurt. Just cry, okay?"

It was so soft and matter-of-fact, so not Aidan-like, that it caught her off guard. So she did. In big, gasping sobs. She soaked his thick khaki shorts. All the while, Aidan kept one hand on the back of her head, moving it just a little, in a tiny circle. He didn't say anything. He just kept her there until she had run out of the big stuff and was reduced to some dribbling and hiccups.

When she felt like she had gained a little control over herself, she looked up cautiously. He was leaning against the armrest and looking down at her, his sharp features still.

"Can I have water?" she croaked.

He slid back down so that he could go to the galley and get her a glass. She tried to wipe off her face. She was a mess—tears dripping down her chin, her nose running. She took the glass looking down so that he couldn't see all of this, but he sat down on the floor next to her, just at eye level.

"Here," he said, passing her a paper towel.

She wiped at her nose quickly, but that just made it run more. It was like a busted pipe of goo. There had to be a way of recovering from this.

"I got smacked," she said, keeping her face in the towel. "Fifty points."

"Smacked?"

"A group of jellyfish is called a smack," she said, her voice cracking a bit. "You know, in Dive!? If you go into one, you get smacked. It costs you fifty points."

Silence. She finished wiping as best she could and sipped her water.

"Why are you being so nice?" she said.

"Don't sound so shocked," he said with a smirk. "Hasn't my natural charm rubbed off on you yet?"

"That was charm?" she asked. "I thought it was a sun rash."

He let out a sigh and shook his head. "Would you stop?" he

said. "I know you're tough. I know you think I'm an asshole. But can we just let it go for a minute?"

Again his directness put her to shame. She felt her face flush. It was impossible to tell if it was embarrassment or if it was just falling in line with the rest of her body.

"Sorry," she finally said. "I thought I was going to drown. I don't know how I made it back."

"Stubbornness," he answered, a little too quickly. "*Or* adrenaline. I think some people *would* have drowned."

A few leftover tears trickled down her face. He rubbed them off with his thumb.

"Thanks," she finally said.

"Don't worry about it."

He sat there, hugging his knees, looking at her. It was strangely calming. There was no need to say anything. His high cheekbones and bright, quick eyes didn't look hard or searching, like they normally did. They just looked . . . good. Reassuring.

"So," he said. "I guess you didn't have a good call to your boyfriend. Is that why you decided to swim?"

"I didn't call my boyfriend," she said quickly.

This was true. She had no boyfriend. And it had been an e-mail anyway.

"So what were you doing?" he asked. "Or is it a secret?"

"Yeah. I'm on a secret mission, just like the rest of you. I was calling headquarters and getting my orders."

He reached out and peeled a piece of hair that had been sticking too close to her eye and set it back in place. A shock went through her body. Maybe it was jellyfish venom, or adrenaline, or maybe an electric eel had gotten her too . . . but it practically crackled. Suddenly, she was very aware that under the comforter, she was lying there in only her underwear and a very wet tank top. And that he had already seen this.

"Whoever this guy is," Aidan said, "he must be a piece of work to put up with you."

He left his hand resting lightly against her head, just one finger lightly running along her hairline. Such a small movement, but Clio had never felt anything like it. It blocked out all the pain or at least made her stop caring about it. Nerves that she didn't even know she had, ones that had never been stimulated before, shot to life.

"I never said—" she began.

"What?"

He was leaning in just a bit. They shared a little pool of yellowy light from the lamp on the end table. At that second, Clio knew that she could have just leaned farther over on the sofa and that Aidan would have kissed her. It was *absolute knowledge* of a variety she had never encountered before.

The other thing was . . . she wanted him to. Very, very badly.

This theory had to be tested. She inched herself slightly toward the edge of the sofa. He leaned just a fraction of an inch closer.

It was amazing. It was like a magnetic field between their faces.

And then, just as she was sliding closer, she caught a whiff of Elsa from the comforter. *Friend,* her brain said. *That smells of friend.*

It did. It smelled of friend. A friend who was getting her help at this very second.

She couldn't pull back from this. He was looking at her. This was her moment. This was what she had waited for so long.

"Never said what?" he asked.

The smell of Elsa was overwhelming her now. She hadn't even known there was an Elsa smell before.

"You and Elsa," she blurted.

He pulled his hand back but stayed where he was.

"Me and Elsa what?" he asked.

But she could see he knew what she meant. She wanted to take the statement back, to make the feeling return, but that was impossible.

"I'm not feeling so good," she said, closing her eyes. "I think I'm . . ."

She couldn't say what she was.

"Yeah," he said. There was an odd note to his voice. It sounded like he was laughing, but at himself. Grimly.

"Yeah," he said again. "You were right about me. I am an asshole. Sometimes you just do things . . . because you can."

She heard him sigh. Another tear trickled out of her eye, but he didn't remove it.

"I'm going to see if they're coming," he said. Then he got up, opened up the glass doors, and stepped out onto the deck.

The Venom

The doctor was a small, polite man in a tan gabardine suit. He sat on the white leather armchair, sweating and making notes on a pad. Then he made a proclamation in Italian, waving his pen like a magic wand.

"He says they have a bad jellyfish problem around here," Elsa translated. "No one should swim outside the swimming area."

"No," Clio mumbled into the sofa. *"Really?"*

Clio's examination was over. It had taken place right there in the living room. The doctor had flipped back the comforter, revealing Clio in her underwear. Martin and Aidan retreated to the deck while this was going on, but Elsa leaned over, like a helpful nurse, translating away.

It was impossible to count the jellyfish stings—they were long, tentacle stings, tangled up on each other. It looked like someone had dropped a knotty mess of unraveled red thread all over Clio's legs and back. They slashed right through the tattoo. The doctor explained that if Clio had been allergic, she would already be dead. So her being alive was a very good sign. Still, he had gone on to say, and Elsa had gone on to translate, it was never advisable to get so many jellyfish stings.

He opened his bag and shook some pills out into a glass tumbler. Then he injected Clio in the arm, set his card on the chair, and left.

Elsa tried to put some clothes on Clio, but the process was much too painful. So Clio was wrapped back in her cocoon of comforter.

"How did you guys get back?" Clio asked.

"We went looking for you. We bumped into Martin on the way. He was about to take the raft back. My mom and your dad were staying out a bit longer."

Nice. Not only were they just left behind—they were left behind so that her dad could go on a date. She had a feeling that this should make her very angry, but the anger didn't really come.

"I think he gave me something . . . interesting in that shot," she said.

"Rest," Elsa said. "Okay? I'll stay right here with you."

She felt Elsa slip her hand under the blanket and find Clio's hand. Aidan stood in the middle of the room and looked at her, then left.

"You know, when I first met you, you sort of seemed like a cheese goddess," Clio mumbled to Elsa. "Did I ever tell you that?"

"I *am* a cheese goddess," Elsa said.

She stroked back Clio's hair.

"You're quite mental," Elsa said. "You know that, right?"

"Yeah," Clio said.

"Why did you run out?" Elsa said. "We were so worried about you."

"It's complicated," Clio mumbled. But her thoughts were getting soft and heavy, like big, sopping-wet bags. Wet bags of thoughts that glowed on the inside like jellyfish, like trapped lightning. She saw Aidan come in from the deck and look at her over Elsa's shoulder, and then she shut her eyes.

When she opened them again, she felt gummy and heavy. Outside, the sky was light and lavender. It was morning, very early. One of the fat armchairs had been pulled up close to the sofa and her father was sitting in it, looking out the glass doors at the sunrise. Clio watched him for a moment, then, unable to hold her eyes open, she drifted back to sleep.

When she woke up again, it was much brighter. The chair was back in its place and her father was gone. Elsa sat in it instead, her knees tucked up under her chin and a magazine balanced on her feet.

Clio was sure she had seen her father there during the night.

It was time for a body check. She lifted the blanket a little and looked down at herself. What looked like red thread the night before had puffed up to the size of yarn. From her ankles straight on up, she looked like some kind of insane road map. She flipped the blanket back over quickly.

"I'm deformed," she said to Elsa. "Hideously deformed."

Elsa looked up and let the magazine slip from her feet as she stood. She lifted a corner of the blanket and looked under. Her eyes widened, and she lowered the blanket softly.

"It's just a little swelling," she said quickly. "It'll go away. Here. Do you want your pajamas and sweatshirt?"

188

Clio could sit up now, and she accepted the clothes. The tank top hadn't exactly dried during the night. It felt sticky and swampy, but she didn't care. The damage was too extensive to worry about something as minor as a humid shirt. She managed to slip on the polka-dot pajama bottoms and pulled on the sweatshirt.

It was time to try to stand. Her legs hurt and they were stiff, but she could support herself. She lumbered over to the glass doors and looked out. She was surprised to find that they were docked.

"We're staying at least another day," Elsa explained. "Your dad doesn't want to leave port until he's sure you're all right, in case you need a doctor again."

"Was my dad here?" Clio asked.

"They went to get some breakfast," Elsa said. "He and Martin. They'll be back in a few minutes."

"I guess they can't survive without me, huh?" Clio said. "They couldn't make breakfast?"

"Not as good as yours," Elsa said.

"I'm sorry if I scared you last night," Clio said. "I came back, but . . ."

"I know," she said.

"You know?"

"I saw you," Elsa said. "You came back to the club. You left because you were trying to help. And you did."

Help? She had been trying to help?

"You saw what happened," Elsa said, unable to contain her smile. "It was good. He's not as useless as he seems. He doesn't do any of the annoying stuff. He's not grabby, and he doesn't force his tongue down your throat. It's just the right amount of pressure. The boy is good."

Clio decided it was time to sit down again, now. Elsa sat next to her.

"For the first night in a long while, I didn't dream about Alex at all," she said. "I think I'm cured. *Cured*, Clio. Cured."

"That's . . . great," Clio said.

Someone was coming up the steps. It was Aidan, freshly showered, with still-wet multidirectional hair.

"What's up, moron?" he asked.

It was the normal Aidan voice. She looked for a hint of the madness of last night, but it wasn't there. It was the old, snarky, arrogant voice. It fact, it was slightly more snarky and arrogant.

"Nothing," she said. "I'm just sitting around, swelling. You know. Like any other morning."

"I'm going to go get my bag," Elsa said.

He nodded and went into the galley, emerging a minute later with a can of soda. Clio searched his face for what she had seen last night, but there was nothing there.

She felt like she had done something wrong. Clearly, she hadn't. She hadn't kissed him. She hadn't cheated on Ollie, because it wasn't possible to cheat on someone you weren't dating—especially not by *not kissing* another guy. Elsa and Aidan weren't exactly dating yet, so there was no betrayal there either.

But she felt wrong. Queasy. It was probably whatever that doctor had given her.

Aidan sat down in the chair and played with the tab of his soda can.

"So," he said. "You feeling okay?"

"Sort of," she said. "It's not my best morning feeling ever."

"No. Guess not."

"Good dancing last night," she said. It sounded very feeble and strange, and he just nodded in reply.

"So," she said. "You're going . . . out?"

"Yeah," he said, squeezing the empty can and making a loud crinkling noise. "Elsa thought . . . well, we're here. So. Yeah."

Then they seemed to run out of things to say to each other, so he got up to throw away his can in the kitchen. He didn't look at her again.

Elsa came back with her bag.

"All set," she said, sitting on the edge of the sofa. "Your dad just called. They're on their way. But if it's all right . . . I'd like to go before they get back. I feel like if we're still here when my mom gets here, she'll make Aidan do something so he can't go."

"It's fine," Clio said.

"I feel bad that you're stuck here," Elsa said. "We'll be back later. You try to rest, okay?"

"I've got that one covered."

Aidan came back in from the galley. His walk was stiff and odd and he kept rubbing the back of his neck, blocking out any view of Clio with his elbow. It had to be deliberate. For some reason, he wanted nothing to do with her now.

As they left, Clio got just a quick hit of the fresh breeze coming in from outside, and then the glass doors slid shut, leaving her in the cool, sterile air-conditioning, alone.

Oyster Girl

The other three returned only minutes later. Clio stared out at them from her little tube of comforter, just a pair of eyes blinking out of seven pounds' worth of down. They brought with them several bags of Italian pastry. And they had all gotten very loud. Maybe just walking around on an Italian street made you loud.

"Kiddo," her father said as he leaned over. "You scared the hell out of me last night."

Clio continued looking up from her little feather cocoon but decided not to speak. She didn't feel like talking anymore. Talking had done her no good. Acting had done her no good. Not acting had done her no good. She was miserable, confused, and swollen. Maybe the solution in life was to hide in a rolled-up comforter and pretend to be some kind of non-thinking, nervous-system-deprived shellfish. She was a sea butterfly, after all. She was related to oysters. It was totally her prerogative.

"I think that stuff the doctor gave her knocked her for a loop," her dad said. "She looks spaced."

He stroked her hair.

They gathered chairs and sat around Clio, like she was a television they were all watching. They went on with their very loud conversation, which was about the pyramid of Giza, occasionally looking over at her to see if she was going to do anything. She didn't. She watched them back.

Julia wore a sunny yellow tank top, and Clio saw her surprising resemblance to Elsa. Though Julia was more skeletal, they had the same wide, brightly awake features. Except that on Julia, they were stretched out flat. On Elsa, there was flesh on the cheeks and an actual blood supply under them to make them flushed and apple-like. In the morning sun, Julia's hair had a high, unnatural sheen. The red had to be artificial. Underneath, she was probably as blond as Elsa—or at least somewhat blond. If she ate a few more sandwiches, she might be as pretty as her daughter.

Not that Clio was one to comment on personal appearance right now.

Martin was chuckling and being his usual friendly, funny self. He was also looking at her slyly. He knew she was choosing not to speak. Clio was certain of it. He communed with her through quick little looks.

"Throw your dad a bone," his expression seemed to say. "He had a bad night."

"What did you get?" she said.

"Almond tarts," her father said quickly. "Cherry tarts and prune, I think. I know that sounds bad, but they're really good."

"Can I have a cherry one?"

A plate with a cherry tart was placed next to her face on the sofa. Clio pulled herself up carefully and took it. The pastry exploded into a crumbling mess the moment she bit into it, showering her with crumbs, but she told herself she didn't care. She was already covered in welts and was hiding under a blanket. A few pastry flakes wouldn't change anything.

It was excruciatingly obvious that Clio and her father were going to have to have another talk, so after they were done eating their breakfast, Martin and Julia decided to go back and "look at that thing." They didn't even try harder than that. They actually said they were going to "look at that thing."

Her father dragged his chair closer. Clio slunk down halfway into her tube.

"I sat here all last night," he said, reaching for another pastry out of the box. So that hadn't been a dream. He *had* been there.

"Is this where you yell at me for swimming and I say I only swam because you left us?"

"That's the idea," he said. "But I feel like we can skip a lot of that, don't you?"

It almost sounded like he was trying to be reasonable, but Clio wasn't so stupid. What he was actually trying to do was get out of any responsibility for his actions.

"You *left* us," she said.

"And we *came back*," he said. "But you had already gone off by that point. So we had to go back and look for you. So the whole thing could have been avoided."

"If you had told us you were going," Clio added.

He let out a long sigh and ran his hands through his hair, accidentally getting crumbs in it.

194

"You know what I wanted more than anything?" he said. "I wanted to give you something nice. It's beautiful here. You don't have to sit around the house all summer, working some stupid job."

"I *wanted* my stupid job," Clio said.

"Instead of this? Instead of cruising the Med on a gorgeous boat?"

"Cruising the Med?" Clio repeated. "You make it sound like I'm on some ship, sunbathing and playing Ping-Pong and stopping at exotic locations. You know what I really am? Your cook on some whacked-out mission that you won't even tell me about. Do you know how *weird* that is?"

"Look," he said. "This trip was set up before I knew you could come. It's based on some research that Julia has been doing for a long, long time. Part of the reason we're doing it this way and not through more-official channels is its highly sensitive nature."

"Highly sensitive archeology?" Clio asked.

"When it came up that you could come," he went on, "I asked Julia about it. Of course, she was dying to meet you. But yes, she was worried about what might happen if you were here and if you were e-mailing people at home. You do live around a major university, Clio. Your mother is there. We just didn't want the details getting around."

"So your solution is that you don't tell me what's going on?" she asked. "Why didn't you just talk to me about it? If you'd told me to keep quiet, I would have."

"Clio," he said. "Look at yourself *right now*. Have you really done what I've asked so far?"

Okay. Maybe he had a bit of a point with that one.

"You have to stop this thing you have with Julia," he said. "If you're having trouble accepting the idea of my dating, just come out and say so. We'll work through it."

"How?" Clio asked. "How do we work through it?"

He leaned down to his knees. Clio noticed a single streak of gray in his floppy, sandy curls.

"Let me be honest with you," he said. "This search, it's been a challenge. We knew it would be complicated, but . . . What I'm trying to say, Clio, is that I think we're a lot more likely to succeed out here if you're on our side. This is a chance for us to be like we used to be. Or something like it. I want you to make a deal with me. Work *with* me, not against me. This whole trip could take months. But it could be a lot shorter if you play along. There's a chance we could find what we're looking for in a matter of weeks. And if we do, you can go home if it would make you happy. I'll work it out with your mom somehow. Maybe you can stay with a friend or something. I'll handle the details."

"What would I have to do?" she asked, sitting up.

"Help with the diving equipment. Take your job as the cook seriously. Follow the rules. No more drinking. No more snooping. You help me keep the boat under control, and you get what you want. I don't want you to do anything against your will anymore—I want us to come to an agreement. How about this? You help us for two weeks and you get to go home."

A trip home in two weeks . . . and all it would take was a little sucking up. She could be back in the aisles of Galaxy and out of this ridiculous place. That was what she wanted, right? To get away from all of this. So why weren't her insides jumping for joy at the prospect of going home? Sure, there had been that whole moment with Aidan—but it wasn't like that meant anything. She didn't even *like* Aidan! He'd never been anything but a jerk to her. And on top of that, she'd already seen him kiss Elsa.

Ollie was the one she was meant to kiss. Clio knew what she had to do. Forget the stupid phone call. Forget the e-mail. What she needed to do was get home as soon as possible and get her kiss from Ollie. The moment with Aidan had been nothing more than a post-jellyfish-attack moment of weakness. And now her father was making an offer she couldn't refuse: help him find his dumb shipwreck or whatever, and she'd be home in two weeks. That was something solid. That was something Clio could do.

"Dad," she said, extending her hand to meet his, "we've got a deal."

Choices

Elsa seemed to have spent every euro she had buying presents for Clio, which she presented to her while Clio flopped on the Champagne Suite bed. There were three magazines in English that cost four times as much as they did at home, a few chocolate bars, and some fancy lemon sodas in glass bottles. The final triumph, presented last, was a box of pastels. Clio knew the brand. They were extremely expensive. She'd never owned a set of them before.

"You said you didn't have these," Elsa said. "I hope I got the right thing. I told the guy in the store all about you and what you did, and he said this is what you needed."

"They're perfect," Clio said. "Elsa, you didn't have to . . ."

Elsa waved her hand and hopped off the bed.

"You are sick," she said. "I am Swedish. I don't *sound* that Swedish, but in my heart, I am. The English just tell you to put your chin up when you're sick, but the Swedish feed you and make you take steam baths. Except I don't know if you should take a bath with those marks on your legs, so I'm just going to make you draw and eat chocolate. So draw! I'm going to take a cool bath, though. It's hot out there."

Clio's sketchbook landed on the bed next to her. Elsa stepped into the bathroom and started running water.

"Also," Elsa said, putting her head around the door, "I'm cooking dinner."

"I heard," Clio said. "Thanks."

"Draw! Eat!"

The head vanished.

Clio stared into the box of pastels. They couldn't have been easy to find, even if they were Italian. Elsa had obviously searched for an art shop (and who'd even known this town had one) and carefully gone through everything in it. She had paid attention to what Clio had said. It was so thoughtful that it almost hurt. Clio picked up a soft bamboo yellow, opened the book to the sketch of Elsa sleeping, and carefully began to fill in the hair. It was such a quality color. It went on the page smoothly. The people who made these pastels loved them.

She didn't deserve these. Elsa had gotten them for her because she thought Clio had run off to help her and had gotten hurt in the process. The truth was that she had managed to betray everyone by doing nothing. No one in history had ever done less and yet been so wrong. Not cheating on a non-boyfriend with the non-boyfriend of a friend. The pressure of thinking that one through made her swollen body ache.

Clio set the pastel back in its box. Now came the real crusher.

She didn't really want to know, but she was morally, legally, and physically obligated to ask.

"So," she called. "Last night. Who kissed who?"

Elsa smiled and cocked her head. She got up and turned off the water in the tub. Great. Now Clio was going to get it in detail. Why was she such an *idiot*?

"Well," Elsa said. "You left. We kept dancing. I think you threw Aidan off a little when you ran out and I was just saying that you looked a little upset, like you had to fix things with your boyfriend. . . . How did that go? With everything that happened, I forgot to ask!"

She looked genuinely upset at this.

"Everything's fine," Clio said quickly. "I think. Well, it will be soon anyway."

"Oh. Okay. So, I thought you were upset, and I was saying that. He looked bothered by that. He pretends he doesn't care, but he really does."

In a strange rush, Clio recalled the touch of Aidan's hand on her head from the night before.

"I just realized that he was cute, smart, fun. And yes, the property of my mum. But you know what? My mum doesn't get to call the shots about everything. She doesn't even know about Alex. She never even asked me what was wrong, even though she had to know I was upset."

This conversation had taken an unexpected turn. Clio hadn't thought of Aidan as Julia's property—but of course that was what he was on this boat.

"Is she nice to him?" Clio asked.

"Nice?" Elsa said. "My mum is not *nice* to anyone. Maybe

200

your dad. Definitely not to her assistants. I don't think she sees them as people. The university gives her an office, a computer, grant money, and an assistant. It's all the same to her."

There was something in this . . . something Clio knew she would want to discuss later. But for now, they had to keep going with this *other* complicated, confusing topic.

"So, you—"

"Right! Sorry. So, it's always seemed clear that Aidan is pretty much there for the taking. Not to sound mean. But he's an engineer. He doesn't get out much. He doesn't have a girlfriend. He's on a boat with two attractive females and has been desperately trying to pretend he hasn't noticed this fact because of my mum. But you know. He's gasping for it. I just leaned in a little, put my hand on his leg. With guys, a little goes a long way when they reach a certain state."

She laughed.

Clio hadn't noticed that Aidan was *gasping* for it. She had been too busy being annoyed at her dad to notice the guy who was there, ready and willing. Could that also explain what had happened— well, almost happened—last night? What was *that* about?

"And so he kissed you?" Clio asked. "After you put your hand on his leg?"

"Not quite," Elsa said. "I had to play with him a little more. You know. Give him a little view down the shirt. Not much— just a little. You know what I mean."

Nope. Clio really didn't have a clue. That was not something (a) that she had ever done or (b) that would have occurred to her to do. Because she was very, very stupid when it came to boys. That much was proven.

"Sure," she lied.

"And I leaned in close. Talked to him a little. It was *fun*, Clio. The windup was fun. And the kissing was better."

"So he kissed you?" Clio asked, trying not to sound too urgent or demanding. This fact had to be established, though.

"Mmmm," Elsa purred.

Clio swallowed hard.

"Today was different," Elsa went on. "We didn't make out. He was being shy. He's worried about my mum finding out. But I can work on that. It will all be taken care of. Now, something more serious."

Elsa jumped off the bed and opened one of the drawers of her dresser. She shuffled through some stuff and produced a single photograph from the bottom.

"I lied to you," she said to Clio. "I told you I shredded all the photos. I didn't—I kept one. Sometimes I take it out when you're not here."

She passed the photo over. Elsa and Alex were sitting on a bed with a deep gray duvet over it and a car poster on the wall. Alex's room. Elsa was her usual glowing self, hugging him tight and looking happy. Alex wore a soccer uniform—a maroon V-necked shirt and long black shorts. He was a smirker. He had a long face, a thick, strong neck, and muscular legs. His hair was almost black and was spiked up along the midline of his head. He wasn't looking at the camera. His smirk was directed toward something just next to whoever was taking the picture. Everything about him said asshole. With a capital *A*.

Strangely, it occurred to Clio that Aidan didn't say asshole. He said something else. Seeing this picture made the difference clear.

"Good-bye, Alex," Elsa said. "You don't know what you're missing. *Wanker*. It's time for that to go. Give it here."

Clio passed it back. Elsa tore it up, then gathered the pieces and pushed them out of the window.

"That little boy caused me a lot of grief. But as they say . . ." She turned from the window and grinned. "Living well is the best revenge. I have a new man now. And I have you."

Temptations and Voices

The prospect of release changed Clio. For the next week, she forced herself to conform, keeping herself on a rigid schedule. She rose very early, getting together breakfast before the morning meeting at eight. She helped move and prepare the diving equipment. She also became the official topside person during the daily dives, waiting on the deck after her dad and Martin had gone under. She forced herself to sit and draw for four hours each day, training her arm to hold steady when the boat lurched. She planned menus and had dinner on the table on time each night. While she prepared these meals, she rehearsed different versions of what she'd say to Ollie when she returned. She tried to recall her beach fantasy, but it was fading, so she threw herself into inventing new ones. The welts on her body gradually went down, leaving spidery traces of red. They itched like crazy for a few days, but she got used to it. In short, she had finally achieved a state of near Zen.

What helped in this was ignoring Aidan. It had become totally, totally clear that Aidan made everything go all weird in her head, like something that messes with the reception of a radio. Her incredibly brilliant solution was a little game called You Do Not Exist.

When Aidan came into the kitchen to get on her case about dinner, she smiled pleasantly and forced her head to repeat the words "you do not exist" over anything else it tried to tell her. When he passed by and leaned over her drawings of Ollie and made more comments about his ironic fashion choices, she thanked him and ignored him. Because he did not exist.

Of course, he did exist. And she felt her pulse race when he sat too close. He was making her nervous. She couldn't tell what he was thinking. She noticed he tended to avoid Elsa too, choosing instead to hide in the workroom and play video games on his computer all night. She knew that was what he was doing because she had listened at the door. (Yes, yes, listened at the door. It's best to know where the source of your irritation is lingering.)

Elsa was the restless one now. Since the day onshore with Aidan, nothing had happened between them, as far as Clio could tell. The calm that she had exhibited in the early days gave way to frayed nerves.

"I need to do somethng about this," she said to Clio one morning after coming downstairs. She stood around in the galley as Clio cleaned up and picked at the leftovers of breakfast.

"You need to what?" Clio asked.

"There must be kissing," she said. "There must be bodily contact. But it's impossible to do anything on this bloody boat.

We're all on top of one another. Everyone knows what everyone else is doing."

Clio scrubbed away at a particularly sticky bit of egg and nodded sympathetically.

"What I don't understand," Elsa went on, "is the fact that he says nothing. He runs off and hides. Every once in a while he looks at me, but that's it. I mean, this is good to look at, right?"

She stepped back and presented herself for inspection.

"*I'd* date you," Clio answered. "But I don't know what's wrong with him. He's always seemed weird to me."

"It's dive time," her father called as he passed by. "Can you come give us a hand?"

Martin was changing into his wet suit out on the deck, stumbling as he tried to get his leg into the skintight rubber. Clio turned her head as Julia helped her dad do the same.

"I think I've gained a little weight out here," Martin said to her. "You cook too well. Oh, would you mind?"

He nodded to his shirt and a key on a lariat.

"Don't lose that," he said with a smile. "It's a master key."

"I'll take care of it," Clio said, slipping the key around her neck.

Aidan joined them, mumbling something about iron. When Martin and her dad had gone in the water, Aidan lingered, slouching down in the corner of the deck with his laptop. He didn't bother to say good morning or look up at Clio.

Elsa trailed out with one of her textbooks and mouthed Italian phrases toward the sun.

And Clio watched. And did some mental math.

Two people on the deck. Julia had gone up to the wheelhouse. Two people in the ocean.

206

And one key around her neck. A key that lay on top of her heart.

Just because she had been well behaved all week didn't mean that she was any less interested in what was behind this trip—it was just that she had chosen not to act on it.

Being given a shiny key is a temptation. Keys open things. And from the moment it was around her neck, her senses were tingling. The same senses that told her what aisle to find Ollie in or what chair Suki was crouched under—these were the senses telling her to take this key and do something with it.

But the place her brain was telling her to go was simply not right.

"I have to go get something," she said to Elsa and Aidan. "Can you keep an eye on them for me? Call me on the com if anyone signals."

"Sure!" Elsa said. Her sunny smile meant that she thought Clio was doing her another favor by leaving her alone with Aidan.

Clio hurried inside. On the one hand, her brain was telling her *no*. No, she was not allowed to do this. This was a serious breach. The other side was forcing her downstairs quickly because there wasn't a lot of time for this, if she was going to do it.

She found herself standing in front of Julia's door, not breathing, holding the key in front of the lock. This was where the answers on this boat were. This was where anything of real interest was going to be found. Something told her that this was absolutely necessary.

But if she got caught, there would be no recovery. It was just an insane whim.

She felt the key slipping into the lock, as if some force was putting it in there and not her hand.

Julia's room was small but very tidy. It looked fairly unused, except for storage. Clio started by just glancing around, but she soon gave it up and started opening drawers. In the small bedside cabinet, there was a baby blue pack of birth control pills. Clio cringed. It sat on a clear plastic box, which Clio could see was full of stones. She gingerly moved the pills aside and took the box. The stones were all different, though most of them looked like they had been chipped off larger surfaces. All were covered in symbols, the same symbols—a bunch of lines crossing each other in meaningless ways. Some were carved deeply, some just scratched. A few bore deep impressions that had probably been made in wet clay and allowed to dry. One was a tiny piece of jade that had been chiseled precisely. The symbols were obviously writing. They repeated, and they were in clean lines. Clio turned the stone around several times. She had seen Greek characters, and Julia knew lots of Greek. But these definitely didn't look like Greek characters.

She set the box back, replaced the pills, and kept looking. There were piles of paper around the room, mostly thick folders filled with printed-out academic articles about languages or translations, a few dissertations. Lots of photocopies of Greek documents. Julia's personal belongings were fairly simple. She had neatly folded clothes, a collection of exotic jewelry, a few thick, very literary-looking novels that Clio had never heard of.

Nothing interesting, really. And she had to be running out of time.

She was about to turn and go when she noticed a black travel file on the floor. She reached down and opened it up. It spread open, accordion style, revealing a few papers. Mostly it was empty. Clio shuffled through the pockets. In the back were many more photocopies of the strange symbols on all kinds of surfaces. It looked like the front pockets were empty until Clio spread them open and had a good look at each one. In the very front was a small piece of paper in a plastic sleeve.

The thing that first caught her eye was the round rubber stamp mark in the corner that read: ARCHIVED, 17 MARCH 1926. The paper was old, and the letter had been written with a loose ink pen that dripped along the page, soaking it in spots, running dry in the middle of some sentences. Clio could see where the writer had had to re-dip the pen and renew the ink. The scrawl was quick but elegant.

My dearest Marguerite,

I write this from Naples, where I am to board the Bell Star in only a few moments.

I'm not sure which will get to you first, this letter or me. Even so, I take the chance. My excitement compels me to write to you and deliver this news.

In the villa in which I have been working in Pompeii, there is a library. But there is something else, something quite extraordinary.

On one of the walls, there is mounted a piece of elegantly engraved marble. Unless my eyes very much deceive me, it is written in that strange script we have been discussing for so long.

Here is the extraordinary bit—the writing is then translated into Latin. I believe the owner of this villa had works written in the script and this was a translation tool. I have found more scraps of the papyrus. It could be that this is a library full of works more ancient and more important than any we have ever known. And now, with the aid of this stone, we can read them.

The marble is white, oval in shape, and twenty-six inches from top to bottom. The craftsmanship is exquisite. Because it is so vital, so lovely, and the key to so much understanding, I have given it the only name that matches it. It is now called the Marguerite stone.

I obtained permission to take it with me. When I reach London, we will take it directly *to Hill and begin our work. Until then, I think only of you.*

Your loving father

Obviously, this letter was important. It was old. It had a plastic sleeve and its own pocket at the front of the file. Important things always go in the front. But unlike the paperwork that was out and around the room, it didn't look like this was frequently needed.

She stood there, reading the letter over and over. A few things stood out. There was a ship in this—the *Bell Star*. They were looking for a ship. There was something important on the *Bell Star*—a stone from Pompeii, a stone that would enable its finder to translate unknown languages.

This was exactly the kind of thing that Julia would want. Especially considering the box of stones with letters on them. Letters that weren't Greek. But the phrase that Clio couldn't get out of her mind was: *It could be that this is a library full of works more ancient and more important than any we have ever known.*

"What is all this?" she said to herself.

Clio took a deep breath in through her nose, then closed the file and pressed the clasp shut, taking the letter with her. As she came upstairs, she glanced out the glass doors and saw that it looked like the divers had already come up. Julia and Aidan were both by the back of the boat. She ducked into the galley for a moment and slipped the letter in between the pages of the

211

Indian cookbook, then continued out. Something wasn't right. There was too much activity. Her father was standing on the deck, but it looked like he was pulling something out of the water.

Except it wasn't some*thing*. It was Martin.

A Kind of Truth

Martin was ashen-faced and sitting on the platform with his head between his knees.

"I'm all right," he said. "Sometimes it just doesn't agree with you, that's all."

"You sure?" her dad asked. "You don't look good. Did you skip a stop on the way up? Are you experiencing narcosis?"

"Should I call a doctor?" Aidan asked.

"No," Martin said. "It's not that bad. I just got woozy on the last bit. Let me catch my breath, and then I'll go and rest for the afternoon. I'll be fine."

Aidan and Clio's dad helped him up and to his room, where he stayed for the rest of the day. That night, Clio made an Irish stew for dinner. That seemed like the kind of thing that might be good for someone who wasn't feeling well. All day long, she was aware of the letter that was right there with her.

When she brought him his dinner, Martin was looking much

better. He sat propped up in his bed in his tiny cabin, reading a book by the light of a little fixture that came down over his shoulder. This room was no Champagne Suite. It was even smaller than Julia's.

"I could smell something good," he said. "And I didn't feel like getting up. Clio, you're a saint."

He accepted the tray and set it on his lap.

"Are you feeling better?" Clio asked.

"Much," he said, picking up a spoon and sampling the broth. "Oh . . . that's good."

Clio reached behind her and shut the door.

"Are you okay enough for me to ask you something?" she said.

"I have never been injured by a question. Shoot."

"Are we looking for the *Bell Star*?"

He smiled and poked a carrot around the bowl.

"What makes you ask something like that?" he said.

Clio produced the letter from the front pocket of her sweat-shirt.

"Who wrote this?" she said. "Who's Marguerite?"

One of Martin's many good qualities was that he saw no sense in wasting time with lines of inquiry that would clearly get him nowhere, like, "Where did you get that?" He already knew the answer.

"The letter in your hand is from Dr. Alexander Magwell," he said. "He was a professor in the late 1800s, specializing in antiquities. He left teaching to work with the British Museum. He worked at Pompeii for a few months each year. He was returning home from an expedition when he boarded a ship called the *Bell Star*. Before he left port, he mailed this letter to his daughter, Marguerite. He never made it home with what he found. That letter was put in with his papers, which were given to the British Museum."

"So, we are looking for the *Bell Star*, right?" she said.

"Right."

"And we're looking for this stone?"

"Right again," he said.

"So, we're not just looking for a boat, which is hard enough. We're looking for a *rock* on a boat."

"Again," he said, "you've nailed it."

"That's . . ." Clio's hands clawed up in frustration. "It's not even insane. It's something else. Insane can be fun. This is just bad."

"It's not impossible," Martin said.

"No, it's not impossible," Clio said. "But do *you* think it's going to work?"

"Stranger things have happened," he said.

"I lost a really cool sock a few years ago," she said. "Can we go look for that next?"

"We actually know a lot," Martin said. "The *Bell Star* was a British-built ship. For the last five years of her life, she ran between Naples, Italy, and Marseille, France, handling passengers and cargo. She left on her last run on May 25, 1897. No one knows exactly what happened, but she definitely went down sometime between the twenty-sixth and the twenty-seventh. She often stopped in Civitavecchia, which is just north of here. They were expected to stop there on this journey. They never did. So, using the spot where the *Bell Star* was last sighted

215

as a point of reference, we've figured out three likely places where she could be. Plus we have a few potential sites that we got from divers and some hang numbers from a fisherman."

"You mean dive coordinates?" Clio asked.

"I mean dive coordinates," he said. "Right. Wrecks are often found in places where the fishing is really good or nets get stuck or lost. We've already hit the first four. We have a few more to go."

"Okay," Clio said. "Maybe we can find the boat and maybe even the stone. It's not likely, but okay. The question is why. Why us? Why do we care? Why is my dad funding this and not Cambridge, or the British Museum, or some big organization?"

"That is a slightly more complicated question," he said. "One I can't really answer."

"And the secrecy," Clio went on. "Why is everyone being so CIA about an old rock?"

"I think that's Julia's request, but your dad is doing it in his normal style. A little over the top."

"Martin," Clio said, leaning in. "I have been in some strange situations in my life, but this is definitely the winner of the Weird Olympics. This letter? It's an original. Not a copy. So how did it get out? My mom works in museums. They're *serious* about keeping their stuff. So how did it end up with us?"

"Julia said that a colleague turned up with it one day, that it must have gotten out of the museum years ago, just gotten lost in the shuffle, sometime back before computers, before there was sophisticated security. They have a lot of documents at the British Museum. Millions upon millions. It's one of the world's largest collections of . . . anything, really. And it's not an especially important letter, as far as the museum is concerned. I'm sure no one ever noticed it was gone. It was just a personal letter from a long-dead academic."

"A colleague?" Clio repeated. "That's not very specific. Someone just walked in one day and handed her this letter, and she showed it to my dad, and then he bought a yacht to go find it? Come on, Martin. It's time to tell me everything."

"I've just told you everything I know," he said. "Really. I wanted to tell you about the *Bell Star* sooner, but I was asked not to. But even I don't know much. I came along because I thought maybe your father was jumping into this a bit too fast. I did have the time, and I thought it would be fun to learn to dive. The boat was an extreme move, I admit. But he *can* resell it. This *might* be very worthwhile."

He reached over to the bedside stand and fumbled around for his key, which he passed to her.

"This is a master key," he said.

"I know."

"I figured you did. Take it and put that letter back where you found it. I'm going to eat my stew."

Martin picked up his fork and started in properly. Clio caught sight of a small bottle tucked behind the alarm clock. It had been hidden until he had reached for the key. She picked it up.

"Nitroglycerin," she said, reading off the label. "Isn't this for heart problems?"

"What," he said with a smile. "Are you a doctor?"

"No," Clio said. "I watch a lot of TV. I've seen commercials for medicines. Plus there's a sticker of a heart on the bottle."

217

"Ah," he said. "Well spotted."

"Martin, are you . . . okay? Really?"

"Just a little chest pain," he said. "I've had it for a while. It's nothing serious."

"Should you be here, doing this? Diving?" she asked. "Does my dad know?"

"The exercise is good for me," he said. "I never got enough before. And the problem isn't serious. I'm on plenty of medication for it, believe me. I'll be fine. I just wore myself out a little today. You worry too much, Clio."

He looked tired and like he wanted his dinner. Clio stood.

"Eat up," she said. "I'll bring you more if you want. Just call me on the com."

"Clio," he said. "Your dad was really down after the divorce. Really down."

"We *all* were," she said.

"I know. But he took it all very personally. I was worried about him. He's like a younger brother to me. I know you don't like Julia. I wouldn't expect you to. I know you think this is all a bit extreme—but that's your dad. This is the first time since it all happened that I've seen him really acting like his old self. I came to make sure he stayed that way. I'm on your side. Both of your sides. I'm not going to let anything happen to him."

This was reassuring, though Clio couldn't help but bristle a little. The divorce *should* have hurt her dad. It was his fault, after all. She was the innocent one.

"I'll bring your key back," she said.

She walked over to Julia's door, put the key in the lock, and then paused. Putting the letter back made sense. It meant that there would be no trouble. But on some level she knew that she couldn't give this letter back, not until she really got to the bottom of it.

She slipped the letter under her shirt as she went to return the key.

A General Malfunction

The next day was Mental and Physical Breakdown Day on the *Sea Butterfly*. There was no real sense of time to the day, either in the sky or in their activity. It seemed to be permanently stuck at a miserable four o'clock. The failures were adding up. That much was palpable.

They didn't go anywhere. They stayed anchored between nowhere and nowhere. No one told Clio why, but she guessed they were planning again, trying to reassess which sites to dive. Not that they really could dive with Martin down. Diving was something that always had to be done in pairs.

The weather was terrible to boot. It didn't storm, but there was a miserable drizzle that made the sky and the water gray and going outside unappealing. The inside of the boat was too cold in the air-conditioning, but when they turned it off, became much too humid.

Martin remained in bed that morning, and Elsa kept to her

usual sleeping habits. Clio's father, Aidan, and Julia holed up in the wheelhouse. Clio put in her earphones and tried to brighten her own mood, but it was useless. Her brain was still churning over the conversation of the night before. She knew the *what* now, but the *why* still wasn't clear. Why the big secret mission for an old rock? Why couldn't anyone know about it? How had Julia gotten the letter?

Clio was in the middle of considering these questions and reheating the strew for lunch when there was a clang, a grinding noise, and the unmistakable sound of water going somewhere that it wasn't supposed to. She looked out in the hall to see soap foam spitting out of the *Butterfly*'s compact washer-dryer.

She picked up her com slowly.

"This is Number Five," she said into it. "The washing machine just mutinied. I think we're about to get kind of wet."

Whatever their plans were for the rest of the afternoon were quickly dropped. The water supply had to be shut down to stop the flow of water, which had gotten foam all through the hall and slightly into the dining room, making the carpet squish.

Her father was getting short-tempered, snapping at the machine and throwing down parts in disgust. Aidan handled it very calmly, sending him up to the wheelhouse and taking over. It was actually kind of impressive, watching Aidan sit on the wet carpet, taking apart the machine. He actually seemed to have some idea of what he was doing.

"How do you know what to do?" Clio asked.

"It's just a washing machine," he said. "It's not that complicated."

"Yeah, if you've fixed one before."

"Appliances are usually pretty basic," he said, looking at a small rubber knob with a puzzled expression.

There was a loud step on the stairs, and Julia came up from below. Aidan was blocking her path into the living room, and she stepped directly into the wet carpet.

"What is this?" she asked. "Is this why there's no water?"

"Yes," Aidan said. "Working on that."

"That's not your job. Let Ben do it."

"Ben tried," Aidan said. "He was losing his patience."

"I'm losing my patience too," Julia said. "We have serious work to do. Get done with that and meet me downstairs."

"She's pissed about something," Aidan said when she was gone. "*Really* pissed."

"Do you know about what?" Clio asked.

"Yup," Aidan said, sticking his head back into the barrel of the machine. Clio found herself staring at his legs and butt as they extended out. Then she shook her head quickly and rubbed her eyes. God, maybe she really *was* desperate.

Up in the Champagne Suite, Elsa was sitting in the bed, writing something on a long pad of paper.

"Know what this is?" she said.

"No," Clio answered.

"It's a letter to Alex. I know I shouldn't be writing letters to Alex, even if I don't send them, but I just wanted to let him know I was better. I wanted to gloat a little. It's *eleven pages long*. And this one?"

She held up another pile of paper.

"This is a letter to Aidan. This one is nine pages long. I think I'm losing it again, Clio. I don't feel cured anymore."

Clio sat down next to her and put her hand on her arm.

"I can't take it anymore," Elsa said, her eyes welling with tears. "I'm so sick of this boat. I'm so sick of Alex. And I want something to happen with Aidan. I don't even know if he likes me. I'm just a mess."

Tears started dribbling down her face. She sniffed and wiped them away with her hand. Clio sat up on the pillows and put her arm around her.

"It's okay!" Clio said. "Believe me. I know how crazy you feel out here."

Elsa dropped her head onto Clio's shoulder and burrowed into her neck. Her hair tickled under Clio's chin.

"Can I ask you something?" Elsa said.

"Yeah," Clio said reassuringly. "Sure."

"You and Aidan," Elsa said slowly. "You don't . . ."

"Don't what?"

"Do you *like* him?"

"What?" Clio said. "Aidan? No. I . . . no."

"It's just that you two are so alike," she said. "Sometimes it feels like you two should be together."

"Aidan?" Clio asked, her heart pounding. "And me? God, no. Elsa, no."

The denials were coming out of her mouth much, much faster than her brain was moving. But even hearing Elsa make the suggestion was intoxicating. Disturbing. Very, very unsettling. It made no sense!

"Good!" Elsa let out a massive sigh. "You have no idea how I was stressing over asking you that. I've been doing a lot of thinking, and I have an idea. I wanted to ask you a massive, massive favor. And you can say no. *Really*."

She was talking quickly now, in one gush of relief. She sat up and faced Clio.

"What?" Clio asked, her mind still reeling. Elsa thought Clio and Aidan were *alike*? That *they* should be together?

"Well," she said. "Clearly, I think something needs to happen. And I feel like we have no chance, you know, for anything to happen stuck on the boat like this. So I was thinking, maybe, would you kind of . . . switch?"

"Switch?"

"Rooms. Just for one night. And it's not like that—I don't want to just sleep with him. Well . . . what I mean is, I just want to have him over. For, like, a date. And there's nowhere else to go but here. I didn't want to ask him until I asked you first."

This landed Clio back in reality. She saw her room, her bed, the coffee-colored rug, the view into the magical bathroom. Things that now seemed like home. Her little universe.

And her friend, who wanted just this one favor. Which was strangely turning her stomach. No, actually. She *didn't* want Aidan in her bed, sleeping with Elsa. Doing *anything* with Elsa.

"What?" Clio said. "Tonight?"

"No, no!" Elsa said. "Tomorrow. I need a chance to plan. I mean it. It's like a date. Really. Feel free to say no. It's *so* much to ask."

"Of course," Clio heard herself saying. "Sure."

"That's what this is," Elsa said, holding up the smaller of the two letters. "The invitation."

"That's a long invitation," Clio said.

"Long but *very interesting*," Elsa said. "I don't think he'll mind. But here's the other favor I need to ask. Could you give it to him? I think he would feel better about it if he knew you were completely okay with it. We'll have to be sneaky, switching around carefully. So it'll really be all three of us conspiring."

"Right," Clio said, a million confused feelings firing off inside her at once. "No problem. No problem at all."

The Exchange

The washing machine repairs went on for hours, being interrupted for a short time when Aidan switched on the water so she could make dinner that night. Clio was sitting in the living room, curled on the leather sofa, pretending to read a book. She had two letters in the pocket of her hoodie. Her nerves were making the remnants of her stings itch.

Elsa was deliberately staying back. The problem was Clio's father and Julia, who simply refused to go to bed as early as they normally did. Clio had to sit through hours of washing machine and archeology talk—which was as bad a mix as anything she had ever heard in her life.

Finally, Aidan gave the all-clear for the water to be switched back on for good, and Julia said she needed to take a shower. The moment her father floated off, Clio went to find Aidan by the washer.

"I need to talk to you," she said. "Outside."

He looked up from his spot on the floor. Up close, Clio could see that his face was lightly glazed with sweat and his eyes looked tired.

"Outside?" he asked.

"Yes. Now. Come on."

He pulled himself up by grabbing the machine. His butt was completely soaked from sitting on the soggy carpet. She couldn't help but crack a smile. It was all so *absurd*.

She took him out to the back of the deck, as far away as she could get from everyone else. She knew that Elsa could see them from the vestibule if she was looking out. She didn't seem to be.

"Going swimming again?" he asked.

"No," she said. "I want to know what you know about the Marguerite stone."

He slumped against the side and met her eyes, the darkness shadowing his face, making his eyes brighter. Just looking at him, his hand resting on the rail of the boat, made her heart do that rapid-beating thing again.

"Did your dad mention this to you?" he asked.

She held up the letter. It flapped in the wind. She gripped it hard. Aidan's eyes zeroed in on it.

"How in hell did you get that?" he said.

"Things get misplaced," she said.

"*That* doesn't."

"Oh no? Then how did it accidentally get out of the British Museum and onto this boat with us? It sounds like this letter has a long history of being misplaced."

He folded his arms over his chest and looked toward the sky, letting out a long sigh.

"Julia is *not* happy," he said. "I didn't think it was you, though. I thought it got misplaced. If she finds out you have that—"

"She won't," Clio said. "It will reappear. But not before I find out what this all means. I know we're looking for the *Bell Star*. I know we're trying to get the Marguerite stone. What I want to know is why. Why is it so important?"

"Clio—"

"Don't 'Clio' me. I have a right to know, and no one is talking. If someone doesn't explain all of this to me, I am *going* to lose my mind. Do you get that? I haven't been trusted from day one, but for no reason."

"So why are you asking me?" he said.

"Because for some reason, I trust *you*," she said. "I think you're honest. And I'm promising you I won't tell anyone that you ever told me anything. I already know the *what*, anyway. I need to know the *why*. I'm asking how we all ended up here together. You, me, Elsa, my dad, this letter. Tell me what it *means*. No one said you couldn't do that."

He took a long, deep breath.

"If we're going to do this," he said, "we're going to need to establish a trust bond."

"Okay," Clio said. "That's fair, whatever it means. How do we do that?"

"I ask you some questions, and you answer them honestly. I'll know if you're lying."

"How?"

"Because I'm good at spotting liars."

"Is that your superpower?" she asked. "We all have at least one."

228

"It's one of them," he said. "Let's get out of public view a little."

"And go where?"

"Down there," he said, nodding toward the back of the deck, toward the water.

"You want to swim? I think I'll pass."

"The platform, genius," he said.

They stepped down the back stairs to the platform. It was just even with the water, occasionally dipping down an inch or two below the surface. They actually had to sit in the orange raft, which was lashed to it. He was already wet, so he didn't care. Clio sat down in the water, making sure both letters were dry.

"You ready?" he asked.

"I guess so," Clio said uncertainly. "What do you want to know?"

"Most girls I know can't stop talking about their boyfriends. You never mention yours. Why not?"

"Why would I tell *you* about *him*?" she asked defensively. Why was he asking her about *that*?

"You don't tell Elsa either. You're very mysterious about him. Where did you two meet?"

"Why does this matter?" she said. "We came down here to talk about this stone."

"I'm not saying it does. I said I wanted to establish some trust. His name is Ollie, right?"

Clio nodded slowly.

"So where did you meet this Ollie?"

"In an art store," Clio said.

"The famous art store. Where you were going to work."

"Right," Clio said.

"So, he's an . . . artist?"

"He's a painter," she said.

"Do you have one of his paintings?" he asked, coming a little closer as his end of the platform dipped.

"With me?" Clio said.

"At all."

He was leveling a gaze at her now as he squatted just a few inches away.

"No," she said. "But lots of painters don't just give out their work."

"Not even to their girlfriends?"

"No," Clio said firmly. "Not when they're building their portfolios. Now it's *your* turn."

That much was true about painters. She hadn't lied about any of this.

"Okay," he said. "Here goes. Everything develops, right? Modern humans have been around for about two hundred thousand years. We can account for about five or six thousand of those years in terms of civilization. We know a little about the activity before that—people were planting seeds and sharpening sticks. But actual civilization doesn't pop up until around 3500 BC. So, a hundred and ninety-five thousand years of chasing deer and living in caves with very little progress, and then suddenly, we have the Sumerians and the Egyptians. Sumerians came first, Egyptians a few hundred years later. Basically, the biggest, smartest, oldest civilization is the Egyptian civilization. Everybody knows they gave us mummies and hieroglyphics and pyramids. Everybody loves them. Following so far?"

Clio nodded. He was getting back into his "I go to Yale *and*

Cambridge" voice a little, but it was strangely bearable this time. Maybe because she was interested in what he had to say for once. Or maybe because it was hard to get too obnoxious when you were crouching in an inch of water in the dark. Clio thought back to the night of her jellyfish smackdown. How Aidan had poured the water all over her body. She shivered.

"Think about it," he said. "Every year, technology gets a little better. Think about how far we've come in just a hundred years. Whole different world, right? Now, let's look at the Great Pyramid of Giza. It's one of the architectural wonders of the world. Most historians date it to around 2560 BC. That's pretty early in human history. And you know what? We *still* don't know how they built it, and we *still* don't quite know what it does."

"It doesn't do anything," she said. "It just sits there. It's a tomb."

"It's way too complex to just be a tomb," he said. "For a start, it's at the place where the longest meridian and the east-west axis meet. It marks *the exact center of the world*—something humans couldn't even begin to identify until a few hundred years ago. It's about five hundred feet high; it's made up of more than two million blocks that weigh between two and fifteen tons each. They're placed so perfectly that the sides are never off by more than eight inches. The inside is engineered and constructed so perfectly that you can't even get your nails in the joins of the blocks. Plus the whole thing was planned out and built with astonishing geometrical harmony. And it's aligned to true north, south, east, and west. How? Why? We have no clue."

"What's that got to do with us now?" Clio asked. "I mean, I'm impressed that you know all of this, but we're not talking about Egypt."

"You asked me to explain," he said. "I *am* explaining. Imagine a little kid going into kindergarten. The kid has to learn his numbers and letters and how to tie his shoelaces because he's *five*. Now imagine that little kid starts scribbling advanced linear algebra equations in his coloring book, then draws up a complete set of architectural plans for a skyscraper. And then *builds that skyscraper*. You would probably think something strange was going on. That's how weird and out of nowhere the Egyptians are. They're so weird that there are people out there who believe space aliens taught them."

"So . . . how did they learn all of that stuff?"

"You want to know the answer to that, you have to tell me a little more about the mysterious boyfriend."

"This is not a game, Aidan!" she said.

"No," he said. "You're right. It's not. And I guess you would know. But if you stopped being so evasive, it might be easier for me to put my ass on the line for you. I'm not asking you for your PIN number and your passwords."

Clio felt her face flush. He probably couldn't see it out here. It was much too dark.

"What do you want to know?" she said.

"I've been stuck on this boat with no TV. I need some entertainment. So, come on. Bring him alive for me."

Her brain was reaching for some meaning in this. Either Aidan was just being weird and messing with her head—entirely possible—or he really was trying to establish some kind of trust. Which was very . . . surprising.

"He's tall," she said.

"Taller than me?"

"It doesn't take much," she said with a short laugh. "But yeah. Way taller than you."

"How much taller?"

"He's six five," Clio said.

Even in the dark, Clio could see that Aidan looked like he didn't quite believe that.

"He's six five," she repeated. "Now, where did Egyptians learn all of that stuff if it's so impossible?"

"Nobody knows," Aidan said.

"*That's* your answer?"

"That *is* the answer. No one knows. Either they were just really, really smart or—"

"Or?"

"Or someone came before them that we don't know much about. Really smart people. This is where it starts to get tricky and people start walking away."

"What do you mean?" she asked.

"I mean that people start to get touchy when you start speculating on ancient history. There are a lot of theories, and some of them aren't taken too seriously."

"Like?" she asked.

"Like that there was knowledge out there that was lost. Knowledge that came from a society that was at least partially destroyed in some kind of cataclysm, like a flood."

"Wait, are you talking about Noah's Ark?" she asked. "In went the animals two by two?"

"Noah's Ark is one of many stories that talk about floods. Name an ancient culture and they talk about it. The flood story appears in the *Epic of Gilgamesh*, the oldest known story. The

Greeks talked about two major floods. The story shows up in India, China, Europe . . . the Mayans, Incas, and Aztecs talk about it. The stories all talk about major flooding, and sometimes the details are similar. And I'm not saying to take the Noah's Ark thing literally. I'm just saying that there's a definite pattern here. Stories about flooding, a lost group of people. From under the water. Are you following me now?"

"Please tell me you're not talking Atlantis," she said, sinking down. "As in Atlantis, the completely mythical lost world. Atlantis, the thing they make theme parks about."

"It's not Atlantis in the way that you may be thinking," he said. "The guy who originally found the stone, *he* thought it was Atlantis. Atlantis was a bit more of a viable theory back then. Now we know that there are no submerged continents. It's more the idea of a world that came before. There have been traces of a language, bits and pieces found all over the globe. That's the weird part. Languages are local. We're finding evidence of something big, something worldwide. A society that could travel around the world long before it's supposed to have been able to. We keep finding evidence of it, but no one can read the writing. That's where the Marguerite stone comes in. No matter what you think about that theory, the Marguerite stone can help us translate an ancient language for the very first time. And that just might change history as we know it. Literally."

"Look," Clio said. "If there was some kind of vast underwater world, wouldn't we have heard a little more about it by now?"

"Maybe. But scuba diving wasn't invented until 1943. Before that, there was no underwater archeology. That's seventy percent of the earth's surface that was inaccessible. And this field . . . it relies on amateurs. People finding stuff by accident. Underwater archeology is actually pretty new. So, no. Now you know what the stone means. Want to know something else I know?"

Clio waited. Her heart was racing again, inexplicably.

He leaned in until he was almost up to her face, his breath against her nose and cheek. Clio could hear her heartbeat echoing in the space behind her ear. The water that was leeching its way up her pajama legs was cold, and she could feel all the nerves in her body again, like on the night of the jellyfish.

"You don't have a boyfriend," he said. "You've been lying. I told you. I can spot a lie."

The information was all coming too fast, and this . . . this was like a smack in the face. She had no boyfriend. She was an insane liar, from a family of general nutcases. His green eyes were boring into her now.

"You're . . ." she started.

But she didn't know what he was.

"I knew it," he said. "From day one, I *knew* it."

He leaned a bit closer. The current, that strange thing she had felt before on the couch when he'd leaned toward her then, it was there again. But his expression was so strange and hard to read in the dark. She could hear the waves slapping at the boat. They seemed to be snickering. Her humiliation was total. He had caught her. He had been laughing at her the *entire time*. She turned and stared out at the dark sea. Then she stood up, stumbling as the boat rolled.

"Here," she said, reaching for Elsa's letter and shoving it at him. "This is for you."

The Date

Clio woke up feeling ill the next morning. Her stomach was tender and her head was pounding. She didn't want to get up. Didn't want to make breakfast. Didn't want to lug around diving equipment or stare at maps in the wheelhouse. She wanted bed, TV, and snack food. And her cat.

But there was no TV, her cat was being watched by a Polish neighbor in Philadelphia, her current bed was partially occupied, and she'd rented out her space for the night.

So she got up. She didn't shower. She put on the skull-and-crossbones pajamas and a black tank top and tied her hair in a knot on the top of her head.

The weather had cleared, revealing a blindingly sunny day. The bad spirits of yesterday had brightened, and Martin was up and about, just like normal. Julia looked happy, presumably because the letter had resurfaced in one of her piles of paper, mysteriously. Clio made toast for breakfast and fell back asleep on the sofa before she had to face anyone else—anyone else being Aidan, who didn't appear. When she woke up, Elsa was leaning over her.

"He's being annoying," she said.

That could only mean Aidan.

"He's down with my mom, so he hasn't answered me. I don't even know if he's read it. Why can't he just say yes so I can go and get things ready? Can you figure out a way to talk to him?"

"No," Clio said. "I really can't."

"Are you okay?" Elsa asked.

"I just don't feel good," Clio said.

"Oh," Elsa said. "I'm sorry. Are you sure you're okay with this?"

"I'm sure," Clio said, not feeling sure about anything at all.

Aidan managed to lay low for most of the day, which was fine by Clio and not so fine by Elsa. She trailed him throughout the afternoon and finally returned with some news as Clio was sluggishly moving away the remains of lunch.

"He said yes!" she said. "We'll have to figure out when to make the switch."

"Whenever you want," Clio said, trying to sound happy. "I just want to go to bed. I'll read or something." *Why?* Why oh why did she even *care* about any of this?

Yet it felt like something that had been alive and flickering inside her—some kind of hope, some kind of something—had just been snuffed out before she could even really know what it was.

Clio packed her bag early in the evening while it was still light out—bunching up her sleeping pajamas, books, her iPod. She picked up the Galaxy name tag. It seemed so long ago that Ollie had typed it up and pinned it to her shirt. It felt like another *life* ago.

All of the downstairs doors were closed as Clio let herself into Aidan's room quietly. He wasn't there—he must have stayed in the workroom.

Clio had seen Aidan's room on the first night, but going into it now was like discovering an entirely new part of the *Sea Butterfly*. It was so much smaller than the Champagne Suite; it wouldn't have held their bed. It was darker, and the carpet was less plush.

It was also entirely full of Aidan. It smelled of boy deodorant. There were wires all over the floor and a small pile of sci-fi novels and two very scary-looking engineering textbooks on the tiny bedside stand. There were crushed soda cans next to the bed. Otherwise, the room was clean.

Clio emptied out her bag and arranged the books and iPod on the stand, pushing aside Aidan's com. She sat on the bed. It was harder than hers, she noticed. And the blanket wasn't as nice. She reached down and pulled it up and put it to her face. It smelled of Aidan, which was to be expected. But tonight she would be sleeping in this smell while he stayed in her bed.

It was much too much to think about.

She got up and was putting on her sleeping pajamas when the door opened. Aidan stepped in.

"Do you mind?" she said, yanking the pants up just in time

"Sorry," he said.

"You can go," she said, getting into the bed and sitting up against the wall. "Have a nice night. *Don't* do anything weird on my bed, although I know there's no point in even saying that."

"We need to talk first," he said, entering the room and closing the door quietly behind him.

"What about?" she asked, flipping open her book. "I'm not going to tell anyone on you, okay? Just go."

But he didn't go. He stood there staring down at her.

"Oh, you must *love* this," she said, her voice crackling. "A girl in your bed. A girl upstairs."

"Why are you *like* this?" he asked. His emotions were so suddenly real that it startled her. "What is your problem?"

They were both speaking quietly so that no one would hear them. As they became more intense, it almost sounded like hissing. She didn't even know why she was still talking to him. She just had this ridiculous need for *him* to understand. She needed to take one final stand and really explain herself.

"You want to know my problem?" she said. "Okay, I'll tell you my problem. Back when we made the game, my dad hired this guy to be his business manager. He was supposed to set up all kinds of investments, do a deal for a television show, all kinds of stuff. And then one day, my mom realized that our accounts were almost empty. And it was all done legally. My dad had signed the papers. It not only left us without money, we ended up in debt."

"And that's when your parents got divorced?"

"No," she said. "My dad took me diving, but he didn't follow the rules. I got hit. Then we go to Japan, and he lets me get this tattoo. Do you know how sick of this thing I am? This. This is the thing that did it. My mom knew she couldn't trust him. She wanted us to have a normal life. I just don't think she felt . . . safe or something. You never know what idea my dad is going to come up with, or where he's going to go, or what he's going to buy. He just does what he wants. And now? Now he's doing it again. Julia knows a sucker when she sees one. This isn't the first time she's used people to get funding."

"What does *that* mean?"

"The only reason Elsa even *exists* is because her father sat on the grant board at a bank that was handing out research money. Didn't you know that? And you have a date with my roommate, in my room, in my bed. So do me a favor and just leave me alone and go do what you want. Just don't mess with my head anymore, okay? I've had enough. I've had enough of *all* of you."

Aidan sucked in his cheeks. He balled up his fist and banged it against his thigh a few times.

"Whatever," he said. "Just, whatever."

And then he was gone.

Clio let out a long breath and put her hands over her face. She tried to make her mind be quiet, to block it all out.

"You do not exist," she said weakly.

Except that he did. A minute later, he returned, shut the door, and continued pacing. Clio looked up in total surprise.

"First of all," he said in a low voice, "*you* broke into Julia's room, and what did you find? An old letter? That's your smoking gun? Look, Julia is a little intense. She's not a lot of fun to work for. But she's smart, and she's a professor, and your dad *found her*, not the other way around. And I've told you why this trip is legitimate and important. Are they going about this a

240

little strangely? Yes, they are. Why? I don't know. But don't blame me for it."

His agitation was totally unhidden. Clio had never seen Aidan like this before—completely raw, not entirely in command of himself.

"Second," he said. "Why Elsa likes me, I *seriously* have no idea. It's probably because I'm the only guy around. I don't know. This is really a first for me. My track record is really, really bad, believe it or not. I should be pissing myself with excitement, but I'm not. She's beautiful, and she's nice, but I don't like her that way, even though my brain is telling me I'm insane. I'm a guy. I'm not supposed to be complex. If a hot girl likes me, I'm supposed to like her. It's that simple. But I don't."

He started to pace in the few feet of space he had.

"The reason I don't is right in front of me," he said. "I like the girl who is on my bed, right now, and who has appeared to hate me from the minute she first saw me. I disgust her so much that she makes up boyfriends to guard against me. She *physically runs away* when I'm supposed to dance with her."

There were almost-audible clicking noises in Clio's head as pieces snapped into place.

"You kissed her," Clio managed.

"I know. I kissed her because . . . because I did. Because I am a guy. Because she was there, and she's gorgeous, and she wanted to. And you really didn't seem to want to be around me. When you got hurt, I don't know . . . it was so weird. It felt like something was happening with us. But then you just shut me down again. So what do I do? Do I accept the invitation, which I am still really confused about? Or do I say no? Do I . . . stay here?"

No, Clio's brain screamed. *He's Elsa's. Remember? Remember Elsa? The girl who thinks she's going on a date with this guy RIGHT NOW?*

Clio opened her mouth, but no words came out. The image of Ollie came into her head, but it was rapidly replaced by what was right in front of her. The guy with the tousled hair and the slightly too-big clothes. Snarky, smart, annoying, handsome . . . He suddenly sat down on the bed next to her and put his hand into her hair. His fingers were just tickling her scalp, making every hair on her body stand on end. Without even knowing what she was doing, she reached out and put her hand against his neck. It was stronger than she'd realized it would be. Immediately, the feeling rushed over Clio that despite everything, this was *right*.

"Stay here," she whispered.

He was quiet for a moment. His finger made a little circle under her chin.

"I was hoping you'd say that," he said. And then he leaned in. He was at her mouth now, and she could feel his breath on her lips.

There was a knock at the door. He jerked a bit. They stared at each other.

"Who is it?" he asked, not moving his face away from Clio's.

The person didn't answer.

"One sec," he called, moving back and standing up.

There was a moment of confusion—bad comedy confusion. There was nowhere for Clio to hide, so she just slid farther under the blanket. He tossed some clothes on top of her. Whoever that was had probably heard them, so this was a complete joke. She peered out from the sleeve of a shirt.

Elsa stood there, looking down at the floor.

"You could have just said no," she said to Aidan. "And *you* could have just told me the truth."

That was to Clio. Or the mass of clothes that was Clio. Then Elsa walked away.

Aidan paused for a second, then carefully slid the door closed and leaned against it, staring at the ceiling. Clio shook herself out of the pile. Her heart was going way too fast to be healthy.

"I do everything wrong," he said.

"I have to go talk to her," she said. "I'll . . . we'll . . ."

"Yeah. Go."

"Do you . . ." She didn't even know what she was asking. She was almost afraid to know. She hurried out into the hall and up the stairs.

Do Not Push the Shiny Orange Button

Elsa had locked their door. Clio stood in the vestibule in the dark with her hand flat against the bedroom door. Locked out of her home, out of Elsa's life.

She turned and looked out the vestibule window. Her father had come out on deck. He was staring at the dark purple sky and the last remnants of the sunlight—the long golden line sinking into the water. He was wearing his ridiculous little cap again, but it was strangely endearing now. After all she had just said, after what had just happened, her insides were so tossed around that her dad was the only thing that made sense.

As unthinkable as this idea would have been a few weeks, a few days . . . maybe even a few hours ago, Clio had the overwhelming urge to go out to him and ask him what to do. That was her *dad*. He could help her figure her way out of this. She needed him.

She hurried down the steps past Martin, who glanced up at her as he sat at the dining room table.

"Clio," he said. "You should—"

"I'll be back, Martin," she said. "Hold on."

She went through the glass doors and out to her father. She was ready—she wanted him to know everything.

"You know," he said as she approached, "it's always disappointing to know that your daughter—the girl you love—thinks you're an idiot."

Clio stopped dead.

"W-what?" she stammered. "I didn't say that."

"You never used to lie to me either," he said, turning around. "A bad judge of character?"

Clio's mind reeled. How did he know that? Even if he'd been somewhere on the deck, there was no way he'd been close enough to hear her say that. How . . . ?

There was only one way, and it hit her immediately. The com on Aidan's bedside stand. Pushing the books at it . . . She must have depressed the side button. It had been on. It had broadcast everything.

"Oh my God," she said. Her stomach felt almost exactly like it did when she drank all of that warm margarita mix two years ago.

"So now I know what you think," he said. "I guess I've always known it. I've just never heard it before."

"Dad . . ." She stepped closer to him, but he held up his hand.

"Hold on," he said. "Let's just be clear about this. Let's get it all out in the open. So you think I'm being conned? You think I'm foolish? I know we lost a lot of money, but we did get some. We got more money than a lot of people see in a lifetime. We had a good run, Clio. And you can't tell me you didn't enjoy those things we did. Half of them were your ideas."

"I was *twelve*," Clio managed to say. "They were a twelve-year-old's ideas."

"They were *our* ideas. Were they that bad?"

"Maybe not bad, but—"

"But what?" he asked.

"Mom wasn't happy," Clio said. "Our life was weird. Then I got hurt—"

"Which I guess you think is my fault. And that's fair. I was in charge. I should never have taken you out there."

"It wasn't your fault," she said. "It was the guy in the boat."

"It was my fault," he said. "I knew it. Your mom certainly knew it. And you knew it too. Do you know how sick I was about that? If anything had happened to you . . . anything more . . . I would have died. You got better, but you always hated the scar. I could see how much you hated it. So I let you get that tattoo. Not just any tattoo, but one drawn by a famous artist. I thought if we covered it up with something really wonderful . . . but I screwed that up too."

Guilt isn't always a rational thing, Clio realized. *Guilt is a weight that will crush you whether you deserve it or not.*

"If you don't trust me, you don't trust me," he said. "I don't want you to be stuck somewhere you don't want to be."

"I want to be here," she said. "I *want* to stay."

"You went into Julia's room. You went through her *things.*"

"Dad," Clio said. "I was worried. You're the one who wouldn't trust me. You wouldn't tell me what was going on. I care. It's really my boat too."

"This is *not* your boat," he said, his voice rising. "You don't understand what this means. You don't understand anything. You think I just left? Your mother told me to go, Clio. You think I wanted to?"

She could hear her father's voice cracking.

"So why didn't you say no?" Clio said. She could feel the tears running down her face now.

"Because she didn't give me any choice. She told me to go. She told me I was ruining everything for you, for us. And she was kind of right, like you said. It's my fault we lost all the money. It's my fault you got hurt. I didn't want to do that anymore."

He seemed resigned now, and he wouldn't look at her. It was obvious and absolutely clear that everyone on the boat could hear them or knew this was happening. Everything had blown apart.

"It's not working," he went on. "I shouldn't have brought you here. I went too far, and so did you."

"What do you mean?"

"We'll go back to land tomorrow. We have to go anyway. I'll see you off the boat there and make sure you get safely to the airport. You'll get on a plane and head straight to Topeka. You can go back to your mom. You'll be away from me. Congratulations. You got your wish."

There was no hug. No grand reunion. He just walked away, leaving her alone. More alone than she had ever felt before.

Mistaken Identity

There was nowhere to go. The bedroom was locked. The bottom two floors had people floating around in them. So Clio went to the dark wheelhouse. She rested across the leather seats and stared out of the darkened windows at even more darkness.

She cried for a while by herself, her face sticking to the leather. Then her body got tired, and there was nothing left to cry. Nobody was coming for her. So she just rested there and let herself adhere. Maybe her face would become glued to the seat. Nobody could make her leave then.

Because that was the kicker. Now she wanted to stay on this miserable boat more than anything. She wanted to make it right with Elsa and with her dad. She wanted Aidan. She wanted Aidan so much. She had no idea when this had happened to her—this want for Aidan. It was nothing like her silly fantasies about Ollie. But who even knew where Aidan was now? Maybe in his room. Maybe in *her* room.

After a while, the ambient lights on the controls came back to life, giving the room a soft techno-glow. Clio felt a sudden affection for the panels, these expensive trinkets that her father had purchased. Only her father would do something like this, on this grand scale. And the truth was, she *had* missed this kind of thing. Yes, it was dumb, and yes, it might ruin or kill him—but no one could fault his style.

It could have been like a fairy tale. But fairy tales aren't real. Things don't work like that. There's a price for everything.

And now she was paying another one. Just as she had found something that she had wanted for so long, it was being taken away. And her own words had done it. What she'd said wasn't wrong or unfair. It was just too hard to hear out loud.

Aside from nodding off once or twice, she didn't sleep during the night. By five, she just gave up. The dawn spread over the ocean, wide and pink, more beautiful than anything had a right to be.

She stumbled downstairs to the living room, where her father was drinking a cup of coffee.

"We're heading back," he said. "We're just plotting course. You'll probably want to get your stuff together."

"Dad—"

"It's done, Clio. It's like you said, that was before. This is now."

Aidan stuck his head up from the stairs.

"I think you should come look at this," he said.

The table in the workroom was covered in maps, images, and printouts. There were several crushed soda cans lined up along the edge. Aidan's eyes were completely red, and he was wearing the same clothes he had been the night before.

"I was up late last night going over some sites in the wreck database," he said. "If we just take a little detour, we can cover this one here, S537, the steamship *Pride of York*."

"And?" her father said tiredly.

"I don't think this really is the *York*," Aidan said, urgency or exhaustion making his voice rise. "It was seen sinking in this area, which is what led to the ID. But I pulled some info on it, and I don't think it matches. I'd made a note of this spot before, but it wasn't really in our search area and didn't seem worth a special trip."

Clio's father looked at him for a moment, as if not quite believing him. Aidan pushed a fuzzy picture forward.

"Have a look. It's pretty similar to the *Bell Star*. Similar kind of vessel, similar time period. But this picture, from what I can tell, shows something longer than the *York* was and slightly the wrong shape."

Clio's father leaned in.

"Hull's there," Aidan said, pointing to a blotch. "It's been driven into the seabed a few feet. Smokestack is there. It looks almost upright, maybe listing to the left a bit. We're in fairly shallow water here. Depth is sixty feet. The ID was done by amateur divers. They don't have any solid proof. And if there was ever anything worth taking, it's long gone. It's just a curiosity wreck. A bunch of dive services use it."

"You think it's worth a look?"

"I think of anything I've seen, this is the closest. There's nothing here that tells me this *isn't* the *Bell Star*. It would take us maybe an hour out of the way, but it's in the right direction."

"I guess it couldn't hurt," her dad said. "We'll head that way. I'll suit up and get a little footage."

He paused at the door.

"Try to control yourselves while I'm gone," he said. "Clio, please start breakfast."

Aidan's face flushed red. He sat back down and stared at the fuzzy outline on the screen. Clio sat down on the floor and picked at the carpet.

"So, I guess you heard," Clio said.

"I heard. *Everyone* heard, apparently."

"Sorry." She practically whispered it.

"It's not your fault," he said, wiping at the screen with his finger. "I don't know what to say. Your dad seems to have made up his mind."

"Yeah," Clio said. "He tends to get like that. Once he's done his dive, he's going to take me back and get me a ticket. I'll probably be off by tonight."

Aidan was still staring at the pictures.

"I don't think you'll be off by tonight," he said.

"You don't know my dad," she said.

"Maybe not. But I do know what I'm looking at. I've been down here all night looking over the data."

"You were down here all night?" Clio asked.

Not that he really would have been welcome at that point, but still . . . he hadn't gone upstairs.

"Your dad told me last night that we were turning around," he said, not looking at her. "He didn't look very happy with me. So I came in here. I remembered flagging *something* I was interested in. It seemed stupid not to take the opportunity . . ."

251

His eyes were still on the table, so it was impossible to get any sense of what he really meant.

"Well," she said, getting up. "Thanks for trying. If you did." She wanted to say more, but how could she?

The morning wasn't entirely cooperating. The water was choppy and the sky was full of clouds. It was almost chilly. Martin was setting up the equipment. Her father must have taken over the driving.

"Listen," Martin said as Clio came out into the cool, misty morning. "I heard about what happened."

"Who didn't?" Clio asked.

"Your dad gets hurt easily. He really values what you think. Your opinion matters more to him than anyone's."

Clio looked down at the deck. Martin, no matter how nice he was, always sided with her dad. He never seemed to get that anyone else had gotten hurt in what happened.

"But he bounces back too," Martin went on. "If he dives today and there's some kind of good news, he may forget all about it."

"Maybe," Clio said. "But that's sort of been the problem all along."

Martin sighed.

"It'll all work out," he said. "Even if you go home. He'll get over it."

She wrapped her arms around herself and shivered. It wasn't supposed to be cold out here. She sat down on the deck against the wall to get out of the wind a little.

"When you went on your fact-finding mission," Martin said while checking a gauge, "did you see anything about Marguerite?"

252

"As in Marguerite who the stone was named after? The guy's daughter?"

"Right. Dr. Magwell's daughter. The stories of her always reminded me of you."

"Of me?" Clio said. "What stories?"

"Dr. Magwell considered his daughter to be his finest pupil. More than that, for a woman of her time, she was really ahead of the curve. She was brave, maybe even a little crazy. After her father's death, she convinced the museum to send her to work at Pompeii. She lived right near where we took off from, in Sorrento. Having read that letter, I'd guess she came here to try to continue her father's work, maybe to try to find another stone. A few years after that, she got interested in underwater archeological work, which was extremely rare at the time. She started off as a free diver, going to the bottom with nothing at all, no diving bell or suit."

"You mean she just jumped in?" Clio asked.

"Yup," Martin said with a laugh. "She was ridiculed at first, but when she started bringing objects off the ocean floor, people really got interested. She became a sort of legend. They called her the mermaid."

"And this reminds you of me?" Clio said.

"Well, I think you have the same streak in you. You make your own way. You're prepared to swim for it. And you're your father's daughter, whether you know it or not."

He patted the tank and rolled it against the side.

"Fortunately for us," he said, "we've pretty much got the diving thing figured out. Our luck is better. Now, do me a favor? Bring up those fins from downstairs? This old man has to get into a wet suit, and that takes time."

• • •

They reached the target spot about an hour later.

"Okay," her dad said. "This is a fact-finding dive. We're going to video the ship to try to get an identifying mark and to get some sense of its condition."

They were loaded down with toys. He'd even brought the handheld underwater scooters with them to help them go faster. They stepped off the back platform and sank under the surface.

Aidan came up beside Clio, a good arm's length away. They both stood looking at the gray sky. The water looked gray as well.

"I'm going to try to talk to Elsa," she said quietly. "Do you want to talk to her first?"

"Let's see what happens," he said. "I have a feeling this day is about to get crazy. We may have to stay out here for a few days. You never know."

"I guess," Clio said. "I have to try now anyway."

The door to the Champagne Suite was unlocked, and Elsa wasn't in the room. Clio looked around and felt a massive wave of sadness. It had been good, being here with Elsa. Elsa was her friend.

She saw a strange blot on the floor, which she soon recognized as her new pastels. They'd been dumped out and stepped on, ground into the coffee-colored carpet. She sat down on the floor and picked up the remains, trying to find any that were salvageable. There were a few pieces. She put them carefully back in the box. Her throat tightened.

Maybe Elsa really didn't want to talk to her. Ever.

She took what would probably be her final shower in the magnificent bathroom, dressed, and went downstairs to the galley. She put on her little paper hat and set to work making breakfast. Strangely, she wanted to hold on to this—everything about it. She had wanted off the boat for so long, she would never have thought it was possible. But she wanted this breakfast to last forever.

She decided to make something like the first morning—a big frittata, and not overcooked. Maybe if she could come up with a really good breakfast, she could stay. Her dad would see how much she was needed, how she was still dedicated. She set to work, tearing the galley apart for ingredients. As she put the eggs into the pan, she heard someone come up behind her. Julia slid around and reached for the coffeepot.

"Good morning," she said. She sounded civil, even pleasant.

"Hi," Clio said.

Julia leaned back against the counter and sipped at her black coffee. This morning she was wearing khaki shorts and a red polo shirt. She almost looked like a normal woman, one who was actually someone's mom.

"Do you know where Elsa is?" Clio asked.

"Asleep in my room," Julia said.

"Oh."

A silence fell between them. Air bubbles in the egg casserole popped slowly.

"What you said was correct," Julia said. "I did meet Elsa's father when he was sitting on a grant board. And yes, your father is funding this work. I'd never made the connection, but that's because I've known people, dated people, in between them. Perhaps I have a fondness for people who support my work, but I think that's natural. Don't you?"

Put like that, it made Clio seem like a true paranoid cretin. What was it that had first drawn her to Ollie, anyway? His love of the inks—his love of art. That he supported her love of art. Also, the jacket. And the bike. And the six-foot-fiveness. But it was the art that started it all.

"I was just—"

"You were looking out for your father," Julia said. "There's nothing wrong with that. I admire that."

Clio looked over. Julia's face was still hard and bony, but the words came out fairly softly. Well, soft-ish.

"I told your father at the time that it might be hard or unfair to bring you out here," she said. "Elsa is long used to my dating. She's never lived with her father, and she usually lives at school. She thinks nothing of it. But you haven't had any time to adjust. So yes. I did think you should have been allowed to stay behind at home. I can understand your reluctance about this entire trip."

All the words were right. It all made sense. But there was something about this that wasn't ringing true for Clio.

"Aren't you mad?" she asked. "About . . . the other thing?"

"You mean Aidan?" she asked. "No. I was seventeen too. I know how that can be. Having the three of you on this boat—it was always a risk."

This sort of made Clio sound like a dangerous, unstable chemical. But then again, maybe that was what she was. It was starting to look that way.

"Can I ask you something?" Clio said.

"Please do."

"Do you have anything about Marguerite?" Clio said.

"Marguerite Magwell? I have a few things. I'll bring them up."

Julia left the galley, and Clio turned back to the eggs. This was all wrong now. Now Julia was being nice to her and getting her things while she attempted to impress her dad with her cooking. Her father's daughter . . . what was Martin talking about?

She carefully layered in all of the goodies she had found. They were a little short on fresh ingredients, but they had ridiculous numbers of things in jars. Good stuff, too. Italian groceries, like peppers and olives in jars. Julia returned with a plastic file containing a magazine article just as Clio was sticking her creation in the oven.

"Here you go," she said. "You can keep this if you're interested."

"Thanks," Clio said. She leaned against the sink and looked at the article. It was from an archeology magazine, with long, glossy pages. The images struck Clio at once. They were very 1920s, black-and-white photos of a woman with a bob haircut and a strange-looking bathing suit that looked like shorts and a shirt, standing on the edge of a large sailboat and preparing to dive. She had a look of utter confidence on her face. And she was beautiful—big and strong, with visible muscles in her arms. Her hair was so blond that it looked almost white in the photo, but her eyes were dark. Marguerite's gaze came right off the page.

There she was again, in a portrait when she was seventeen. Even though this was an extremely old picture, taken in one of those formal settings that always looked so contrived, her face had that same fierceness. The emotion came through even though she sat demurely wearing a little sailor-style dress, her hair arranged in a pile of very thick curls looping over the top of her head, a little bouquet of flowers in her grip.

"She was a remarkable woman," Julia said. "A revolutionary. Totally devoted to her work."

"She was a diver, right?"

"Yes, she was. And long before there was safe equipment. She began the search that we're on now. She was looking for her father's boat when she had her accident."

"Accident?" Clio said, looking up from the pictures.

"She died during a dive," Julia said crisply. "She was trying out a new piece of diving gear, but something went wrong. She was dead before they even got her back up onto the boat. But now we're continuing the work, and we won't fail in the same way."

There was something cold about the way she said this, whether she meant it that way or not. Something shockingly practical, as if you could just step over someone who died and take over what they were doing. As if an equipment failure during a dive was Marguerite's fault.

Or maybe it was just the English accent. It was hard to tell. But Clio felt her eyes narrowing a bit in reaction.

There was a sound on deck. The divers were coming up. Clio hurried out of the galley and joined them. Her dad was out first. Martin sat on the platform, still halfway in the water.

"How did it go?" Clio asked.

They didn't answer. Her dad was leaning over Martin, taking off his mask. Something was wrong.

"Clio," Martin said weakly, "that bottle . . ."

It took Clio just a second to remember the nitroglycerin on

the bedside stand. She started off running for it, swinging down the circular steps by holding the rails. Her sudden appearance, running through the downstairs hall, drew Aidan's attention. He leaned out of the workroom.

"What are you—"

"It's Martin," she said.

She was back up with the bottle in less than a minute, Aidan right behind her. Martin took the bottle, removed a pill, and swallowed.

"Should I radio for help?" her dad said. "Should we get you to a hospital?"

"It's just chest pain," Martin said. "I just need to . . . sit down."

Clio's father and Aidan helped him off the platform and undid the top of his wet suit.

"We should get you in," Aidan said. "You're not looking good."

"I'm all right," Martin said, his voice gruff. "This has happened before. I'll be fine once this pill kicks in. Go have a look at that."

He half pointed to the video camera dangling from Clio's father's hand. The camera was passed to Aidan.

"Yes, take a look," her dad said. "I think we may be on to something."

Impulsive Decisions

In the light of the camera, the water was a messy green, with gold and brown flecks flying in all directions. Little blobby jellythings and fish poked in and out. The wreck itself was covered in pod-shaped sea creatures, hundreds of these little circles, distorting its form and making it look puffy. But it was there. It was encrusted, but it was a ship.

"There's a lot of damage to the front," Aidan said, pointing to where the ship seemed to melt into the sea bottom. "The metal is twisted. They hit something."

Aidan sat at his computer, Julia leaning over his shoulder. Clio stood off to the side, her eyes going between the image and Aidan's face. He had never looked so intent before. His eyes were lost, deep in the footage.

"Aidan," Julia said. "Is this our boat?"

Aidan still didn't answer. He twisted around toward the table and began shuffling through the pile of papers scattered there, eventually pulling out a technical drawing of a boat, one that looked quite old. He looked at it, then the screen, then massaged his eyebrows with one hand, pinching them together.

"There's no ID." Aidan paused. "Or there's another ID. A wrong one, I think. There's something about this boat. I'm going to call it. I'm going to say this is it."

This hit Clio harder than she expected. Her knees gave a little and she leaned back. Aidan started to laugh a bit, and Julia cracked the first genuine smile Clio had seen on her.

"How do you know?" Clio asked.

"I've been staring at pictures of this damn boat for months. And I can read the sonar images. This is what I do."

"Let's go tell them," Julia said. She kept her voice calm, but just barely.

Upstairs, things weren't looking so good. Martin was out of his wet suit but was slumped on the sofa. He was still insisting that he didn't need a doctor.

"What have you got?" her dad asked as the three of them approached.

"A hit," Julia said.

"You're kidding."

He had to sit down next to Martin. His face contorted oddly, either on the verge of laughter or tears. Neither came. His face just stayed like that.

"First thing we need to figure out," he said. "Martin."

"I'm *telling* you, Ben. This is not new. It's just pain."

"But you're not diving again," her dad said. "There's no way."

"It probably wouldn't be smart," Martin admitted. "I'm not quite feeling up to that."

261

"You can't dive alone," Clio said quickly. "First rule of diving."

"I know the rules," her father said. "I'm not crazy."

Clio could see the debate raging in his eyes. Here they were, maybe sitting on top of the *Bell Star*, and they couldn't dive. This wasn't a position she wanted to be in. And yet . . . yet she knew that she was going to do it anyway.

"But I can go with you," she said.

"No," he said quickly. "No way."

"I'm the only card-carrying diver here besides you guys," she said.

"That's probably expired."

"You know what I mean. And I don't even know if they *do* expire. And no, I don't have it *on* me, before you even say it . . . but come on. We're sitting on top of it. And trust me, I'm careful."

This drew looks from everyone.

"I am!" she said. "I can do it, Dad. And you know I can. It's not even that deep."

"It doesn't need to be deep to be dangerous."

"You taught me for a reason," she said. "I learned. I can do this. I'll go with you. You won't let anything happen."

Even as the words were coming out of her mouth, even as her gut instinct was seconding them, her ears couldn't quite believe it. She was agreeing—no, *insisting*—that she go diving with her dad.

"I think she's right, Ben," Julia said. "She can handle herself. You even told me her accident had nothing to do with anything she did."

So her father had told Julia about the accident.

"You're sure about this?" he asked.

"Completely."

No one said anything for three or four entire minutes, which is a lot of silence. Aidan sat down at the dining room table and stared into the galley, his lower jaw set off on an angle. He was deep in thought about something, and he didn't seem to like that thought very much.

Finally, her father took a deep breath, then sat up.

"Okay," he said. "We make a plan—a detailed plan—and we stick to it. We do this *conservatively*. Aidan, I need you to map that boat, give us a way in and out, plus backups."

"You're doing this?" Aidan asked.

"We'll see," he said. "Maybe. Let's get the plan together. Look at those cargo holds. If this is the *Bell Star*, anything that Magwell was carrying was probably in that area, in crates. Clio, you go with him, and you watch. Get the picture of that boat into your head."

"You're serious about this?" Aidan asked Clio as they went down the stairs.

"Totally serious," Clio said.

"Think about this," Aidan said, turning around on the steps and blocking the way. "Don't pretend to be tougher than you are."

"Are you worried about me?"

"I'm just—"

"Look," she said. "My dad spent a ton of money on my training. I had a private instructor. I did hours of class time. I did penetration training with some wacko who used to be in the Greek navy. I know what I'm doing. I just haven't . . . done it in a while."

Aidan sighed, then turned and kept walking down and to the workroom. At the table, he pushed aside most of the papers, selecting a few and arranging them in the middle.

"Meet the *Bell Star*," he said, pointing to several grainy photographs and a few of the structural drawings. "These drawings are actually of a ship called the *Daybreaker*, which was a sister ship. Completely identical, except that it was two feet longer. It's not a huge boat. There were three cabins for first-class passengers. The next level down had twelve second-class cabins and other rooms for the captain and crew. Just below, to the front and the back of the boat, were the cargo spaces. The one in the front was much larger. The back one was next to the engines and the coal hold."

He turned back to his computer monitor, where the blurry image of the wreck was on the screen. With one hand, he reached over and grabbed Clio by the shoulder, pulling her down close. She tried not to think about the fact that mere inches separated their faces again.

"It looks to me like that's the rip that brought them down," he said, pointing to a shadow on the screen. It took Clio's eyes a second to get used to the focus and find what he was talking about. "It's not huge, but it's definitely big enough."

"What could do something like that?"

"There's no way to know exactly, but it looks like they went into something hard. A rock, a fishing boat. No idea."

"You said they knew the route."

"The captain should have, yeah. But there was a storm that night. Something obviously went wrong."

"Do you think they knew they were sinking?" she asked.

"On a boat this size?" he said. "A hit like that? Probably. The people on the *Titanic* didn't know they were going down because the ship was massive. Some of them felt the bump when the ship hit the iceberg, but most of them paid no attention. A few of them even took the ice from the deck and put it in their drinks. But that was the world's biggest, most unsinkable ship, and the night was clear. The *Bell Star* was no *Titanic*. It was a small passenger boat. And it was clearly hit hard enough for a hole to open in the bottom of the boat. Don't you think you'd feel that?"

"Yeah," Clio said. "I'd feel it."

"Okay," he said standing up and turning back to the drawings on the table. "The *Bell Star* carried both passengers and small amounts of cargo. The manifest said it was transporting tiles and mail. The tiles were worth some money. They may also have weighed the ship down. You probably saw on the image that the bow is farther down into the seafloor."

No. Clio hadn't seen that at all.

"My guess is that's where the tiles were," he said. "The boat could have been a little unbalanced in the way things were stored. Just a guess. Another guess: the tiles would have been packed in advance, long before the passengers or the mail. My hunch is that passenger cargo, like the stone, is in the back of the boat, here."

He drew an invisible circle around a section of the diagram with his finger.

"That's where I'm going to plot you guys to," he said. "You'll have to go down a few levels. And frankly? Yes. That thought scares me. There are going to be all kinds of edges and metal bits that can slice tubes and lots of weird corners and shifted stuff that can trap divers."

"You were going to send my dad there," she said.

"It's not the same thing," he said. "You need to think about this. Look at that picture on the screen. That is a rusted mess, sixty feet down. Is that really what you want your first dive back to be? You told me yourself that sometimes your dad isn't too careful. And at this point, you and the water don't have a very good relationship. I don't want to sound like grandma here, but this isn't a joke."

No. It wasn't a joke at all. He was right about the issues. Going deep down into a boat like that—down levels of stairs, past torn bits of metal, completely in the dark. Clio felt a bubble of fear catch in her throat. But more overwhelming was . . . a lightness in her head. She liked this idea. She had *loved* diving. The only reason she hadn't gone back was that her arm was hurt and her mom was freaked out. And then her father was gone. But she would have. Wouldn't she?

And if they were right and this stone was all it was supposed to be, nothing was going to stop her from doing the dive. A stone that important . . .

"Wait a second," she said. "Why are you looking in the cargo hold?"

"We're looking for a large historical item, which would have been boxed up. It's the definition of cargo."

"How big is the Marguerite stone supposed to be?" she asked.

"The letter says about two feet long."

"Right. So you're Dr. Magwell, and you have a stone that can help you translate a language no one has ever been able to read

266

before. You're on a boat that's sailing to France, and you're going to be on it for days. *You're* on a boat now. It's boring, right?"

"Not always," he said.

"You know what I mean. So, if you were carrying something like that and if you were stuck on a boat, what would you be doing? Would *you* put it in the cargo hold? Or would you keep it with you and study it?"

Aidan drummed his fingers on the table and thought about this.

"Okay," he said. "Purely speculating, let's say that the stone is in his cabin. We have no idea which one was his."

"He took this boat a lot, right?"

"Every year."

"And was he rich?"

"He was well off," Aidan said.

"That puts us up here," Clio said, pointing to the cabins with the windows. "First class. That's going in, but it's not that bad. And it's only a few cabins. That's where we start."

She could *see* Aidan thinking this over. Under the fringe of overgrown hair, his green eyes flicked back and forth from image to image, and he pulled his long, thin lips into a taut line.

"You may be right," he conceded. "I'm going to model these and figure out ways in and out. Are you still sure?"

"Are you really worried?" she asked.

"I have to be," he said.

"Why?"

"Because if you die, Julia will probably make *me* do it, whether I know how to dive or not. So it's in my best interests to keep you alive. Also, I think you're nuts."

"I *am* nuts," she said, feeling her eyes widen. "I'm my father's daughter."

It looked like Aidan was about to do something—she wasn't sure what. Reach over for her. Jump up and down. But instead he sat at his computer with a very definite effort.

"Yeah," Aidan said. "Maybe you want to skip anything that sounds like famous last words right now, okay? Please?"

The Diver

First, there was a quiz.

Every single bit of gear, every hand signal, the use of the dive computer, questions about decompression stops, what to do if she had to switch to the secondary breathing regulator if the first one ran out. Clio had been trained well back in the day and managed to get almost every single question right. The one she got wrong wasn't very serious but still got her a lecture.

Martin wasn't a huge guy, so his suit wasn't such a bad fit. She had forgotten how unpleasant this part was, getting powdered up, dragging the rubber up her legs inch by inch. Her father loaded her down, putting the backpack-like buoyancy compensator over her shoulders, the weight belt around her waist. They did a trial dive to make sure she could handle herself under the surface.

Getting in wasn't a problem. It involved taking one very wide step off the back platform, one hand holding her mask and regulator in place. She looked out, not down, just like she was supposed to, and watched the horizon drop away suddenly, only to be replaced by a greenish-tinted, very quiet world. The weight she carried pulled her down a few feet. She cleared her ears, looked around for jellyfish, and took a thirty-minute swim with her dad around the boat, descending about twenty feet.

The second she went under, it was if the intervening years without her dad just went away and they were exactly where they were before. There was so much freedom under the water. As she came up to surface, she could see Aidan leaning over the edge of the platform. He looked very tall from down here, very grave. He still didn't like the idea. As for Clio, it felt really good to be worried about.

They rested a bit before the actual dive, going over the plans that Aidan had worked up.

"We're using pony bottles today," her dad said as they geared up to go. "We're going to be carrying way more gas than we need. And you're going to be carrying a second knife."

Clio was covered in her weight in equipment. Three bottles on her back, knives on her thigh and arm. A spool of guide rope. Artifact bags, weights, camera, light. There was something hanging off every part of her body that could withstand the weight. It was almost impossible for her to move.

"One more time," her dad said to Aidan.

Aidan pulled out the plans and held them down against the breeze.

"Okay. Your access point is here, this doorway under the intact funnel. It appears to be an open passage, nothing you have to work to get through. It leads to stairs that go down to the passenger cabins. There's one bend in the staircase, after the fourth step. It's not really wide, but I think you should be able to get through without too much trouble. From there, you have a hall with a series of six doorways. Magwell's cabin was likely along this hall. If you follow this hall all the way back, you'll end up in the dining room."

"Nice and simple," her dad said. "But even simple things can look confusing underwater."

"I know," she said.

"First sign of trouble, you give me the up signal and we come back."

"I know."

"All right," he said. "Let's do this."

Clio took the one big step. Being so much heavier, she went down much more quickly. It took her a moment to stabilize herself, then get over to her father. She was light now. Free. Physical reality changed in an instant.

They slowly descended along the anchor line. The visibility was good, with the sun cutting down through the water and making everything glow. But at about ten feet, it started to get darker. At thirty, they switched on their lights.

At about forty feet, she saw it clearly—a massive, tilted thing below her. Things that have been underwater a long time cease to look normal. There are no straight edges on the bottom of the sea, just undulating forms with puffs and fronds coming off them. You could get some sense of the boat's shape, but it was squashed and confused.

They went down farther, making regular stops to check the monitor that was connected to her tanks, which told her when she had to stop for a few minutes and let her body get used to the pressure.

At fifty feet, she was looking at a rusted smokestack. They kept going.

Clio hung, suspended, just a few feet above the deck of the boat and watched her father inflate a lift bag—a kind of underwater balloon. He released it and it gently floated to the surface, trailing a rope that he had already tied to the bow. He was marking their position so that the *Sea Butterfly* could guard them from any boats in the area. Then he tied the anchor to the wreck, securing everyone above, and attached a strobing light to the line. It winked at her, like the hazard light on a car. It seemed to have a repetitive message for her: *Warning, warning, scary, scary, death boat, death boat.*

A strange, to-the-bone fear made her want to shoot right back up to the surface, rip the gear from her body, and cower in her bed, as if the duvet could protect her from the weight of eternity. Her breath was catching in her chest. She had to keep it even. She couldn't breathe through her nose—she had only the respirator to suck from, and it was up to her to drink in the air evenly.

She closed her eyes and allowed herself to hang there, standing on nothing. Just floating. She imagined that the cool hiss of air was a drink, a slow, refreshing drink. She was drinking life. One sip of life. Swallow. Relax. Two sips of life . . .

Someone was slapping her arm.

Her father gave her the "are you okay?" underwater signal. She'd forgotten about the hand signals. She indicated that she was.

They went farther. Now she was at eye level with the top part of the ship, peering in the encrusted windows into the utter blackness. That was where she was going—into rooms that had been the property of the sea for more than a hundred years.

Her father waved her along, down what had been the deck, to a pitch-black opening. He secured another line just outside this and tested it for strength. That would be their guide if they lost their way. Inside the opening was the staircase.

In normal life, staircases weren't something that Clio gave a lot of thought to. This staircase, in addition to being filled with water, was incredibly narrow. And she was *not* so narrow, with all of these tanks on her body. There was no turning in this staircase, only moving forward. And there was no stepping, because her finned feet were too large for the steps. She had to hover with one hand on each wall, carefully working her way down, turning, and going down farther. It was too much work for her even to be frightened.

There was more tying of rope and signaling okay once they were in the hallway. At least she assumed it was a hallway. It didn't look like much of anything, and it felt small. At least here, though, she and her father could face each other. There were, as reported, six doors. Three of them were closed. They started with the three open ones. The rooms felt a bit different. They were scrambled, but she could see that they had been bedrooms. There was a light fixture, a bit of chair, a piece of glass. There was a dark form that had probably been a bed. Someone had stayed here, and this was where they had died.

She had a huge worry that she would see a spooky doll's head. She had seen pictures of the *Titanic*, and there was a spooky doll's head in one of them. But the worst she saw here was a comb that had been permanently stuck to the floor under some kind of rust formation.

These three rooms produced nothing. Back in the hall, her father signaled that he was going to work at one of the doors and pointed Clio toward another.

She looked down into the impenetrable darkness at the end of the hall. In her light, it looked like the view of a snowstorm by car headlights, with mysterious flecks. The water was very *full*. Every part of it sustained smaller and smaller forms of life.

She turned back into the first room—the broken, rusty mess that surrounded her. Running her light along the walls, she was just able to make out a small lamp on the wall. It was twisted to the side, but the glass shade was still intact. That was the only familiar object. But where there was a light, there was likely to be a bed. That could have been the lumpy mass next to her. She worked her way around, trying to mentally place objects and make sense of this world.

Clio didn't know how she saw it. Something with just a little bit of shine to it. A tiny circle of white. A tiny circle of white that didn't belong in the composition around her.

Oh no, her brain said. *It's the eye of a doll.*

Maybe it was her own fearful disgust that made her look, to assure herself that it wasn't the lone, staring eye of a doll peering out at her from watery darkness. Whatever it was, it was under a pile of half-rotted wood. She picked up the remnants of a metal pole whose original function was a total mystery and poked deep into the pile, dragging at the white spot. A few small fish skittered out, causing her to jolt. But the massive eel or toothy fish she'd been expecting never came. She smacked at the wood a bit, shoving some of it away. It was hard to maneuver the tiny object with the clumsy pole.

She was obsessed now. Whatever little piece of junk this thing was, she was going to get it. She pulled out her ankle knife and speared at it, knocking it closer. She got closer to the floor and shone her light down.

It was then that she saw something slightly larger but also white. It was about three inches thick but clearly smooth. It could have been many things. It could have been the collapsed marble top of the table that this appeared to be. But it was under the rotted wood. It couldn't be the tabletop.

She picked up the pole again and poked farther, not caring about any potential critters she was going to stir up. She moved the rotting wood away.

Whatever it was, it was about two feet long. And it was oval.

The Stone

The *Sea Butterfly* barely rocked as they sat in the Mediterranean. The Marguerite stone sat out on the back of the deck in its tub of water. Like a newborn, it had emerged covered in goop. The goop, in this case, was partially alive and couldn't just be scraped off. It would have to be done carefully, by an expert.

There had been some screaming, some jumping, and a lot of enthusiastic hugging from Clio's dad. Clio even managed to stand a Julia-dad kissing moment. She was feeling generous for not wanting to barf. A bottle of wine was found and opened, and everyone on deck had a glass. Even Clio got a little. Martin was sleeping, so the good news would have to wait. Elsa didn't emerge. They would have to join in later.

The cameo sat on the table, its creamy peach alabaster background standing out against the white lacquer. Clio studied it.

"This," she said. "This face. It's Marguerite."

Julia came over and had a look for herself.

"I think you're right," she said. "He must have had this with him when he died."

"Then it only makes sense that the person who found the stone should get to wear this," Clio's father said, coming around. The chain was badly blackened, but it held as Clio's father slipped it over her head carefully. The cameo landed right in the center of Clio's chest and stuck to her skin.

"We have to consider that more might be down there," he went on. "We need to at least look to see if Magwell brought anything back that he didn't mention. We need to go back to land first, though. I think Martin should get checked out by a doctor. And we need refills for the tanks."

"We're on our way to Civitavecchia," Julia confirmed. "We might as well go there."

Clio was starting to feel the effects of a sleepless night, on top of her dive. She collapsed in a chair in the living room, but never quite fell asleep. She just let herself be lulled by the movement of the boat as it headed to the shore. She had just nodded off when they stopped, having reached the town.

"Bad news," her father said, stepping back in after a consultation on the dock. "This place is full. There's no slip available for us. We're going to have to anchor farther out. A few of us can disembark here. We can get a doctor to give Martin a once-over, and we can pick up the things we need."

"Come on now, Ben," Julia said. "We all need to celebrate. We can all ferry in on the raft. Proper dinner. Champagne."

Clio looked over in surprise. There was an odd look in Julia's eyes as she suggested this. Julia wanted them all to go ashore . . . *to have fun*. There was definitely something strange about this, but Clio was too tired to think it through.

"No," her dad replied, shaking his head. "We can't leave the boat unattended. It's a good idea, but someone is going to have to stay behind. Aidan? Do you mind? You could drop us off and take the boat out."

"No problem," he said.

"Okay. Everyone else can get out here. We'll need Elsa too, to help us find the doctor. I'm going to get the tanks ready. Some guys here will help me move them over to a dive shop."

Clio followed her dad out onto the deck.

"Can I stay?" she asked groggily. "I'm exhausted."

"Aidan's staying," he said. "You're coming."

"I didn't really sleep last night. And the dive today was so amazing . . . I'm crashing. Please."

"I'm not an *idiot*, Clio," he said. "And I haven't forgotten last night."

"Does that mean you're still sending me back?"

"Don't you want to go back?" he asked.

"No," she said. "Especially since you're going to need me."

"Clio—"

"Anything I've done that you really disagree with—it was only because you wouldn't tell me what was happening. I only swam because you stranded me. I went into Julia's room to find out what was going on."

He picked up a tank and lifted it off onto the dock. Clio kept at his heels.

"Okay," she said. "I need to say this. I'm seventeen. I'm a girl. Which means that yes, Dad, there may be dating involved. *You* do

278

it. And you know Mom does it. I get to do it too. It's reality. I grew up. But tonight? I'm really, seriously just tired. Please, can you please trust me enough to be alone with a member of the male species for a few hours? And it's Aidan. You have to trust him too."

He said nothing, but she could see there was some confusion in his mind now.

"Dad," she said, "we *dove* together today. We *found* it."

Usually, repeated attempts to convince her parents of something failed. But this time, the logic was inescapable, the day simply too good. He paused midway to reaching for the next tank.

"Come on," he said.

She followed him back inside, where Julia was leading Elsa down from the Champagne Suite. She didn't look at Aidan or Clio. Her bearing wasn't mean. It was embarrassed and sad. Clio wanted to talk to her so much, to explain herself, to make her feel better.

The keys were passed over to Aidan.

"Aidan and Clio are saying here," he said.

Elsa looked down at the floor. Clio felt a pang in her chest. There was so much to be repaired between them.

"Aidan," Julia said as she prepared to go, "if you're going to be here, please write up a report of what happened today. We'll want a record. Have something ready by the time I get back. And maybe prep some of the video footage."

"It's like it would kill her to give me a night off," Aidan said after the boat had pushed off, "even after we *find* the stone."

"How come you get to drive the boat?" she asked.

"Because they showed me how to do it," he said.

"Well, then you can show me," she said.

Up in the wheelhouse, the turn of a single key brought to life all of the little panels. Clio wasn't paying the slightest bit of attention as Aidan explained what they did, and she could tell his mind wasn't exactly on the task. He was comfortable around machines and didn't have to think very hard when discussing them. There wasn't very far to go, but he let her take the steering wheel for a few seconds. It felt like a steering wheel.

They reached a spot not too far out, yet away from any traffic that might be going along the shore. Aidan flipped some switches to release the anchor, then killed the engine, and the lights on the panels went off. The wheelhouse was silent.

"This isn't right," he said, looking out of the tinted glass.

"What isn't right?"

"I don't know," he said. "There's just something really eerie about getting what you're looking for."

"Eerie as in bad?" she asked.

"Just, you don't expect it," he said.

He drummed his finger on the panel, examined his shoes, then looked at Clio.

"I thought you were tired," he said.

"I woke up."

Neither of them moved. They stood in the middle of the wheelhouse, looking at the panel. Something had to happen. Clio could feel the space between them. It was practically throbbing. One of them would have to *do* something. Even a large pile of dynamite needs a little spark to set it off.

"You hungry?" he asked.

"Starving."

They left the wheelhouse and went back down and inside,

leaving the glass doors open to catch the evening breeze. In the galley, they gathered up whatever leftovers they could find. Aidan's plate ended up being entirely filled with meat, while Clio's held a strange arrangement of small items—tiny marinated mushrooms, squares of cheese, ends of bread loaves, bunches of salad.

"Since you're here," he said, "you can help me work. Come on."

It was almost like a game they had silently agreed to play: a test to see how long they could draw this out. A few minutes later, they had settled themselves in the small room downstairs, each on one side of the table.

"You were down there," he said, pushing a pad in her direction. "Give us an account. I'm going to put together some of this data."

He flipped open his computer and set to work.

"So," Aidan said, not taking his eyes off the screen. "What happens next with you?"

"Maybe I stay a few days. Maybe go back home. Maybe we all go back to England."

"You have a lot of maybes in there," he said.

"I guess life is full of maybes."

Clio looked at her com. She switched it off very carefully and quietly pushed it across the table.

"What was that for?" Aidan said, his green eyes flashing over the top of the screen.

"Just moving it out of the way."

He looked over at his own com out of the corner of his eye, then continued typing. He rocked forward on his chair, and his knees bumped against hers under the table, quickly, once. And then again. Clio drilled her eyes into the pad of paper, willed her hand to stay steady. She leaned in slightly and kneed him back.

He never even blinked. She heard him typing away. But his foot reached out and hooked her ankle, drawing her slightly closer.

One of them would have to look up. One of them had to act. Slowly—very, very slowly—she unwound her foot.

"Do you want to see what I wrote?" she asked.

"Yeah," he said. "Sure."

She turned the pad upside down to face him but didn't move it any closer. He lowered the screen of his laptop.

"What did you promise your dad?" he asked, smiling slowly.

"That I would lock my bedroom door," she said. "And that I wouldn't pull any funny stunts."

"Define 'funny stunts'," he said.

It was unbearable now. She leaned into the table just a bit. He pushed his laptop over. Then he half stood, leaning in. He draped himself over the table, leaning on his elbows. And then he did something that Clio couldn't quite recover from—he reached out and, just with the tips of his fingers, touched her right under the chin.

"You know," he said, "it's really hard to say the words 'you're pretty' without sounding like a mental patient. But you're pretty."

He brought his face closer, just touching his lips against hers but not pressing. Just touching. And then . . .

And then something happened that wasn't quite what Clio was expecting.

The boat lurched to life and started moving backward at a

high rate of speed, throwing them both backward. Clio grabbed the edge of the table, but Aidan couldn't secure a hold on anything fast enough. He was tossed back into his chair and then back against the wall, where his head landed solidly with a thud.

"They must be back," he said. "I didn't hear them. Did you?"

"No."

There were footsteps above. Clearly, everyone had come back. The boat angled itself, then switched to rapid forward movement.

"We dropped them off," he said. "How did they get back without the launch?"

The sudden cutoff of the moment, combined with the movement, left Clio thrumming. She felt a little woozy.

"I don't know," she mumbled. "My dad—"

"This isn't right," Aidan said. "I don't like this."

Clio was just recalling that he had said the same thing earlier, up in the wheelhouse, when the door opened. A man in a Nirvana T-shirt stepped inside. A stranger. He was a fairly small guy, with slightly tufty brown hair. He looked lost. He stared at Clio and Aidan. He looked around at the maps and laptops. He spoke to them in Italian. They looked at each other.

"Who the hell are you?" Aidan asked.

The stranger cocked his head, then in reply pulled a gun from his pocket and pointed it right at Clio.

Prisoners

Clio was having an epiphany. It was exploding across her mind, as epiphanies do.

Movies won't help you now, it said in its all-consuming echo. *See how wrong they are about this? That's a gun, and it's pointing at you, and does this seem at all like something from a movie? No.*

Her brain flipped the gun into a few other objects. He was holding a stapler. He was threatening them with a hand blender. That was a wrench. A garden hose.

"Hey," Aidan said quickly. "It's okay. You don't . . . You don't need to do that."

His words only seemed to confuse the man. The intruder noticed the com on the table and grabbed it. Then he glanced around and behind him, peering out into the hall but keeping the gun trained on them at all times. Then he stepped out and shut the door.

Clio couldn't even move.

"What," Aidan said, "the hell was that?"

She managed to back toward Aidan a little, and they stood together in the corner, looking at the door.

"Okay," he said. "Apparently the boat is being stolen. What are you supposed to do? What's the rule?"

"Do you think he's coming back?" Clio asked, her eyes darting around the room.

"No idea. Probably?"

There were voices in the hall. The door opened again, and the man stepped back in. Another man glanced around the door. The two men conferred. Then they waved Clio and Aidan out of the room and up the stairs. They sat them down on the living room floor against the sofa.

Both men seemed nervous. One kept grimacing and laughing, walking around the room and picking things up. He was deeply tan, wore an Italy World Cup Champions T-shirt, and played with his lighter a lot. The other, the one who'd found them, was the smaller of the two. He sat at the table and watched them, tapping his fingers relentlessly. He held his gun loosely with his other hand, almost with the casualness that you might hold a cigarette. Neither, it was clear, spoke any English. Clio got the impression that whoever these men were, they hadn't been expecting to find anyone on board.

Of the many strange places she had been in her life, Clio had never been in the path of a gun. And the truth was, it was so completely scary that it almost ceased to be scary at all. Her mind seemed to have short-circuited on fear, leaving her unable to do anything but stare at the leather armchair and take in its every detail. It was kind of like they had invited very weird, awkward guests onto the boat. Guests who brought guns instead of snacks.

For at least an hour, Aidan never moved his eyes from the glass doors. Then Clio heard him speaking in a very low voice when neither of the men was looking.

"Look upset," he whispered.

She mouthed the word, "What?"

"Look like you're upset."

Clio tried her best to arrange her face in something that resembled extreme unhappiness. This should have been easier than it was. Her face didn't really want to move. Aidan slipped his arms around her and pulled her comfortingly close.

The guy at the table looked back, but this seemed to make some sense to him. They were still harmlessly on the floor, and he had the gun.

Aidan's face was right up next to her head now.

"No matter what I say," he said. "Just keep looking upset, okay?"

She nodded.

"I don't think these guys know what they're doing," he mumbled into her hair in a sort of cooing voice. "I think we've been heading due west. Maybe slightly southwest. And we're going pretty fast. I have the feeling they're heading for Corsica or Sardinia. There's nowhere else to go unless they're taking us to the middle of the Mediterranean Sea."

Looking upset got a little easier.

"If you were a boat thief," Aidan said, singsonging away and rocking her a little, "and you had just stolen a million-dollar yacht loaded down with expensive toys, what would you do with two people you found hiding belowdeck?"

"I don't know," she mumbled, keeping on her sad face.

"People will shoot you for your wallet on a dark street. I think they might be prepared to do that for an eighty-foot yacht. They look nervous. Nervous is not good for us. So I suggest we make a decision before it comes to that."

"What decision?" Clio said, managing a few tears.

"The kind of decision I've never anticipated making," he said. "We need to get off this boat. And I think that means jumping off."

"This sounds like a really bad plan," she said.

"It's horrible, but it's the best I can do. We don't have a lot of time to debate this. Are you in?"

Clio pressed her head into his chest even harder.

"Yeah," she said. "Actually, I think I've heard worse."

Tears were nothing now. He rocked her some more. The second guy returned to the room and looked at them, then started to laugh.

"If we can distract them," Aidan said, "we can get through the doors to the deck. Do you know if there are any flotation devices out there?"

Clio went back in her mind to the day that Martin showed her around.

"A raft," she mumbled.

"The raft is good," he said. "But we'll need to seriously get them looking away for a few minutes. Cry harder and think how we could do that."

She buried her face in his chest and let her mind race. She walked it all around the main floor. The most logical place to go was the galley. That would be a logical spot. When people were attacked, they grabbed knives, right?

She wasn't going to get into a *knife fight*. No. There had to be something better than that. But nothing was coming to her. She ran her mind over all the useless and stupid things in there. The orange press, the fancy toaster, the stupid crème brûlée torch.

The stupid crème brûlée torch.

A fire. There was a fire alarm in the galley. That would definitely attract attention.

Now that she had something to focus on, a plan started to assemble itself in her head. She mentally found the torch. It was in the cabinet with the mugs. It had a safety on it, and the only way it worked was by depressing the catch. If she could wrap something around it to hold it down . . .

Like a ponytail holder.

"Pull the band out of my ponytail," she managed to gasp in what were supposed to be sobs. "Play with my hair. Give me the band."

Aidan reached up and slipped off the band. It pulled and snagged a bit on the way, but he managed it. He shook her hair loose and rubbed her head. Then he nudged her forward and pushed the band into her palm.

"I'll be back," she said. "When the alarm goes, we go."

She stood, her legs shaky.

What's the international symbol for "vomit"? she thought frantically.

She clasped her stomach and pointed in the direction of the bathroom, holding a hand over her mouth. The laughing guy watched her, and the gun guy stiffened. But she must have looked harmless enough. The laughing guy followed her but allowed her to go.

As she passed the galley, she stopped and motioned for a glass of water. She stumbled in before she even got a look of permission. She went right for the sink, turning it on and putting her mouth under the spigot. This made the guy chuckle a little.

Laugh away, you bastard, she thought.

She dropped against the edge of the sink, then weakly pointed at the cabinet, as if asking for a mug in total defeat. He nodded but watched her carefully. He came around behind her a bit, but there was very little up there except cups and spice jars. And one stupid crème brûlée torch.

She managed to get her fingers around it as she pulled out the mug. Now it needed to go down the sweatshirt. That was fairly easy. She pressed her arm into her stomach to keep it from coming out of the bottom.

Now she had a mug and a stupid crème brûlée torch down her shirt. Wonderful. She filled the mug and stood there, drinking. She needed a moment to get the thing on.

But the guy had had enough. He grabbed her arm and forced her out of the galley. It looked like he wanted her back in the living room, but she lurched forward, throwing herself into the bathroom and shutting the door.

Panic set in. Her head started to spin. She backed herself up against the door, whacking her head into the towel hook. That felt good. It was solid, reassuring. She banged it again.

She was trying to fend off two men, at least one of whom had a gun—with a crème brûlée torch.

She flicked it on. A tiny blue tongue of flame flickered out. It was hot, but pathetic and small. She released the catch and closed her eyes.

They were going to be expecting barfing noises or something. She attempted some hacking and retching sounds and looked around. How did you set fire to a bathroom? It wasn't exactly the most fire-friendly place. There were two thick hand towels. Toilet paper. That was about it. She felt the towels up and down. They were perfectly dry.

From her limited experience making fires, she knew that they usually needed something that would burn fast and high, which would set the slower-burning things alight. The toilet paper would go up very quickly, but it probably wouldn't burn enough to take out the towels. So that wasn't really enough.

She made a few more barfing noises while she looked around the tiny compartment in despair. What else would burn? Not the floors or walls—they were tile. There was nothing else.

Her sweatshirt. That would burn. She ripped it off.

Now she just had to assemble this. She took the toilet paper off the spindle on the wall and set it down. Then she bundled the two towels and the sweatshirt loosely around it.

There was a knock at the door.

This was it. Now or never.

She pulled out the band that had held up her ponytail and wrapped it around the catch of the torch tightly, keeping the tiny flame lit. She slid this carefully along the floor into the center of the pile, tucking the edge of towel around it.

Then she flushed the toilet, splashed some water on her face, and opened the door. The guy looked at her, glanced inside, but didn't see the towels. The bundle hadn't gone up . . . yet.

He brought her back into the living room and pushed her in the direction of the sofa, where Aidan put his arms back around her. This time, the embrace felt very real. She hugged him back. He was shaking a little.

"Well?" he whispered.

"It's done," she said.

Well, something was done, anyway. It was either going to work or it wasn't.

Five minutes passed. There was no smell of smoke. No noise.

Then the laughing guy decided it was his turn to use the bathroom. This was it. Considering there had been no alarm so far, this would undo them. He would find the fire, and they would be shot, and the whole summer would be punctuated by a bullet. A period. The end. Worse than she had imagined at the beginning, but—she almost laughed—not that much worse.

Bullets seemed quick. They would pop you like a balloon. She tried to get herself used to the thought in the time that she had left.

The man was at the door. In a moment, he would notice. He would yell.

The door opened. No cloud of smoke.

Clio could smell it. He stood there, looking down. He said something in Italian, which stirred the other guy, who stood up and turned toward him. He walked a few steps toward the bathroom.

Then the alarm went off. It was in the hall. All of a sudden, Aidan was shoving her forward.

"Now!" he said.

In the space of two heavy heartbeats, they were at the glass doors. The whole thing was dream-like. They were passing through them before the two guys had even quite figured out why they would want to go out on deck or if they cared whether they did.

Aidan yanked the doors closed. He already had the key in his hand to lock them from the outside. The men rushed for the doors now, but Aidan was halfway through locking.

The man pounded on the glass. As Aidan moved away, he shot blindly at the glass, puncturing but not shattering one of the thick panes.

There was no time to think about it. Clio pulled the orange box from under the back wall, her hands shaking as she released the four metal clasps that held it there. It dropped at her feet. She picked it up and threw it over.

The door to the wheelhouse opened and a third man looked out. The man inside took another shot at the glass doors, breaking a large hole in them. Aidan pushed Clio toward the steps. She stopped. She could hear the boat's motor now loud in her ears. Without thinking twice, she lunged toward the tub and lifted the stone, wrapping it in her shirt.

"Clio!" Aidan shouted over the rushing water and the motor beneath them.

She stood, her shirt soaking wet, the stone wrapped tight in her arms. It was heavy, like a small child.

And then she tipped herself off the side of the boat, the stone dragging her down.

The Great Beyond

Here was another occasion today when life seriously deviated from the movies.

There was nothing graceful about jumping off a moving boat. Clio tried to control her fall but lost it when she dropped directly into the boat's wake, which tossed her onto her back and down underwater. She slammed hard as she hit and opened her mouth and took in water. The force of the blow bounced her several times along the water's surface like a skipping stone. Long before she could even tell which way was up or down, she was sinking under the surface, her nose and throat burning with salt water.

Underwater is a strange place to be. The world suddenly goes quiet—a frightening loss. The water, which seemed so bright and clear at the top, rapidly darkened. She had nothing now. No tanks. No mask. Nothing to block her nose.

The stone, which was on top of her now, pulled her down.

She managed to get out from under it and spread out her legs to slow her descent. It took a lot of effort, but she was able to kick herself up, her nose burning as she gagged on the water.

If she just dropped the stone, she would get there. Just dropping it would fix everything.

But she held on, forcing her legs to pump like they had never pumped before. When she finally broke the surface, her lungs ached, and Aidan was nowhere in sight. The *Sea Butterfly* was a white speck in the distance.

She screamed for Aidan. After a moment, she saw him flapping in the distance. He swam toward her with choppy, uncoordinated strokes. He was badly out of breath and coughing.

"Let's . . . not . . . do that again," he gasped when he had regained control.

"Do you have *any* idea where we are?" she shouted.

He came a bit closer, his legs bumping into Clio's as he treaded water viciously.

"I would say . . . somewhere off Italy? That's only . . ." He paused for breath. ". . . about twenty-one hundred miles of coastline to cover."

Clio rotated around in the water to give herself a full view. Unfortunately, all she saw was ever more water. Except in the distance, there was a tiny lump with what appeared to be a light on it.

"I see something over there," she said. "Maybe a light. Look at it. What do you think?"

"It could be land," he said, gasping. "It could also be a freighter a hundred miles out to sea. And that means we swim into rougher, deeper waters. And then we die."

"We won't die. Someone will find us. Besides, if we can find that orange box, we'll have the raft."

They looked around, but there was no orange box.

"It must have drifted," she said. "We'll have to swim for it."

"Swim which way?"

She squinted. The *Sea Butterfly* was still just in sight; she turned in the other direction.

"This way," she said. "Can you handle the swimming?"

"I'm not sure," he said.

"I can do it," she said. "Can you tread water with this?"

"I can try."

"If you feel weak, drop it," she said. "Drop it before you lose all your energy, all right?"

"I'm not dropping it," he said, accepting the stone. It pulled him under a little, but he fought it.

"I'll be back," Clio said. "And maybe slow down a little. Only tread as hard as you have to to stay up, okay?"

He slowed a tiny bit but not much.

"I'll be here," he gasped. "Try not to run into any jellyfish."

Aidan didn't drop the stone in the half hour it took Clio to retrieve the box. They took turns just leaning against it for a while until they had regained some energy.

By dusk, their kiddie-pool-shaped orange raft was bouncing somewhere off the twenty-one hundred miles of Italian coastline. It had a metal frame that needed to be snapped together, a tiny pump to supply the air. None of this was easy to accomplish while treading water.

The contraption was actually fairly sturdy when it was up. It kept them at least a foot and a half out of the water, and it had a tented roof and many built-in pockets that they had already emptied of their contents—three flares, two very small paddles (some assembly required), six seasickness pills, a whistle, a signaling mirror, two pints of water, and a miniature first aid kit. They'd sent up two of the flares, to no avail. The third was in Aidan's hands. There was a tiny self-powered light on the inside of the raft that came on as soon as the roof was popped open. It gave the space a weak but intensely orange glow.

They lay inside silently, recovering from the ordeal. A thin layer of seawater rested in the bottom of the raft, just enough to keep them damp and cold. Aidan didn't seem to care that he was lying in it. The Marguerite stone rested in it comfortably. Clio peered out of the tiny access flap at the white moon hanging over the ocean. She tried to focus on that and not the utter terror of the blackness that spread out in all directions around them. From this angle, the whole world was dark water of unknown depth, with lots of things living in it. It was right below her now, just about a foot. She could reach her hand out of her tiny orange joke of a raft and touch eternity.

"It's a really nice view," Clio said, trying to sound cheerful. "Want to see? The moon is amazingly huge and white over the water. If this was a hotel room, it would cost a fortune."

"Not really," he said. "It's been about two hours."

"Can you tell that from the sky?" she asked.

"I can tell that from my watch."

"Oh," she said.

Aidan wasn't buying the cheerful act. She closed the flap with the zipper and shifted herself farther inside. Aidan reached into a pocket and took out a bottle of water and the seasickness pills.

He popped two of them with a careful drink of the water, which he tightly resealed and set carefully back in the pocket.

Something bumped against the side of the raft.

"Did you just feel something?" Aidan asked.

"Let's not talk about whatever that was."

"Okay."

"How long do you think we'll be out here?" she asked.

"It depends on how soon they realize the boat was stolen. We're just hitting the time that they were supposed to get in touch. They'll probably try the coms for a while."

"So what do we do?" Clio asked.

"We don't *do* anything," he answered. "We wait."

It was later.

How much later was unclear. Aidan had taken off his watch and thrown it into the water because they'd become so obsessed with looking at it. It was better not to see the hours tick by. Night on the ocean only gets bigger and darker, the moon looking down from higher and higher. At one point a fish landed in the raft. The screaming that came out of the two of them when this unforeseen event occurred could easily have been heard on the coast of Italy, wherever that was. Clio tossed it back.

Now they were both lying in the pool of tepid water, arms loosely locked around each other. Either it had warmed from their bodies or they had simply gotten used to it. The waves had gotten a little higher, tossing the orange raft unpleasantly along. Clio had taken one of the seasickness pills as well, but she wasn't sure if it would really help. All that mattered was resting here, keeping as warm as possible. She could feel Aidan's breath on the top of her head as she kept her face pressed into the curve of his neck.

"I spy, with my little eye, something that rhymes with *pee*," Clio said.

"Is it *sea*?" Aidan answered.

"Yeah."

"Okay. I spy, with my little eye, something that rhymes with *potion*."

"We should stop," he said.

"Yeah," she said. "You're right. My bad."

Something stirred Clio. It wasn't a noise or a movement, just a feeling, maybe the subtlest of ripples in the water.

"Something's coming," she said, sitting up and balancing on one hand. The raft wobbled with the sudden movement.

Aidan sat up instantly. They opened the flap of the raft wider and looked around.

"Where?"

"I don't know," she said. "I just know it's something."

They kept looking until a small red light appeared in the distance. They watched it as it grew bigger and other lights clustered around it, and it finally became a shadow in the dark. An extremely big shadow. A cruise-ship–size shadow, which was headed straight in their direction.

"It's like . . . a cliff," Aidan said. "A *cliff* is drifting at us. How do we get out of the way of that?"

He had a point. The sheer massiveness of the ship made moving in any direction a bad idea. Whichever way they went, the ship would be there too. There was simply no way that the raft could dodge this boat. It filled all directions.

"I don't think we do," Clio said. "I think it either misses us or goes over us."

Aidan turned to look at her.

"Oh, come on," he said, his voice cracking in despair.

Clio shrugged. There came a point when certain realities were inescapable, simply too big to spaz out about. A cruise ship bearing down on them was one of those kinds of realities.

"Come *on*!" he yelled. "No! This isn't fair!"

He reached for the tiny paddle.

"What do you think?" she asked. "Are we going to make it?"

"How am I supposed to tell?" he asked.

"Eyeball it."

"Fine," he said. "Fine. I'll *eyeball* the cruise ship."

The white menace came closer. They could see individual port windows now, hundreds of them, like the little eyes that flies have.

"Jesus, that thing is big," he said. "That's our boat five hundred times over. Okay. If we go to the right a bit, I think we *might* make it."

"Are you sure?" she asked.

"I have no idea. You're looking at the same thing I am. What do *you* think?"

It was bearing down hard now, getting bigger and bigger. Its massive anchor, easily the size of a Hummer or three, was in clear view.

"I think . . . maybe," she said.

"Decide!"

"Right! Right!"

He paddled frantically. The tented kiddie pool responded by going in a circle.

It didn't really matter anyway, because as the ship came closer, it became obvious that they were clear of the side by thirty or forty feet. It was a staggering view, easily thirteen or sixteen stories of sheer white monster boat with a great, hulking bow that sloped out of the water and peaked at about the five-story mark. The lifeboats that dangled from the sides and looked so puny probably weren't all that much smaller than their boat.

"Back!" Aidan said. "Scream!"

They screamed. They flashed the lights. They waved their arms.

A man in a large, cone-shaped hat was leaning over one of the lower decks, waving at them frantically.

"He sees us!" Clio said. "He sees us!"

Except he didn't. The ship continued on its massive way, spitting out a monster wake that shook them so badly it almost felt like the raft was going to flip. When it was all over, they ended up on opposite sides of the raft, clutching their stomachs, making a concerted effort not to vomit.

"In case we die . . ." Clio croaked.

"Can you not say that?" he answered, just as hoarsely. "This is a *life* raft. *Life* being the operative word."

"In case we die," Clio continued, "there's something I need to tell you."

"What?"

She crawled over to him carefully, not wanting the world to tip or move any more than necessary.

"My secret," she said. "My one true secret."

"Please let it be that you have the ability to turn into a helicopter."

"No," she said. "Listen to me. I'm only telling you this because I just saw my life go past. And if you laugh, I'll make this thing rock again. I'll take us both down."

He pulled his head up from between his legs to look at her.

"I'm not laughing," he said. "I don't think I ever will again. I think I can only barf from now on."

"Good," she said. She reached for a bottle of water, which rolled up next to her, and took a careful sip. He waved away the bottle.

"You guessed right about my boyfriend," she blurted. "That I didn't have one. But I never lied. I never said he was my boyfriend. It was just something that Elsa thought. He *might* have been if I had stayed." Clio stopped herself for a moment. *He might have been.* Ollie. She had wanted him all summer. When had that changed? She looked Aidan in the eyes and took a deep breath. "But that's not my secret."

"Okay," he said. "What is it?"

"I've never been kissed," Clio said quickly.

This caused him to raise his head a bit higher.

"What?"

"I don't know why," she went on, shaking her head. "I think something *happened* to me. When I was a kid, everything was so . . . amazing. Seriously. I had this kind of perfect life. My dad and I made the game. Everything worked for us. Everything was exciting. And it blew up in about one day. It all ended. My dad left. Life came crashing down. I just didn't want anyone *near me*. I can't explain it more than that. I had friends. Friends were good. But if a guy even looked at me twice, I would just start being . . . really mean."

"You know," he said, "I noticed that."

"I don't know why I do it," she said.

"Maybe it's a test," Aidan said. "To see who can take you." He was looking at her closely.

Clio looked up. "To see who can *deal* with me," she said. "Do I hate myself that much?"

"Maybe," he said. "Or maybe you're choosy. Maybe you don't want to get hurt, so you want to see who's really worth the risk."

"Maybe," she said, staring into his eyes. She felt the feeling again, like the night she was hurt—that energy radiating from Aidan. That feeling she could barely understand. The warmth that almost felt like champagne, except champagne was nowhere near as fine. Champagne made your head buzz. This made everything buzz. She pushed herself closer, back over to his side.

"Would you have said something like that if we weren't in a life raft?" she asked.

"I doubt it," he said. "I would have said something meaner but funnier."

"Doubtful. You're not as funny as you—"

It really didn't feel like anything that she had ever heard described. She felt it in her mouth, of course. She felt his lips on hers. They were softer than she would have thought. She also felt his hand reaching around into her hair, cradling her head as she fell back. Aidan didn't taste woody or have berry-like overtones or any of that. He just tasted like Aidan, and it was better than any taste she had ever experienced. A massive rush went over her head. It was like she was both dizzy and as

302

steady as she had ever been. It shook her body too, rocking everything. Everything was shaking. Everything was shaking a *lot*.

And there was a voice somewhere deep in her head saying, "Clio! Are you in there? Aidan?"

"Dad?" she said into Aidan's lips.

"Okay," he said. "Later we're going to discuss why you should never say that, like, when we're doing this."

He started kissing her again.

"Did you hear that?"

Aidan looked dazed, his hair sticking up in its most extraordinary formation yet. The voice came at them again. It wasn't in her head at all, and it *was* her father's. It was coming closer. The raft was shaking a lot now, and a light was penetrating the industrial fabric walls of the raft. They both jumped at the flap and pulled it open, just in time to be nearly blinded by the searchlight coming from the white-and-orange boat that was stopping in front of them.

The Guardia Costiera officers hauled them up quickly. In a few bright, loud moments, they were standing on a deck being draped in blankets that looked like they were made of tinfoil but were immediately warming. And just another moment after that, Clio's father was hugging her as he had never hugged her before, pulling her close.

"How did you find us?" Aidan asked.

"A cruise ship radioed in," one of the boat's officers said. "A passenger saw something in the water. They said he was drunk, but what he described sounded like a raft."

"The boat," Clio managed to say into his chest. "I'm sorry.

There was nothing we could do. I don't know if you insured it or not. . . ."

"The boat?" Her dad looked shocked. "You think I care about the boat?"

"Also, it's a *little bit* on fire," she went on.

"Clio," he said, taking her face in his hands. "I don't care what happens to that boat. I couldn't care less if I tried. I've got you. *Nothing* else matters."

Her dad was holding her so tight now, he didn't even notice when one of the ship's crew removed the piece of marble from the raft. She leaned into his shoulder and smiled.

The Truth

The Guardia Costiera boat sped along the shadowy coastline, a mere ten-minute ride away. They continued up until they reached a small, official-looking port with three other patrol boats docked there.

They were greeted on the dock by a man who was almost as tall as Ollie, wore sunglasses in the dark, and smiled as if he was being presented with his very own miniature pony instead of a few bedraggled Americans.

"Now you'll come this way," he said, his English thickly flavored by Italian, but pronounced with great precision and pride. "We will have an interview. Yes, all right?"

They were escorted into a low, long building covered in small plaques and signs. The inside was one stretch of hallway that they squelched down in their saturated shoes. The building wasn't air-conditioned; it was nicely warm and sticky, and smelled comfortingly of heavily rubberized safety equipment.

There were two figures on a bench farther down the hall. One was leaning against the other. As they got closer, Clio could clearly see the blond hair.

"Elsa?" she said.

Elsa had clearly been crying. Her face was puffy all over, even around her mouth. She was also, Clio noticed, tucked under the arm of a good-looking Guardia Costiera officer who seemed very content with his night's assignment. She stood up and stared at them both for a long moment and then embraced each of them, causing their Mylar blankets to crinkle loudly.

"I'm surprised you didn't want me dead," Clio said, trying to sound light.

"Don't say that," Elsa said. "*Never* say that. No matter what. And especially . . ."

"It's okay, Elsa," Clio's dad said, quickly stepping forward.

"This way," the officer said. "Interview now. Just you two."

Aidan and Clio were ushered into a small room with no windows, filled mostly by a square black table. The officer sat down with a very straight back, removing his hat and placing it on the table in front of him in a studied, exacting manner. His hair was very dark, and cut in short but frizzy curls that sprang up toward the ceiling when they were released. He did not take off the sunglasses.

"First," he said, smiling broadly, "we will get for you coffee and pasta. Hot food."

He picked up the phone and spoke in machine-gun-fast Italian, then hung up and regained his smile and slow, measured pace.

"We start at the beginning, all right, yes? And you will tell me how this has happened to you. You tell everything. Nothing is boring to me. And now, I switch on this tape device, in case I miss something."

So Clio and Aidan began to recount the story of the robbery, the fire, their escape, and their time in the raft. They were asked to repeat several details over again. Many questions were about the stone as well. They were only interrupted by the arrival of two trays of steaming hot pasta, which they wolfed down as they spoke.

"Can we have the stone back?" Clio asked as they reached the end of their story. "We risked our lives to get it off that boat. We *swam* with it."

The officer spread his hands and made one of those "these things are hard to say" grimaces.

"This is a very unusual thing," he said. "If it came from Pompeii, as you say, maybe one thing will happen. But if it belongs to the British Museum, even so long ago, maybe another thing will happen. Maybe it will go to them."

"It's better than nothing," Aidan said. "At least they'll look at it there. They may not take it as seriously as Julia would, but still."

"We will see," the officer said. "I am sure something will come of this. Now, I must go for a moment. Do you need more food?"

Aidan nodded vigorously. Clio sucked on her fork in thought and shook her head no. The officer left the room, shutting the door.

"What did you just say?" Clio asked as Aidan used his fork to scrape up any remnants of sauce from his tin takeout container.

"I didn't say anything."

"No. A minute ago. About how Julia would take it more seriously than the British Museum."

307

"That's what I said, then," Aidan answered, reaching for Clio's empty container with his fork.

"Why isn't Julia in the hall?" she asked. "Why is Elsa crying so hard?"

"You're asking me all this stuff I don't know. Why?"

"When we got to town, Julia almost *insisted* that we all get off the boat and go to dinner. Which is crazy, right?"

"She was happy," he said.

"It's Julia," Clio said. "You think she cares if we all get a fancy dinner if it means leaving the boat alone? It's weird, right?"

"I guess now that you mention it, yeah. But she's wanted this stone for a long time. Maybe she was feeling happy and generous for a change."

"Right," Clio said. Pieces were snapping together in her head, making a perfectly clear picture. "She's wanted it for a *long time*. So, there's only two of us on the boat, and we take it out and anchor it, and some guys find us and take us. We couldn't have been that easy to see from shore. Either someone followed us, or someone knew where we were going."

Aidan stopped mid-scrape.

"What are you saying?" he asked.

"I'm saying, what if she made a grab for it? Maybe when she went to shore she got some guys to come out to the boat and lift the stone. But instead, when they saw how pimped out the boat was, they decided to take it."

"Why would she steal something she already had?" he asked.

"Because the story would be all about the Dive! family making a real-life diving find. It wouldn't be about her and her work. So if she had it taken from the boat, she could claim she found it anywhere. It would be about her again. This whole trip was unofficial. The only proof we have is the video footage, which she asked you to gather. Don't you see?"

"You've had a long night," Aidan said. "Maybe you should ask for more pasta."

"Aidan, I'm serious," she said. "Where is she now? Why isn't she in the hallway right now, with her crying daughter and her distraught boyfriend?"

"I don't know," he admitted. "Maybe with Martin at the hospital?"

"Does that sound likely to you?" she asked. With every word, she felt her internal temperature rising, her brain working fast. "Wouldn't Elsa have stayed? She's the only one who speaks Italian. I know you can't believe it because she's your boss. I'm sure of this, Aidan. I have to tell this guy. I at *least* have to tell him what I think."

"I don't think that's a good idea," he said.

The door opened again, and Clio got another glimpse of Elsa with the sailor. They were deep in a conversation in Italian, and he was wiping tears from her face. The officer ushered in Clio's father, who hurried in and sat down next to her, putting his arm protectively around her. He clasped Aidan on the shoulder.

"Where's Julia?" Clio asked innocently. "Why isn't she here? Is she with Martin?"

"No," her father said. "She's gone."

Clio shot Aidan a wide-eyed "told you" look. In reply, Aidan's eyebrows rose and locked in position, and he fixed her with a silencing stare as she started to open her mouth.

"I deliver news," the officer said, going back to his seat. "And

I must ask some more questions to all of you. Do you know a Jeffrey Fox?"

"No," her father said. "Never heard of him."

"Not the owner of *Foxy Lady*?" Clio said.

Her father's face lit up in recognition. He started pointing at Clio in agreement, pointing his finger toward her.

"Sure," he said. "Fox. I bought the boat from an Angela Fox. Clio's right. It was called the *Foxy Lady*."

"Things become clearer," the officer said, opening a file. "We have written here that Jeffrey Fox is a banker from London who works in Rome. Our records show that he had a boat called the *Foxy Lady* docked here in Civitavecchia."

"What about him?" her father asked. "I bought the boat. It's all legal."

"Yes," the officer said. "This I know. We get the name Jeffrey Fox from three men we find just now."

"So, you found the boat?" Clio asked quickly.

"No," he said, still smiling. "It is sank. Do I say this correctly? It hit a rock after a fire broke out on board. They were not watching where they were going. We pull these men from the water. It is a busy night for us. Jeffrey Fox wanted his boat back. He told people at the dock to watch to see if it ever returned, and when it did, they called him. He hired these three men to take the boat back."

Clio felt herself slumping. Just a second ago, Julia's guilt had been the clearest thing in the world. That reality had been swept away. She couldn't even bring herself to look at Aidan.

"Already, police in Rome are finding Jeffrey Fox," the officer went on. "And surely, a boat like this, it is insured. All ends happily."

Clio's father sank a little in his chair.

"Well," he said. "I didn't expect to have it that long, and I could only get a policy for a year. And it was really expensive."

"This boat is not insured?" the officer asked, looking aghast. "I see. I must go and make arrangements for these men. I will leave you here for a few moments."

"Where *is* Julia?" Clio asked her dad.

"She called her contacts in Rome," he said. "There are people there who understand the importance of the stone. They asked her to come there at once and help them gather up everything necessary for the transport. She got on a train. It's a quick ride. She'll be so crushed. . . ."

He trailed off, shaking his head.

"I can't really care," he said. "About the boat. About the stone. I have you two. But it's hard to know that we had it. We actually *had it.*"

"Dad—" Clio said.

"It would have changed so much," he went on. "We could have opened a window on a whole part of the ancient world that we know nothing about."

"Dad—"

"It's okay, Clio," he said. "Like I said, it doesn't matter."

"Ben," Aidan said. "We—"

"You two!" her dad said loudly. "Let's just forget about it and think about getting you guys—"

"We got it!" Clio finally yelled.

"Got what?" he asked.

"It. The stone. We got it off the boat."

It took him a minute to catch up with what she'd said.

"It's not gone?" he managed to ask. "How?"

"It was an interesting swim," Aidan said.

"You two . . . got away. *And* you took the stone? You had to have put yourself at risk to do that. I don't know whether I should hug you or yell at you."

"It couldn't really get any more risky," Clio said, accepting another massive hug. She smiled as Aidan was similarly crushed.

Kos, Greece, March 1905

What probably first drew Marguerite's attention was the fact that a naked man was standing on the very lip of a small boat. He held a small net in one hand.

"There's a naked man," she mentioned to Jonathan. "With a net."

For the last eight years, Jonathan and Marguerite had worked side by side in Pompeii. There was always much to be done. It was a massive city—a site on a scale unlike anything in the world. And every day they found more.

She had become physically stronger over the last few years, used to bright sun and long days. She wiped two thousand years' worth of ash and dirt from mosaics and frescoes. She found jewelry, money, and, occasionally, human remains. She learned the technique of putting plaster into gaps in the ash, preserving the form of the bodies entombed within.

It was good, hard work. And nothing made her happier than

working with Jonathan. Still, she couldn't help but feel that she was letting her father down. In eight years of labor, she hadn't uncovered anything as important as the stone that bore her name. Something gnawed inside her. There was something more she needed to do.

She didn't know what it was until she saw the naked man on the side of his boat.

The man took a flat, bell-shaped stone and dove headfirst off the side. There was a rope connected to the stone. She watched it slither into the water as he sank.

"A sponge diver," Jonathan said, flushing a bit. "You would think someone might have mentioned that there were naked men leaping about."

The nakedness did not bother Marguerite in the slightest. She understood its function at once. It was to make the descent quick. That was what the stone was for too. How else did you get what you wanted from the bottom of the sea? You had to drag yourself there.

In that moment, everything fell into place for Marguerite. Everything that she had ever wondered about was under the sea. Maybe even the Marguerite stone itself.

She started the very moment they arrived home in Italy. Marguerite was an exceptionally strong swimmer for a woman, but the traditional swim outfit was holding her back. So the first thing to go was the baggy, heavily skirted swimsuit she was supposed to wear. She had her dressmaker design a special one-piece suit that bared her legs, which meant she had to practice carefully, where she couldn't be seen.

The other thing that she needed came from a stonemason in

town. She had him make what she had seen in Greece—a *skandalopetra*, the bell-shaped stone with the hole for rope.

The first time she landed on the seafloor, Marguerite knew she was in love. She had no mask to protect her eyes, no fins to help her swim. Her lungs burned painfully. But she was ecstatic—a woman standing on the bottom of the ocean, where there was an entire world waiting to be explored.

It was so stunning that she almost forgot to keep her count until the panic of airlessness racked her body. She gave the rope a firm pull, grabbed the diving stone hard, and felt herself rising. She was rising slowly, but she was rising. She exhaled slowly.

Marguerite was feeling like she could go no longer when the sunlight appeared through the surface of the water, She kicked for it, and then she broke the surface, gasping and giddy. A massive cheer erupted from the boat.

There was no going back.

The Worst Summer of My Life

Three days later, four members of the group sat in the airport in Rome. Checking in had been easy. None of them had any suitcases, which raised an eyebrow or two. They had only whatever they had picked up to wear in the last few days.

Clio caught sight of herself in a reflective surface. She'd had to make do with the slim offerings in the local tourist shops, so her outfit was a pair of sweatpants with the word *Italy* written down the leg in big red, green, and white letters and a T-shirt that said, *Ciao!*

At least people won't ask me where I've been, she thought.

Aidan had made out slightly better in the pants department, with a long pair of surf shorts. His shirt was worse, though. It had a picture of Michelangelo's David on it holding a tiny Italian flag. Elsa's clothes hadn't been soaked in seawater and messed up in an escape attempt, so she had washed them.

Martin was given a clean bill of health but a warning to be

more careful and to avoid strenuous activity. He was resting at the hotel. Julia had remained on in Rome once she heard everyone was safe, and was battling through the many layers of red tape to have the stone released back into their custody.

With nowhere to stay, and so many ends to tie up, it only made sense for Aidan and Elsa to go. Clio's mom had yet to be told the full story, but she knew that something had happened. So Clio was going as well. The group was split up as quickly as it had been thrown together.

Elsa's flight to Stockholm was the first to leave. After hugging everyone good-bye, she hooked her arm through Clio's.

"Walk with me to security?" she asked.

"Sure," Clio said.

They walked in silence for a moment, dodging the luggage carts and people running for planes.

"We should talk," Elsa said. "I want things between us to be settled."

"Me too," Clio said.

"I was upset," Elsa said. "It wasn't what you did. I could see what was happening between the two of you. You're good together. It's just that you didn't tell me the truth. If you had just told me, I wouldn't have gone after him like that."

"I know it sounds ridiculous, but I didn't know I liked him then," Clio said. "I swear."

"I know," Elsa said. "I'm still sorry I wrecked your drawing crayons."

"You *bought* them, too," Clio said.

"True, but it's no excuse."

"So," Clio said, "you don't want to stay here? Go to Rome?"

"No," Elsa answered. "My mom is tied up now in work. I might as well go and see my dad and his family. I like Stockholm."

"You won't try to contact Alex, will you?"

"Ah," Elsa said. "Now, there is good news on that front. I don't think I've shown you this."

She held up her phone and showed Clio a picture in a text message. It was of the sailor from the dock making a kissing face. There was some Italian written under it.

"No way," Clio said.

"He's coast guard," she said with a little giggle. "He gets time off, just like a normal job. He's going to come up to Sweden to see me in two weeks. He already bought a ticket. Alex is going to die when he hears that my new boyfriend is an Italian sailor. I can't wait to walk him around the football pitch someday while Alex is playing. It'll *kill* him!"

Elsa took the phone back.

"Not that I even care," she added quickly, shutting it. "But there's always a silver lining."

"You can come visit me," Clio said. "My house is kind of a serious violation of most safety codes, but it's really big. It's easy to get to Philadelphia. And you'd love my cat. You always have a place to stay."

"Maybe I will," Elsa said.

There was an announcement in Italian.

"That's me," she said. She wrapped Clio in one more hug, squeezing hard.

"Keep the boy," she said. "He needs you."

And with that, she was gone. She left much like she'd

appeared—head held high, smiling no matter what happened to her. Still every inch the goddess, drawing looks from about half the people she passed.

When Clio got back, Aidan and her dad were hungry. They returned to the restaurant where the whole trip had started. Without Elsa, they were a bit helpless. Clio's dad just pointed to a pizza and held up three fingers. The only topic was the stone. Clio could see that her dad wasn't ready to talk about Julia yet.

"What time is it?" Aidan said, looking at the spot on his wrist where his watch used to be. "Right. Need a new watch."

"Probably close to time," Clio's dad said. "We'll pay and walk you over."

It was time. In fact, it was past time.

"Last call," Aidan said, looking up at the screen. "I guess I should . . ."

He pointed a thumb at the mass of people at the security checkpoint. Clio's father nodded and extended his hand for a shake.

"Make sure to keep in touch," he said. "You have my e-mail."

"I will, Ben," he said. "I need to hear how this all ends."

Aidan turned to Clio. Her stomach bottomed out.

"Dad, could we . . ."

Her father blinked. No comprehension at all. She was going to have to spell it out for him.

"Dad," she said. "Look at those gorgeous silk ties at that store over there. Don't you need a tie?"

"A tie? I . . ."

There it was. The look Clio had known would come someday. He got it.

"I'm going to go look at ties," he said, forcing his face into an overly serious expression. "Aidan, have a good flight."

With one more shake, he went off and vanished deep into the tie store.

"He'll probably buy one," Clio said. "He can't do anything halfway."

She felt her eyes starting to fill, so she quickly looked down at the shiny gray tiles on the floor.

"Will you miss Cambridge?" she asked.

"No," he said. "After England, New Haven weather actually sounds nice. And the food is good. I could really go for a cheeseburger at the Doodle. Did I ever tell you about the Doodle?"

"No," she said.

"Good cheeseburgers. We should go."

He looked at her, half smirking. The eyes were still analyzing. But there was a seriousness about them now.

"Want to make it a date, haircut?" she asked. "As soon as I scrape together the cash for the train ticket?"

"What's with the 'haircut,' *kiddo*?" he asked. "I thought we were past that."

"We'll *never* be past that," she said.

"What about Ollie?" he asked.

"Ollie's a nice guy," Clio admitted. "But he's not my boyfriend."

Aidan tried not to smile.

"Well," he said, stretching himself long, exposing his stomach as he pulled up his arms in a supremely bored gesture. "I *guess* that's okay, then. Maybe I'll even come to Philly. I heard you guys have good cheesesteaks. I've always wanted to be in a relationship based on local sandwiches."

Clio tried not to openly gape at the word *relationship*. She swallowed hard.

"So," she said. "Does that mean I don't have a fake boyfriend anymore?"

"Have you drawn my picture?" he said. "That seems to be the sign."

"Actually . . ."

She pulled out her sketchbook and opened it up to the new sketch that she had worked on in the last few days. This time, he had no reply at all. He just stared at it.

"I've never torn anything out of a sketchbook before," she said. "But if you want it . . ."

"Yeah," he said. "I want it."

She squatted down and carefully ripped the page out, pulling it away from the spine. She passed it to him.

He took a step back, then rocked on his heel.

"It's time," he said. "I'd better . . ."

He moved so fast, Clio barely saw it coming. He bent down and took her face in his hands and kissed her long and hard. She had to grab onto his sleeve to keep from toppling over.

"See you, rich girl," he said, tucking a strand of hair behind her ear.

"Later, snob."

And then there were two.

When her father emerged from the shop, a full fifteen minutes later, he didn't have a tie with him. He was shutting his phone.

"Good news from Julia," he said. "The stone is being released back to us. And she's already been contacted about it. The story is getting out. All of a sudden, everyone's interested. This thing is getting big already, Clio. The news wires have picked up the story. Everyone wants to know what we're going to find. And it's all possible because you are stupidly brave."

"And you have idiotic ideas," Clio added.

"Of course," he said. "What do you think, kiddo? Are you ready to get back into the game? We always made a good story."

"You never stop, do you?" she asked.

"No," he admitted. "I guess I don't. I guess I did it again. Why am I always putting you in danger?"

"You didn't," she said. "Jeffrey Fox did."

He tried to smile, but she could see he was finding it hard.

"You know what?" she said after a moment. "I thought Julia sent those guys. I really did. I thought she wanted the stone for herself. I was about to tell the police that and everything. Aidan stopped me."

"You thought *Julia* did that?" He laughed. "Can you imagine Julia going to the dock and hiring thugs? In that voice of hers?"

"It made sense at the time," Clio said weakly. "I'm sorry I didn't trust her. I guess she's nice. I'll try to like her more."

"Well, I could have introduced her to you under better circumstances," he said. "Why have we had such a rough time? Is it me?"

"We're just interesting people," Clio said. "We're both very difficult."

"Is that it?"

She looked up at the screen of multicolored flight names and times. One of them meant home—not that she wanted to go there as much as she had before.

"You should go, kiddo," he said. "You know what security is like."

"Right," she said with a sigh.

She gave him one final hug, then started on her way toward the throng of people at the gate being checked and frisked and metal-detected. Halfway there, she turned around and walked back to where he was standing, his hands buried deep in the pockets of his new white shorts, another tourist shop purchase. They were worse than the cutoffs she had first seen him in, but the effect was different now. And at least that little captain's hat was gone.

She reached up and took the cameo of Marguerite that she still wore around her neck and placed it in his hand.

"Here," she said. "She'll keep you company while I'm gone. I mean, she was finishing her father's work. And then we finished hers. We're practically family."

"Yes," he said, looking down at the cameo and then up at Clio. "Yes we are."